Praise for David Hagberg

"*The Expediter* involves a standoff between China and North Korea that threatens the world, and it is terrifying in its very plausibility. A brilliantly realized novel of heart-stopping action, slick hardware, down-and-dirty characters, and fast international settings. David Hagberg is *the* grand master of the contemporary espionage thriller."   —Douglas Preston, *New York Times* bestselling author of *Blasphemy*

"It's fun to watch professionals at the top of their game, which in this case means not only the characters in this great story, but David Hagberg himself as he creates a world-spanning crisis that only Kirk McGarvey can save. The nonstop action races the clock with the fate of millions waiting for the winner."

—Larry Bond, *New York Times* bestselling author, on *The Expediter*

"Hagberg is known for being prescient about terrorist events, and the finale sets up the terrifying challenge McGarvey will face in the next installment. One can only hope America's real-life enemies haven't thought to study this series."

—*Publishers Weekly* on *Dance with the Dragon*

"David Hagberg runs in the same fast, high-tech track as Clancy and his gung ho colleagues, with lots of war games, fancy weapons, and much male bonding."

— New York *Daily News*

"If you're looking for thrillers with international intrigue, Hagberg is a major find."   —Dean Koontz

WRITING AS DAVID HAGBERG

Twister
The Capsule
Last Come the Children
Heartland
Heroes
Without Honor
Countdown
Crossfire
Critical Mass
Desert Fire
High Flight

Assassin
White House
Joshua's Hammer
Eden's Gate
The Kill Zone
By Dawn's Early Light
Soldier of God
Allah's Scorpion
Dance with the Dragon
The Expediter

WRITING AS SEAN FLANNERY

The Kremlin Conspiracy
Eagles Fly
The Trinity Factor
The Hollow Men
False Prophets
Broken Idols
Gulag

Moscow Crossing
The Zebra Network
Crossed Swords
Counterstrike
Moving Targets
Winner Take All
Achilles' Heel

WRITING NONFICTION WITH BORIS GINDIN

*Mutiny: The Inside Story of the True Events That Inspired
The Hunt for Red October—from the Soviet Naval Hero
Who Was There*

BURNED

•

David Hagberg

A TOM DOHERTY ASSOCIATES BOOK
New York

This is a work of fiction. All of the characters, organizations, and events portrayed in this novel are either products of the author's imagination or are used fictitiously.

BURNED

Copyright © 2009 by David Hagberg

All rights reserved.

A Forge Book
Published by Tom Doherty Associates, LLC
175 Fifth Avenue
New York, NY 10010

www.tor-forge.com

Forge® is a registered trademark of Tom Doherty Associates, LLC.

ISBN 978-0-7653-5751-9

First Edition: June 2009
First Mass Market Edition: February 2010

Printed in the United States of America

0 9 8 7 6 5 4 3 2 1

This is for Lorrel, as always.

ACKNOWLEDGMENTS

•

Although this story is based on an incident that actually happened, all of the names and most of the characters are completely figments of the author's imagination. The character of David Monroe, the husband, bears absolutely no resemblance to any person living or dead, nor did the scenes in which he appears here, actually ever happen.

The character of Patti Monroe is inspired by a real woman, Yvonne Bornstein, who not only lived through her own horrible kidnapping ordeal, but survived intact by her grace under pressure, by her indomitable courage, by her spirit and fortitude, and by her belief that a woman should never, never give up.

Yvonne's message, which is the inspiration for this novel, is: where there is life, there is always hope.

This is her book.

BURNED: an intelligence service term for someone who has been picked up by the opposition.

THE BEGINNING

August

A mountain pass on
Pakistan's northern border

•

A battered Russian jeep topped a rock-strewn rise. Above ten thousand feet, even this high mountain pass was dominated by snow-covered peaks towering in every direction.

Behind the wheel, Sergey Lysenko stopped the jeep, got out with a pair of Steiner mil specs binoculars, and glassed the rugged valley two thousand feet below.

At first he saw nothing. No movement, no signs that any human had been here in a millennium, in ten thousand millennia. These were the Hindu Kush, the tallest mountains on earth. But Lysenko, a Chechen-Russian by birth, raised and educated in London, was a patient man. Here on the border with Afghanistan, where there was no rule of law, save one—al-Quaeda—it paid to be careful, to be deliberate, to be smart.

He was forty-one, just under six feet, dark with short-cropped steel gray hair and deep-set eyes. He was husky, but he had not turned to flab. A non-practicing Muslim, he was nonetheless bin Laden's main conduit to the west and a dedicated *jihadist,* though not a fanatic. Women in London found his weathered face and probing eyes dangerously exciting. He could have passed for a desert nomad, a Bedouin. He was a man who never questioned himself.

After five minutes he was rewarded with a tiny flash of light from below, probably the reflection off the lenses of a pair of binoculars, or from a riflescope. Bin Laden's entourage was always cautious.

I have arrived, he had told them by stopping.

And they had replied, *Ay-wa,* yes, we see you.

He tossed the binoculars on the passenger seat, got behind the wheel, and drove the rest of the way down into the valley. He was conscious of a hundred pairs of eyes on him: Kalashnikovs, RPGs, and 7.62mm Russian-made Dragunov sniper rifles following his progress.

At the bottom he parked under a low overhanging mesh canopy and got out of the jeep, keeping his hands in plain sight. He was dressed in Russian *Spetsnaz* camos, and was unarmed except for a Heckler & Koch room broom submachine gun and a 9mm Steyr GB automatic pistol in the *GAZik.* He'd been given these weapons, plus his clothing, at Peshawar before flying on to Chitral, Pakistan's most northerly airstrip, where he'd picked up the jeep.

A pair of *mujahideen* armed with Kalashnikovs stepped out from behind a big boulder about twenty feet above the camouflage net and watched as Lysenko came up the steep slope.

When he reached them they stepped aside. "May Allah be with you," one of them said.

"And with you," Lysenko replied in Saudi Arabic, although it was all stupid mumbo jumbo as far as he was concerned. His passion was killing and not some useless religion. Sometimes he would stop to wonder what, if anything, he did believe in, other than his own survival, which was the only thing that mattered since his childhood in England, where his boarding school had taught him how to hate.

The entrance to bin Laden's cave complex opened behind the ten-foot-tall rock. Lysenko climbed past the guards and ducked inside. Immediately he could smell the distinctive odors of electronic equipment, and something unpleasant—perhaps mold. This sort of a place was never meant as a refuge for very long, yet bin Laden and his loyalists had been living in mountain caves since before 9/11. Living like animals; the thought came to Lysenko as it did each time he came here.

Fifteen meters in, Lysenko felt a chill as he passed through a low opening, on the other side of which was a fairly large chamber, perhaps eight or ten meters on a side. Persian rugs were scattered on the dirt floor, halogen desk lamps illuminating single sideband radios, weather fax machines, and laptops, one of which was streaming Al Jazeera, the television network from Qatar, and another a CNN feed from London. A couple of earnest-looking young Saudis in traditional dress were busy at the machinery and didn't bother to look up as Lysenko walked by.

Here al-Quaeda was connected to the world, and anyone who didn't belong could never get this close.

Three chambers farther into the complex, Lysenko ducked through another opening, this one into an even larger room, the floor and the walls carpeted.

Osama bin Laden, his legs folded under him, was seated on cushions in front of a low table, two young mujahideen on either side looking fierce with Kalashnikov rifles clutched against their chests, pistols stuck in their belts. They stiffened and pointed their rifles at Lysenko.

"It's all right, my children," bin Laden said softly. He was gaunt, his eyes sunken, his face pale, beard and hair pure white now. When he raised his right hand in greeting

6 · David Hagberg

it shook with a palsy. "This is the butcher of Grozny. You remember. He is a friend."

"Papa, how can we be sure?" one of the boys, who couldn't have been more than fifteen, asked respectfully.

Bin Laden chuckled good-naturedly. "Go now, kittens. Leave us."

The boys left reluctantly. They felt important here.

Lysenko approached bin Laden and the two men embraced.

"Sit, and we'll have tea," bin Laden said.

When Lysenko was settled, bin Laden filled small handleless cups of tea from a pot on a small electric brazier. They sat in silence for a long time. A waste, Lysenko thought. All of this—the caves, the fighting, the hiding, the *jihad*—yet he never felt more alive, more free, more in command than he did in the middle of an operation. Nine/eleven had been the most sensual day of his life, and he suspected that the next attack would be even more emotional. But it was all for nothing; they could never win. Bin Laden didn't understand the West like Lysenko did. The al-Quaeda leader had been once, briefly, to London, but never to New York or Chicago or Los Angeles. He had no real conception of the vastness of the infidel West. Bringing down the twin trade towers had been a blow to the American psyche, but it had been nothing more than a pinprick against the empire.

Yet Lysenko could not give up, not now. Not ever, he suspected, unless the demons that had chased him since he was a child in London finally caught up with him.

"The plans are complete?" bin Laden asked.

"Yes."

"All that lacks is the money. And thou wouldst not

have taken the risk to come all this way unless you had good news."

"The nuclear demolition device will be delivered across the border from Tajikistan when we have the money."

"Ten million dollars."

"Yes, and we will have the money within six months."

Bin Laden's eyes suddenly brightened and he sat forward so quickly he spilled some of his tea. "Tell me." This last spectacular attack against the U.S. would be much greater than 9/11, and most likely bin Laden's last before his failing kidneys finally killed him.

"You remember the American couple doing business with the company I set up in Moscow and Vladivostok. The Monroes."

"Yes, but stealing their money with a few business deals will not work. It's taking too long."

"Mrs. Monroe's family is wealthy."

Bin Laden moistened his lips. "How wealthy?"

"Rich enough so that the parents would spend ten million to rescue their daughter from her kidnappers."

Bin Laden sat back. "Ah," he said. "Americans would spend that much to save a daughter? No Arab would. A son perhaps, but never a daughter."

"January," Lysenko said, his blood already rising with wonder at how interesting it would be *before* he allowed her to make the first telephone call. According to Aleksei, who ran the business for them in Moscow, the husband was a blowhard, and the woman was a typical American bitch—spoiled and strident.

He would teach her respect. And a great many other things that he'd been taught at Oxford by his Iranian professor of Middle-Eastern studies, who'd taken him under his wing and into his bed.

It was a long way from his roots in Lebanon and his Chechen engineer father and Lebanese mother, who'd moved to England to avoid persecution. In three months, that winter at Oxford, he had become so radicalized that on a spring break home he and his parents had gotten into a tremendous row over his jihadist conversion, and in a black rage he had slit both of their throats and fled to Saudi Arabia.

THE FIRST DAY

January 2nd

ONE

•

The landing at Moscow's Sheremetyevo Airport in blowing snow on an icy runway had been rough. Patti Monroe was on edge, in part because of the dull knot of fear that had formed in her gut the moment they'd boarded the aging Aeroflot jet in Frankfurt, which she worried would crash. But mostly it was David. She was at her wit's end, and she didn't know what to do to save her marriage.

She was a slender, small boned woman, just thirty-two in five days, with long dark hair up in a bun, frazzled now after nearly eighteen hours in the air. She was dressed in plain designer jeans, soft Italian boots, a vibrant pink short-sleeved turtleneck cashmere sweater, and a Gucci leather jacket. A large Louis Vuitton bag was slung over a narrow shoulder.

A nasty weather system had stalled over most of Eastern Europe, and here in Moscow snow fell vertically in sheets, temperatures hovering around the zero mark, the late afternoon already getting dark. Everyone in the terminal seemed to be in a nasty mood.

David was a few steps ahead of her, as usual, with his long-legged stride, bulling people out of his way. At just over six feet he towered over her. Three years ago, when they'd married, his height and bulk had been reassuring; he was her Rock of Gibraltar. Somehow his size and rotten attitude had become intimidating; he was still a rock, but now it was around her neck, dragging her down.

Maybe her father and Uncle Tobias had been right about him, but she didn't want to believe it even now. David had fallen in love with her for herself, not for her family's money. If that had made her a romantic in the beginning, she was becoming a realist finally, a role she didn't know if she could play. Or if she would be very happy playing it.

They turned left along a filthy corridor to the customs hall where they were among the first off the flight. Men in shabby uniforms waited behind battered desks. The terminal was incredibly hot.

David was a handsome man, in Patti's eyes. Narrow face, nice lips, expressive eyes, and when he was in a good mood, or when he was trying to con something out of somebody, especially a woman, a devastating smile. He handed their passports to the officer without a word.

This was their fourth trip to Moscow, and they'd come to expect delays at this point, sometimes more than an hour, while everything in their two hanging bags was unpacked and handled, and dozens of questions asked. Once, three customs inspectors had become involved. Patti suspected it was a national sport, and she prayed that David would hold his sharp temper in check. They were in enough trouble as it was.

"Business, Mr. Monroe?" the agent asked, his English thick. He opened the passports and glanced at the photographs, but he didn't look up.

"Yes," David said.

The agent stamped both passports and handed them back.

"What the fuck?" David muttered.

They headed across the hall to the rusty carousel where their bags had already arrived. On the other side of a wire fence was the terminal, packed with people waiting for passengers off the Frankfurt flight. Some of them held up small hand-lettered signs.

Patti tried to spot their business rep, Aleksei Voronin, but he wasn't in the front rows, and the terminal was dimly lit, unlike airport terminals in the West. And she had forgotten how bad it stank—cigarette smoke, unwashed bodies, and stale vodka.

She was sorry they had come, but for the past couple of weeks she'd kept telling herself the trip was necessary. David was in trouble to the tune of 1.5 million dollars U.S. They'd been making barter deals through a company called SovAustralTech. They'd acquired a million and a half dollars' worth of Chinese cell phones in Hong Kong for one million, which they traded for 1.5 million dollars' worth of Russian fertilizer that they'd planned to sell in Taiwan for two million, making them a nice profit of one million.

But David hadn't paid attention this time. The fertilizer was half sand and was rejected by the buyers. Most of the cell phones were reconditioned units and didn't work. Aleksei said his backers wanted their money back. All of it, and an explanation if they were going to keep doing business.

And it had to be in person, which worried Patti, because Aleksei was almost certainly connected with the Russian Mafia and they killed people who got in their way.

David laid their bags on a low counter in front of one of the agents and handed over their luggage receipts, customs declarations, and passports. The Russian seemed tired and bored.

"What is the purpose of your trip to the Russian Federated States?" he asked.

"Business," David replied.

"What is the nature of your business?" The agent glanced at David's customs declaration, which showed nothing. "Mr. Monroe."

"We're partners in an import/export firm."

"And what do you import to Russia?"

"Stuff," David shot back. "Shit that you people can't produce for yourself."

Christ, Patti said to herself.

"What do you export?"

"Shit you people can't use."

The agent flipped through the passport, stamped with Russian entry and exit permits. He looked up again. "You have been here many times."

Patti stepped forward before David could say anything else.

"We have friends and business partners here in Moscow." She smiled, as warmly as she could, although her stomach had tightened into a knot again. "But maybe we're not prepared for a Moscow January."

The agent hesitated for just a beat, glancing again at David, but then he managed a slight grin. "Moscow is best for Muscovites in the winter," he told her shyly. "We know how to live with it." He stamped their passports and handed them to Patti. "Have a pleasant visit, Mrs. Monroe. Be sure to keep warm. Perhaps a good fur hat would be wise."

"*Spaseeba.*"

"*Pazhaloostah,*" you're welcome, the agent said.

Hefting their bags, David and Patti passed through the barrier and headed into the terminal, the first passengers from the flight. Welcome to Moscow.

TWO
•

P atti had always thought that the toughest parts of a trip to Russia were getting into the country, and then getting back out. But this time they had to face Aleksei and solve the problem so that everybody would be happy. And she didn't know if it was possible. Not now. Their bank accounts in Hong Kong and Sydney had less than three hundred dollars between them, and after paying for their air tickets they were just about maxed out on their credit cards.

"Stop brooding," David told her sharply.

"Maybe you should be worried," she said. "We don't have the money to pay them."

He stopped in midstride and turned on her. "I wouldn't pay the bastards even if we did have it. They fucked us. The fertilizer wasn't worth the shipping costs. On top of that we've screwed at least three of our Taiwanese contacts. I've been trying to explain it to you ever since we got out of there. We've got bigger troubles than the mil five."

The situation in Taipei had been tense. Chris Liu, their trading partner for all of southeast Asia, had tossed a handful of the bad fertilizer in David's face. If three of Liu's gunmen hadn't been standing right

*there, Patti was sure David would have started a fight,
which would have landed them both in a Taiwanese
jail.*

*"You will fix this problem, Monroe," the man had
shouted. "You will go to Moscow and straighten those
bastards out. Otherwise you will never do business in
Asia again." He'd stepped closer, his face inches away
from David's. "If you come back with empty hands I
will personally kill you."*

Passengers coming out of customs flowed past them,
no one paying them the slightest bit of attention, but
Patti could feel heat rising to her cheeks. She hated
when she got like this. Her father had taught her to stand
on her own two feet, take responsibility for her own
actions, and not to cry, while her mother had simply
shaken her head at their tomboy daughter. She never
cried, but lately David could embarrass her; and when
that happened she wanted to strike out at something.

*Her instructor at the Chicago dojo where she'd be-
gan her martial arts training had told her to channel
her feelings of aggression.*

*"It is a useful energy; direct your anger where it
will do the most good."*

*At first she hadn't even been aware that she was
angry, or why. But three months into her training,
her instructor had paired her with a third-year student against whom she had no chance. It was to be a
test. The instructor had planned on kicking her out of
the dojo because of the chip on her shoulder unless
she learned to handle her attitude.*

*Thirty seconds into the bout she'd realized that she
was fighting her father for trivializing her all of her
life. He'd wanted a son, and he'd been disappointed
that Patti was a girl.*

The boy's name was Paul, and he was a senior at her high school. After the fight, in which she had coldly and efficiently taken him apart, her instructor never questioned her anger again. In fact he'd taken her under his wing, grooming her for international competition, she'd been that good. Paul dropped out of the dojo and avoided her the rest of his senior year.

But that seemed like five lifetimes ago.

"Let's save this until later, okay?" she asked. "Let's talk to Aleksei, then get to the hotel. It's been a long day, and I'm tired."

"I'm going to do a hell of a lot more than talk to him," David shot back. "But I want you to keep quiet this time. If he wants to think that you're still connected to your dad's money, we're not going to tell him anything different. He owes us a mil-five worth of good fertilizer, and I'm going to get it from the bastard."

"What about the cell phones?" Patti asked. Supposedly they were in a warehouse somewhere in Moscow. "These people don't screw around."

"When we get the fertilizer, I'll replace the phones," David told her. He started to walk away, but then stopped suddenly and turned back. He was smiling. "Look, sweetheart, I want to get us out of this mess as badly as you do. But we've made some good money here, and I don't want us to screw the pooch over some small shit like this. I'll get Aleksei straightened out, we'll go back to Liu and make him a happy camper, and when we get home we'll take a cruise. Someplace warm. Maybe Rio. Maybe St. Kitts. Maybe the Riviera." His smile widened, and he suddenly was the old David, the man she'd fallen in love with the first time she'd laid eyes on him. "How about Monaco? Give you a chance to spend some of our money."

"You'll have to take it slow," Patti warned. Aleksei had visited them at their home in Baltimore last year, when business was good. They had just signed a million-dollar mortgage for the big house, and he'd been impressed.

"Very nice," he'd kept saying the whole five days he'd been with them. *"In Russia we have to kill someone for something this nice."* He smiled in his diffident, almost effeminate manner, as if he'd never had any need to lie about anything, or brag.

"Just let me handle it, okay?" David said angrily.

Patti could feel her temper flare, but she held herself in check. Lately David had been doing and saying things that she was sure were meant to hurt her, and she didn't know why. Sometimes she felt lost.

The one lesson her father, who had almost never been there for her had taught her was never give up. *"Don't let the bastards get to you. Fire away and keep firing until they back off and give you a little respect. Just because you're a woman doesn't mean you have to take shit from anyone."* Like her mother had taken it; the thought came to her often.

"Let's not argue, okay?" she said. "I'm a part of this business, too."

A pained expression came over his face, the same as always when he thought that she was reminding him whose money paid the bills. It was a look she'd never forget.

"Fuck it," he said, and walked away.

Patti hurried to catch up with him, but when she reached his side he wouldn't look at her. "I'm sorry," she said. "I didn't mean it the way it sounded."

"Right," he said tight-lipped.

Patti groaned inwardly. He was in one of his martyr

moods, and she knew exactly what he would say next. *I'm just trying my best here. It may be your money but they're my contacts.*

"Look, Patti, I know that it's been your money from the start, but goddamnit I've been cultivating these people since Chicago, since before I ever met you."

"I didn't mean to bring up old wounds, sweetheart. Honestly. But right now it's just as much my problem as it is yours. We're in this together. We'll work it out, you'll see."

"That old man of yours is a son of a bitch. I should have told him that to his face from day one."

David was her third marriage, and he'd been the straw that broke the camel's back as far as her father was concerned. He'd given her a $500,000 check for her wedding present and that was that. He was washing his hands of her until she came to her senses. "Divorce the bastard and everything's yours," he'd told her flat out.

She had no sisters or brothers, and her father's hundred-million-plus fortune would be hers if she jumped through the hoops.

At the time it was a no-brainer. David didn't know just how rich her dad was, or so she thought. And with his plans and her half mil they couldn't fail.

But that had been three years and a lot of very bad, stupid deals ago. Now they were here.

Aleksei Voronin's familiar round face appeared out of the crowd, a serious, patient look in his eyes behind the wide glasses. He was dressed in a nice pale gray overcoat and Russian sable hat.

"Finally," he said, his voice soft, his English heavily accented but educated. He'd graduated from Frunze, the Soviet Union's most prestigious military academy, akin to West Point and Annapolis rolled into one. He embraced Patti and put out his hand to David, who ignored it.

"We've got some shit to work out," David said harshly.

"Yes, I understand. But you must understand our position, too."

"Bullshit," David said, stepping closer. "Fertilizer laced with sand? I even had to pay to have it unloaded from the ship, trucked out into the mountains, and dumped. Where the fuck was your head?"

"You inspected the sample before the deal was made," Voronin reminded him, reasonably.

The fact of the matter, Patti thought, was that David hadn't bothered. Nor had he bothered to check the cell phones.

"The sample I had tested was fine," David said. "Someone must have added the sand later to make the weight."

"It was up to you to have the shipment inspected before you attempted to deliver it," Voronin said. "Standard business practice. I inspected the cell phones and rejected them before they were sent east. If you had done the same with the fertilizer our deal could have been adjusted."

"That's why I'm here. To get it *adjusted*."

Suddenly, Patti had an awful feeling, almost overwhelming, that they were heading into a very bad place from which there would be no escape. Considering the deal gone bad, Aleksei was being far too pleasant. His mood versus David's was ominous.

THREE

•

Patti followed David and Voronin through the terminal to the departing passengers' doors and outside to the three-lane driveway where cars, taxis, and buses waited. When they stepped outside, the cold took her breath, and she had to turn away, her eyes instantly watering. She wasn't dressed for this kind of weather, not after Baltimore, but she had forgotten all about Moscow winters.

"Everything is fine with operations," Voronin said. The cold didn't seem to affect him. "I don't want you to worry about the other deals on the table, just this one needs to be straightened out." He raised his hand.

A lot of traffic clogged the driveway, but there were very few cops. The air stank of diesel and gas fumes, and something else, something foul that Patti couldn't identify.

A long, black Zil limousine pulled away from where it was parked, twenty meters away, and glided up to them.

"What the fuck is this?" David demanded. "Did we buy a new car?"

"It belongs to a friend of mine," Voronin said calmly. "It's more comfortable than the Benz. Trust me."

A heavyset man with a thick dark beard was behind the wheel, while another man, craggy with short-cropped hair, wearing a thick fisherman's turtleneck sweater, riding shotgun, got out and opened the rear door.

Patti got the impression that he was a soldier because

of his close-cropped hair and crisp bearing. She thought he was handsome in a dark, dangerous way, and she smiled.

"Good afternoon," he said. His English sounded British and cultured.

"This is my friend, Sergey Lysenko, who's come from London to meet you and perhaps arrange a few deals," Voronin said. "If we can work out our little problem."

"We'll definitely resolve the problem," Lysenko said, smiling.

"I'd like you to meet David and Patti Monroe," Voronin said.

"Of course I've heard so much about you," Lysenko said smoothly. He took Patti's hand and kissed it, then turned to David. "Mr. Monroe. Or may I call you David?"

David ignored Lysenko's outstretched hand and turned instead to Voronin. "I just spent half the day in a sardine can," he said. "Let's get going."

Patti touched her husband's arm, and he turned on her. He was pissed off, and it worried her.

"What?"

"Take it easy, David, please," she said. "And could we get in the car, it's cold out here."

"Christ—" David said, but Lysenko motioned her to get into the limo.

The Zil was huge. It had served the same purpose in Russia, as a limousine for Soviet government bigwigs, as the armored Cadillac did in the U.S., the Rolls-Royce in England, and the Citroën DS19 in France. Only, in the old Russia, most people associated the Zil with the KGB. When this car pulled up in the street in front of your apartment, and four men in long leather coats jumped out, you understood that life as you knew it was at an end.

The interior was stiflingly hot. Patti was almost immediately too warm, and she unzipped her jacket.

The driver had gotten out, taken the bags from David, and was placing them in the trunk as David slid in beside her. Voronin pulled down the jump seat facing them and sat down.

Lynsenko closed the door and got in the front passenger seat. A few moments later the driver got in behind the wheel and they headed away from the airport, the windshield wipers going full speed to keep up with the snowstorm.

Nothing felt right to Patti. At this moment she wanted to be anywhere else but here. Voronin had frightened her ever since he'd come to the States to visit, and his friend was hiding something from them. She'd seen it in his eyes when he'd looked at her. It was as if he had been undressing her, and the impression gave her the willies. The man was dangerous, she was sure of it.

"I want to go to the office before the hotel," David told Voronin, as he unbuttoned his overcoat. "And turn down the heat."

Lysenko switched the fan off.

"Thank you," David said.

Patti wanted to tell him to calm down, but if she said anything else at this point he'd probably go ballistic. She knew his moods. All she wanted was to get to the Metropol so that she could take a long hot soak, then have a drink and dinner. They could work out everything in the morning, with clearer heads.

"I want to see the books," David said. "I want to know what you paid for the fertilizer. My connections in Taiwan are exploding."

"If you will share with me your cost for the cell phones," Voronin said. "I have nothing to hide, do you?"

"I also want to know about payroll and expenses," David said.

They'd passed Khimki, but instead of staying on the highway south into downtown Moscow where SovAustralTech's business office was, the driver got onto the outer ring highway that circled Moscow and headed east.

For a minute David wasn't aware that they were no longer heading into the city, but Patti knew that something wasn't right, and a little thrill of fear tickled at the edges of her thoughts, the same as the first moment you lose your balance and begin to fall into the path of an oncoming train.

"Those records have always been available," Voronin said. "We have nothing to hide here. But when I came to visit, you never gave us the chance to get to know each other. Little chats over a beer in the afternoon; the way business partners get to become friends."

The snowstorm was intensifying, but traffic on the major highway was heavy and no one was slowing down. Patti thought it was crazy. Her thoughts were starting to jump all over the place.

David suddenly looked out the window. "Where are we going? We're on the ring highway. This isn't the way to the office." He looked out the window again. "We're not even heading into the city."

Voronin stared at him, but said nothing.

Patti thought that she was caught up in a strange movie where nothing was as it seemed to be. Everything was out of joint, sounds and voices discordant, jangling her nerves.

"What do you think you're doing?" David demanded. He sat forward and punched the driver in the shoulder. "Where are you taking us?"

The driver didn't react.

"What's going on, Aleksei?" Patti asked.

Voronin simply looked at her, his eyes wide behind his glasses.

FOUR
·

Patti didn't know all of David's past, but from what she gathered he was ashamed of his family, his Midwestern working-class roots. "I'm not one to look back," he'd told her three months after they'd started going out.

"Something might be gaining on you?" she'd suggested.

They were in a swank restaurant at the top of the Sofitel Water Tower, with a view of downtown Chicago and the lakefront steaming in the late December weather like a pot of slowly simmering stew. A slight look of irritation momentarily darkened his expression, but then he'd smiled and Patti had melted.

"Nope. I'm thinking about the future. With you."

He took out a ring box and laid it in front of her.

That night, the ring, the proposal—she said yes with no hesitation—the dinner and, afterwards, the suite he'd booked where they made long, slow love were the happiest hours in her life, up to then, and now.

Nothing was ever quite the same again, not her, not David, not life. He was a hard-charger, as bad as her father was, and there never seemed to be much time for each other. They never took normal vacations, though they traveled a lot, mostly to Russia on business deals.

Now this, and Patti was frightened because David wouldn't keep his mouth shut, and Lysenko wouldn't look back, although Aleksei tried his best to get him to calm down.

"This isn't what you think, David," Voronin said.

"You don't know what I think," David shot back angrily. "I want to know what's going on. Where're you taking us?"

He was shouting now, and Patti touched his sleeve. "You're not helping," she said.

"Bullshit," he said, his face so screwed up into a mask of rage that she had to turn away.

They had turned off the ring highway and were traveling down a narrow road that ran through a birch forest that was cold, bleak, and desolate. Snow lay in long drifts, and in the distance she could see what looked like the ruins of an old factory. She had no idea where they were, except that they had to be heading away from Moscow. No other cars were on the road and Patti had the feeling that they'd been transported to another planet, another time. Civilization had never seemed so far away as it did now.

"I want some answers," David shouted.

Patti touched his sleeve again. "Give it a rest, sweetheart."

"Good advice," Voronin said.

Lysenko said something to the driver, who slowed the car and pulled off the pavement to the side of the road. He turned again to David. "Let's go for a little walk. I want to explain something to you. But not in front of your wife. Just the two of us, man-to-man."

"David?" Patti said. This wasn't right.

"Everyone needs to stay calm," Voronin said.

"Good idea," David said. "We need to get some shit straight here." He looked at Patti. "This is long overdue." He opened the door and got out, an icy blast of wind-driven snow instantly cooling down the inside of the car.

Lysenko got out, said something that Patti could not hear, then he and David started up the road, the snow swirling around them in the Zil's headlights.

"What's happening, Aleksei," Patti asked.

"He wants David to calm down. We can't negotiate in good faith this way."

Voronin's voice wasn't right. He'd become hesitant, which wasn't like him.

David and Lysenko had headed into the woods about twenty meters up the road. They disappeared then reappeared in the darkness. Entering a narrow clearing, Lysenko pointed toward something in the distance. David spoke. Patti saw his frozen breath swirl around his head. He was looking toward the factory and the distant woods, his back to the road.

It was getting harder to make out details because of the blowing snow and gathering darkness, but she thought she saw Lysenko pull something from his belt under his sweater.

David started to turn back when Lysenko raised his right hand, and David's head snapped forward violently. She heard the pistol shot an instant later as David fell forward.

"My God," she cried. She scrambled for the door handle but Voronin lunged off the jump seat to stop her.

"Don't be a fool," he shouted.

She lashed out, hitting him on the bridge of his nose with the heel of her hand, blood instantly gushing

down his face and the front of his gray cashmere overcoat. He reared back, clutching his smashed nose with
both hands.

She leaped outside into the searing cold and raced
into the woods, slipping and sliding in the snow, her
open jacket flapping, her heart hammering.

Lysenko turned toward her, a look of indifference
on his dark features.

David's body lay face down, a large halo of red
blood splattered out two or three meters ahead of him.

Patti tried to get to her husband's body, but Lysenko
reached out and almost gently took her by her arm.

Patti attempted the same attack she'd used on Voronin, but Lysenko casually batted her hand away.

Shifting her weight she tried to side-kick his shin, but
again he was too quick for her. It had been too many
years since she'd last competed in Boston and New
York, and too long since she'd studied ballet at her instructor's insistence.

*"You must learn to be nimble. Balance is the key to
winning."*

Putting his Austrian-made Gock-17 semiautomatic
to her head, Lysenko said: "There's nothing you can
do for David."

She could not fully grasp what had happened
here. But David was dead, and that fact burned in her
stomach.

"Your husband was a foolish man. Would you like
to join him?"

Someone would discover David's body and report the
shooting to the police. Even in Moscow some crimes
did get solved, especially crimes against wealthy Americans.

She looked up into Lysenko's lifeless eyes. "Why?"

"You'll see."

"Before this is over with I'll see you in jail or dead." Her voice sounded flat in her ears, the words unreal.

Some flicker of emotion crossed in front of his eyes. Patti couldn't read it, but the man was moved, she could see that much, though he showed no fear whatsoever.

She looked again at poor David, then turned, spat in Lysenko's face, and headed back to the limousine, a million conflicting thoughts snapping off inside her head like fireflies on a summer's evening.

For the very first time since she could remember she wanted to cry, not only for David and the indifferent brutality of his murder, but for all the little bits and pieces that had brought them together three years ago in Chicago, and had finally led them here to this god-forsaken spot.

FIVE

•

When Patti got into the back seat, Voronin was holding a bloody handkerchief to his nose, a bleak look in his eyes. Lysenko got into the car a couple minutes later, said something to the driver, and they pulled back up onto the highway and headed away.

She turned and looked out the window as they passed David's body lying in the snow, alone now in an alien land.

"I'm sorry, Patti, but this should never have happened," Voronin said, his voice hoarse.

"You'd planned it all along," she said dully, amazed at how calm she was. She nodded toward Lysenko.

"You hired that son of a bitch to kill him," she said without emotion.

She didn't know exactly what she was feeling. Horror, grief, loss, she suspected it all would come crashing down on her later tonight, or in the morning, and every morning afterwards when David wasn't there.

Voronin pulled the handkerchief away, the blood from his nostrils just a trickle now. He looked at her, but then shook his head.

Patti tried to pull herself together. She felt that she was on the verge of disintegrating. It wasn't possible for her to accept that David was gone. Just like that, in one instant. Sooner or later she would have to face the fact that he was never coming back, but for now she held on to one thought that was brilliant, sharp, hard, hurtful: David had been murdered, and she was going to make sure that his killers paid with their lives; if it meant sacrificing everything she was or ever wanted to become, she would kill them.

But first she would have to get hold of herself. Play a new role. One that they would accept, until the opening presented itself. She turned again to Voronin. "Now what?"

"Make sure that the same thing doesn't happen to you," Voronin told her.

"How do I do that?"

"Talk with us. Come to an agreement."

"Money's more important than a man's life?"

"Here?" Voronin asked. "Yes."

"It was just business."

"Illegal business, Patti. You have bank accounts in Hong Kong and Sydney, why not a legitimate one in Baltimore?"

"Taxes," Patti said.

"*Da,*" Voronin nodded. "You hide the money to avoid taxes. It is the same for us. It's illegal."

"Not as illegal as murder," Patti said.

"Here the distinction between the two is not so clear. Here is more like your inner cities where boys murder boys for Nikes."

Closing her eyes, Patti could see her father looking across his desk at her in his study at the Boston house, a stern, admonishing expression on his face. He was lecturing her on the responsibilities of family.

"What you do reflects on me, on your mother," he was saying. "Because of who we are, because of our position in society, the public expects—no, demands—a certain level of behavior from us. We must set examples so that others, less fortunate than us, know how to behave."

She was twelve, and even then she thought she could see the flaw in his argument. In school she had read about Mother Teresa, the nun in India who was an example to follow, and it had nothing to do with money, power, or position.

Patti had gotten into trouble fighting with some girls in Grace Academy for Young Women. A strongly worded letter had been sent to her parents that such behavior in the future would result in her expulsion. She suspected that the other girls weren't threatened with dismissal, in part because their parents were even wealthier than hers, but at least in some measure because they had won the fight.

"I expect more from you," her father had told her, but at the time she wasn't quite sure what he'd meant.

A few months later she enrolled in a karate dojo downtown, in secret and with money from her allowance. She would never be beaten again.

They entered the outskirts of a manufacturing town, passing a train station and a few narrow side streets, and came to a two-story brick house behind a tall concrete block wall. The neighborhood was shabby; trash and junk were piled here and there, great mounds of firewood and sawed-up railroad ties alongside nearly every house, a heavy pall of smoke and soot in the air, swirling in dirty clouds around chimneys, icicles hanging from the eaves.

The driver pulled up and honked twice. A couple of minutes later the tall wooden gate swung inward and a woman was there in a faded housedress, tall rubber boots on her feet, a scarf covering her head.

"What is this place?" Patti asked.

"Noginsk," Voronin told her.

Lysenko said something sharp in Russian that Patti didn't quite catch, and Voronin looked away.

They went through the gate and pulled up at the back door of the house, which looked as if it were ready to crumble. Roof tiles were missing, dirty gray stucco covering the concrete block had fallen away in large patches, some of the windows were cracked, and two on the second floor had been boarded over, while a third had been fitted with bars. Snow lay in large dirty piles, and against the back wall, three pit bulls stared out from their doghouses, but strangely did not bark.

Lysenko and the driver got out of the car and went inside, leaving Patti alone with Voronin in the backseat. She thought that she could kill Voronin, steal the car, and get out of here, but the woman in the scarf and boots had already closed the gate. She walked past the car, her shoulders hunched, and went inside.

"We need to go inside now, Patti," Voronin said. "They're waiting for you."

"Then what?"

"Sergey will explain."

"He's not just a friend, then, you're working for him. Is that it?"

"We all are."

Patti got out of the car and, preceding Voronin, went through the back door, down a short hallway, through another door with a beautiful stained glass window, and into a large kitchen, a round table with ten chairs, old fashioned cabinets and shelves and cupboards, and an old crone of a woman using a huge butcher knife to cut potatoes into a pot steaming on an ancient coal-fired range. The babushka looked over her shoulder at Patti and laughed.

The room was terrifically hot and stank of cooked cabbage, urine, and mold, unwashed bodies, and maybe a backed-up toilet.

Lysenko said something to the driver and the woman who'd opened the gate, and they immediately turned and left the kitchen.

"Okay," Patti said, her throat parched from the extreme cold, from the screaming, and now the extreme heat. "What do you want?"

"You'll be told in the morning," Lysenko said. He was maddeningly calm.

"Now!" Patti screeched. She was sick with remorse, her insides roiling, her fear so strong and so close to the surface that it was hard to keep on track.

Lysenko walked over to her, and Voronin stepped aside. "In the morning," he said, an oddly gentle expression in his eyes.

Before Patti could move out of the way or defend herself, Lysenko hit her in the chest, driving her backward against the door, her head slamming against the frame. Spots danced in her eyes from a pain worse than anything she had ever imagined was possible.

She started to drop into a defensive crouch, her hands coming up, but Lysenko kicked her in the stomach, and her legs collapsed out from under her, all her breath gone, sharp daggers spiking into her forehead.

Voronin dragged her across the filthy linoleum floor and she couldn't do anything about it, except look up into his eyes.

"Money?" she croaked.

The old grandmother held open what looked to Patti like a long, narrow trapdoor, a toothless, malevolent grin on her weathered, cracked face.

"You need to cooperate, Patti," Voronin said. "It's the only way you will be able to survive. Trust me." He seemed to be genuinely sad.

"I did, you son of a bitch," she whispered.

Voronin gently rolled Patti through the opening. She fell one meter down to the dirt floor of the near-freezing root cellar, and as the trapdoor was closing over her head, plunging her into absolute darkness, she threw up the lousy food and cheap vodka from the flight, then passed out.

THE SECOND DAY

January 3rd

SIX

•

Patti phased in and out of consciousness for most of the night, huddled in a fetal ball to conserve her body heat and protect her breasts, which were swollen and on fire. Dreams came in flashes, as if a strobe light blinked on to reveal a scene then went out. She saw David at their wedding. She saw her father and mother sitting in the conservatory, having their Sunday morning tea and reading the newspapers. She saw her second husband dying of leukemia in the St. James hospice. She saw David's body in the snow.

She could hear people walking around above in the kitchen, hear muffled voices and the smells of breakfast being cooked. She thought that she might have heard a child's laughter, but then she wasn't so sure.

Someone was at the trapdoor, and suddenly the root cellar was flooded with a blinding light. Patti had to turn away and shade her eyes.

"Dawbruyeh Ootrah," good morning, the old babushka called down, and cackled as if it was the funniest thing she'd ever said.

Squinting, Patti looked up. The trapdoor was still open but the grandmother had disappeared. From where she lay huddled on the dirt floor, Patti could see light streaming through a window between cupboards. It was morning, the sky an intense blue, smoke or fog blowing. It looked very cold.

She managed to push herself to a sitting position, but she had to stop until her head cleared. She wanted to be sick to her stomach again, but there was nothing left to throw up.

The steep wooden ladder had four steps, which she managed one at a time, her head rising above the level of the floor. After the root cellar the kitchen seemed like a blast furnace to her, and she was dizzy and intensely nauseous again. All she could smell was burned grease.

The babushka was at the stove, and three school-age children were seated at the table eating breakfast. The woman who'd opened the gate last night was at the stone sink washing dishes. She looked over her shoulder and spotted Patti half up from the root cellar. She dried her hands on the front of her filthy housedress and came over.

"Let me help you," she said, her English difficult but not impossible to understand.

"Why are you doing this?"

"It's not me," the woman whispered. She took Patti's arm and helped her out of the root cellar to a place at one end of the large table. The children were eating what looked like oatmeal, and they didn't look up.

The woman brought Patti a large mug of hot tea. "Drink this, it will help. My name is Lana."

Patti raised the mug with shaking hands, but when she tried to drink she burned her lip and spilled half the tea on the table, her stomach doing a slow roll.

The babushka was suddenly there, a thick leather razor strop in her hand. She pushed the woman aside and brought the long leather belt down hard on Patti's shoulders, the end cracking like a bullwhip against Patti's left breast.

The old woman raised the strop again, but Patti leaped unsteadily out of the chair, a deep black rage overcoming her. She grabbed the babushka's arm and started to pull it back and around, which would have broken bones, but Lana was there urgently talking in her ear.

"You cannot do this, Mrs. Monroe! They will kill you! Believe me, you have to cooperate!"

Patti turned and looked into Lana's careworn face. It was impossible to guess her age. Maybe twenty-five, maybe forty-five. But she looked used up, tired, frightened.

Slowly Patti turned to the babushka and released her grip. "Don't ever do that again."

The babushka stepped back, and started to raise the strop again, but Lana put her arm around Patti's shoulders and led her out of the kitchen, down a broad corridor to the front hall and a flight of stairs.

"That old woman is crazy," Lana said.

The sudden anger had drained Patti. "They killed my husband."

"Yes, I know. So you have to cooperate, or they will do the same to you. It makes no difference to them."

"Is it just money?" Patti asked as she and the woman started up the stairs.

"Yes, it is very important. You can't imagine how important. Your life is meaningless. It's only money they want."

Patti almost laughed out loud despite the intense pain in her breasts. If they only knew how long she had felt that her life was meaningless, they might have passed her and David by. Her father had been too busy making his fortune to pay her much attention. Nothing she ever did was good enough for him. And her mother, who'd wanted a proper young lady, had been so disappointed she'd left Patti's upbringing to the house staff, none of whom gave a damn. She wasn't enough of a boy for her father, and too much of a tomboy for her mother.

At the head of the stairs, Lana helped Patti down another corridor to a sitting room furnished with a dilapidated couch and a couple of easy chairs facing a large-screen television set on a low table. A very large man with filthy jeans and a thick sweater, dark hair on the backs of his hands, looked up at them with pig eyes. He was drinking vodka and sweating heavily. Patti realized that he was the driver last night.

He said something to Lana in a Russian dialect that Patti couldn't understand, but Lana ignored him, steering Patti through a doorway covered only by a long brown wool blanket into a small bedroom, bars on the only window.

Patti's and David's hanging bags lay in a heap on the floor, but they'd been opened and ransacked.

The only furnishing in the room was a small bed, with one thin blanket over a bare, filthy mattress. The light fixture hanging from the ceiling had no bulb, the plaster walls were dirty and cracked, bare lath showing in some spots, and it was so cold that Patti could see her breath.

This was a prison, she thought all of a sudden, and she was going to die here. She turned to Lana, but another woman pushed aside the blanket and stepped into the bedroom.

"My name is Raya Kiselnikova," the woman said, her Russian accent thick but her English good. "I think you and I can be friends." She smiled.

She was Patti's age or a few years older, not very

tall, with a figure that was nice if a little on the muscular side. She wore dark sneakers, what looked like skintight black Armani jeans, and a khaki shirt with pockets and epaulets, the long sleeves rolled up above her elbows. Her face was round and attractive, but her hair was cropped as short as a man's, and with her smile there was no humor in her dark eyes. She looked to Patti like someone in the military, someone who had killed people and enjoyed it.

"I understand that you aren't sure why you are here," Raya said. "You have been kidnapped, Mrs. Monroe. And until you pay us what we require you will remain here, as our guest."

"I don't have that kind of money," Patti said.

Lana stepped away.

"We think you do."

"I'll show you my bank accounts. A million and a half dollars is impossible."

"Your husband didn't cooperate, so we killed him. Now it's up to you, but this time we want twenty million dollars, U.S."

Patti laughed. "That's impossible."

Raya said something over her shoulder and the large man from the television room came in. Without warning he shoved Patti violently back against the wall, her head banging hard enough against the plaster that she temporarily saw stars, and before she could do anything he pulled a long strip of duct tape from a roll, and taped her wrists behind her back.

"I thought we could be friends," Raya said reasonably.

The big man yanked Patti away from the wall, and held her in a vise grip so that she couldn't move.

Raya pulled a clear plastic bag out of her shirt pocket and all of a sudden Patti understood what was about to happen to her, and she tried to rear back, but she couldn't move.

Raya stepped closer and put the bag over Patti's head, the thin plastic immediately wanting to cling to her mouth and nostrils, making it almost impossible to breathe. The woman wrapped duct tape around her neck, sealing the bag, and all at once she was suffocating, struggling to break free, but it was impossible.

"You have a minute or two now before you pass out," Raya said. "I suggest you use the time to find peace with your maker. This place is the last thing you'll ever see."

Patti tried to scream, but couldn't. She struggled a little longer, spots in front of her eyes, until the big man shoved her aside.

For a seeming eternity she stood in the middle of the room, her hands taped behind her back, looking at Raya and the big man, and Lana at the doorway. She was going to die here, right now, the thought crystallized in her head, as the floor came up in slow motion to hit her face.

SEVEN

•

MVD Sergeant Feodor Bokarev sat on the dilapidated couch in the living room of his apartment nursing a bad cold the Russian way, with hot vodka that had been laced with a lot of pepper.

It was getting late, but the girls were still up and raising hell, while he tried to watch a replay of the German-British soccer finals of last fall. He'd seen the game a half-dozen times but he never got tired of it.

Only this evening his head was splitting, he was running a fever, and every bone in his body ached as if he'd been run over by a truck.

"*Pizdec,*" shit, he swore. "Yana, get the kids to shut up."

His wife came to the kitchen door, wiping her hands on a dish towel. She was his exact opposite: tall, slender, narrow hips, nice ass. She was from St. Petersburg, where her father was a medical doctor.

Feodor on the other hand was a short fireplug of a man, with close-cropped hair that had turned gray last year, before he'd turned forty-one. His father, Vladimir, had worked as a welder in the navy repair yard in Baltisk until he had been killed in an apparent accident five years go. But investigators found out that the accident had probably been staged by a Mafia enforcer because Vlad hadn't been willing to sell tools and materials to the mob, like other workers did to supplement their incomes.

Even for the funeral, the morticians hadn't been able to clean the grime from his hands, so they had put white gloves on him. That picture had stuck in Feodor's mind. His father had given his life for the State, and yet no arrests had been made. In the end all he received were the white gloves. It was the reason Feodor had stuck with the anti-crime unit, sticking it to the Mafia every chance he got.

"How are you feeling, sweetie?" Yana asked. "Do you want something?"

"Get the kids to quiet down, would you?" he asked.

She was instantly sympathetic, and she came over, kissed his cheek, and held a cool hand against his forehead. They'd been married sixteen years and had four children, aged five to eleven, who adored their father. But from the beginning Yana had been an indulgent mother. Noise and disruption never seemed to bother her, and she couldn't understand why, even sick, Feodor was upset. But she loved him.

"You have a fever," she said.

"I know," he said. "Put the kids to bed, please, Yana. Otherwise I'll have to get my gun and shoot them."

She chuckled good-naturedly.

The idle threat was as far as his discipline ever went, and the kids knew that he was as big a pushover as their mother was. The fact that he had been a top sergeant in the army's training base at Sevastopol, and that for the past five years he had worked as assistant to a chief investigator in the Counter Insurgency Directorate of the MVD—which was an offshoot of the old KGB—didn't mean a thing. To his wife and children he was a teddy bear who made them laugh. Tania, his oldest daughter, who had just turned eleven, sometimes called him Spy Smasher, the Russian James Bond from television, which made even him laugh. He had never spanked them. In fact he'd always been afraid to do it lest he hurt them. As gentle as he acted around the house, he was a strong, capable officer who was known for being fearless. There was a lot of respect for him in the gangs around Moscow.

Yana sat down on the arm of the couch. "You don't feel good, I know that," she said. "But something else is bothering you."

He shrugged. He never liked to bring his work home with him. If Yana or the children knew what he had to do sometimes, they would never look at him the same way again. He'd killed men—bad men—and he'd enjoyed it.

"When you picked me up at the airport yesterday I could tell something was going on. What is it, Feodor? Seriously."

Her eyes were very large and chocolate brown, under highly arched eyebrows. He'd fallen in love with her face even before he'd fallen in lust with her perfect body.

He had planned on filing an encounter report this morning, but he'd never gotten to the office. He'd awoken with a fever and chills, and Yana'd insisted that he stay at home, something that he never did. As soon as the children found out that their father was sick and wouldn't be going to work, they insisted that they stay home from school to help take care of him, and he hadn't the heart to say no to them.

He figured that he might have had a better chance of getting well at work than here, but he didn't mind the attention, it was just the noise that got to him.

"You've been brooding all day, like an old milk cow ready to give birth," Yana said, and the girls who'd stopped shouting and had come to the door to listen, suddenly shrieked with laughter.

"Get my gun," he shouted.

The children laughed even louder, but then they trooped in to give their father a kiss goodnight. They were all washed and in their pajamas and in high spirits. Missing a day of school *and* having their father home, even if he was sick, was a rare treat.

"We love you, papa," they each said and quietly went off to bed.

"See, they were afraid that you were about to shoot them," Yana said. She took his glass. "I'll get you another vodka and then you'll tell me what's wrong."

She went into the kitchen and he turned up the television sound a little, as Germany made its final, winning goal, and the crowd in Berlin went wild.

Yana had flown to St. Petersburg for three days to visit her parents and her sister, something she did a

couple times each year. Feodor had gone out to Sheremetyevo to pick her up yesterday afternoon, when he'd
spotted one of their old adversaries, Aleksei Voronin,
and some hard case meeting a pair of American tour-
ists. Voronin had been a pain in the ass for several
years now, but he had connections and he was very
careful. To this point they'd never been able to put a
viable case together based on evidence that they could
bring to the Moscow district prosecutor.

But it had gotten him wondering what a Mafia-
connected guy like Voronin was doing picking up a pair
of Americans.

By rights he should have followed them, but then
Yana had come through the gate, all smiles, and smell-
ing like Prada, which her father gave her each time she
visited, and he forgot until this morning. Voronin was
back in town and up to something. Maybe this time he
would make a mistake.

Yana came back with his hot peppered vodka in a
tea glass with a silver holder. "What's the matter Feodor? Did you see a ghost?"

"We may get lucky and bag one of the bad guys," he
said.

"A spy story?"

"Better than that," Bokarev said. "I have to call the
captain tonight."

"First I want to hear," she said.

He never told her everything, of course, but what he
did confide in her he usually dressed up as a melodrama.
And more often than not the children would be listening just around the corner to one of Papa's stories.

"His name doesn't matter, but he is a bad man who
we've been trying to catch for a long time," Bokarev
began.

EIGHT

•

The uniformed old man at the fashionable Leningrad Apartments, in Moscow's Arbat Street, downtown, opened the glass door for Alexander Kampov, who'd parked his Mercedes C230 at an odd angle on the street and staggered up the walk.

Kampov was drunk, as was usual on most nights, by seven. In the old days, when he drank too much, he'd become everybody's friend, the guy ready to sing a sad Russian folk song and shed a tear with everybody else. But since Nina's death on the operating table at Moscow's Municipal Hospital N4, he'd become a biting, nasty drunk. Not physical, just sarcastic, his comments aimed toward the jugular vein, toward whatever weakness of character he could perceive.

"Good evening, Sir," the doorman said warily. "A cold evening."

"A cold evening for all of us. You go to church. Have you said your bedtime mumbo jumbo yet tonight? Mary Mother of God. Or is it Allah beseech us?"

Kampov didn't wait for an answer; he never did. He lurched across the entry hall to the elevator, which the doorman had thoughtfully brought down, stepped aboard, punched the button for number sixteen, the penthouse floor, and when the door closed, laid his head against the cool metal and closed his eyes.

A pair of Mafia hit men had kidnapped her just before Christmas two years ago. They demanded that Kampov call off an investigation into one of the mob-operated gasoline and diesel fuel distribution scams and she would be returned unharmed. When he did just that, she was dumped in front of this building, but it had been two hours before anyone had noticed her lying semiconscious in the cold. She had been horribly beaten.

January fourth, exactly two years from this night, he'd brought her to the emergency room, but it had taken the doctor four hours to decide that Nina's appendix had ruptured and had to come out. Three hours later he walked out to the waiting room, his gown splattered with blood, to announce that Mrs. Kampov had bled to death on the operating table. No help for it, actually. Wasn't her appendix after all, it was her gall bladder.

Kampov hadn't killed the man, though to this day he wondered why not. But then he'd been in shock. No children, just twenty-three years with a rare woman who made him know love, gone because of a misdiagnosis and a botched operation.

At fifty he had risen to chief investigator in the MVD with the rank of captain, and, because of his attitude, it was as far as he was going to go. It didn't matter that Nina's father had been one of the *Gasprom* multimillionaires and pals with Putin, nor that his own father had been one of the heroes of the Cold War, Captain General Valery Kampov, Deputy Commander of the Soviet Rocket Forces.

All of that was gone, Nina's father in a plane crash, and his own father of cancer two years ago. Nina's kidnappers had never been found. The Moscow Prosecutor General's Office had decided that the case was of too low a priority, which meant money had probably changed hands. All that was left were his nightmares, and French cognac.

A whore's drink, he thought, getting off the elevator,

his leather heels making an empty tapping on the marble floor across the hall to the huge apartment that Nina had furnished from the best stores in Helsinki, Stockholm, and Copenhagen. A whore's drink for the whore he had become, serving a state he no longer believed in.

He tossed the keys on the hall table and crossed to the living room sideboard, where he poured a large cognac from a crystal decanter and, despite the cold, went out onto the balcony that looked toward the Kremlin, all lit up in the night.

Kampov was a tall man for a Great Russian, around six feet, with a good build and a square face. It was marked by childhood smallpox scars, but nonetheless it was interesting and expressive. Nina had said that the window to a man's soul was not in his eyes, but in the symmetry of his face. And his, she'd said, was in perfect balance. It was nonsense, of course, but since she'd believed it, so had he.

He'd been his Army unit's boxing champion, and had gone all the way to division before he'd been knocked out in the first round by a monster from Novosibirsk. He'd been drafted into the GRU, Army intelligence, where he'd worked until the Soviet Union collapsed, when he'd gone over to the MVB, which was a division of the old KGB. His job was catching bad guys inside Russia. Not just spies and Chechen terrorists, but Mafia pricks as well.

Since Nina's death, and especially just in the past year, after Putin had become prime minister and had started to go back to the old ways, Kampov had taken to his work with so much zeal that despite his insubordinate attitude his superiors tolerated him.

He took a sip of his drink, but the liquor suddenly tasted sour to him and he threw the glass as far as he could. It hung in the night air for a long time until it rocketed to the street below. Going back into the apartment he had the vicious hope that the glass had hit some stupid bastard walking along the sidewalk, maybe the doorman out to take a piss in the snowbank.

He turned on the television set to the end of last fall's Germany-UK soccer finals. A rerun of a Bolshoi performance of *Giselle* was coming next. He and Nina had seen it live a few years ago, just before she got kidnapped.

He took off his overcoat, tossed it over a chair, and walked into the bedroom, shedding his suit coat, tie, and shoes. Pulling off his shoulder holster, which held an American-made Wilson Tactical Super Grade 9mm auto-loader with an eight-round magazine, he draped it over the bedpost on his side. It was an expensive weapon that he'd bought for himself and his sergeant. The pistol had good stopping power and a fantastic accuracy and reliability.

He took a long, hot shower, then ice cold, and afterwards put on a Japanese silk kimono, another of Nina's many presents to him, and went into the kitchen, where he opened an Extra Lager 9 beer and made an omelet with onions, which he brought into the living room just as the ballet's overture began.

The telephone rang almost immediately.

He resisted answering, trying to concentrate on the music instead of the noise, but after the third ring he slammed down his beer and picked up the telephone.

"Even if this is a matter of life or death, it's not important enough to be calling me at this hour," he snarled.

"It's me," Bokarev said, his voice nasal because he was sick. "Just get in?"

"Yes. How are you feeling?" Kampov asked. Feodor

was one of only three true friends he had left. Their difference in rank meant nothing to him, though he suspected it meant a lot to Bokarev.

"Like shit. Next question?"

"Why are you calling me this late?"

"I ran into an old friend of ours yesterday afternoon when I was fetching Yana from Sheremetyevo."

Bokarev had been with Kampov for nearly five years, his career stagnating as well. But he wouldn't quit, he wouldn't accept a transfer, and Kampov didn't have the heart to fire him.

"Who's that, Pope John all the way from Vatican City?"

"His brother, Aleksei Voronin."

Kampov's head suddenly cleared as if a bucket of ice water had been tossed on him. They'd been trying to get something on the prick for the past couple of years. But he was slippery, and well connected, always one step ahead of them. He'd dropped out of sight a couple of months ago. "What was he doing out there? Coming or going?"

"Neither, he had some hard case with him—looked ex-military. They met a man and woman—either American or Canadian. I just caught a glimpse of them as they walked past me."

"Why didn't you follow them?"

"I told you, I was out there to pick up Yana. She was visiting her parents again. Anyway Voronin has popped up, this time with the American or Canadian couple, whoever they were. We can check the airline in the morning."

"They won't be the only Americans or Canadians."

"No, but the list will be short. I can check it against hotel records. And once we find them, we might have something we can use to nail Voronin. I'd love to get my mitts on him."

Voronin was suspected of bringing heroin in from Afghanistan, which in itself wasn't such a bad deal in Kampov's estimation. The druggies would get their fixes, one way or another. If the supply were easy there'd be little or no trouble. But Voronin, or some of his scumbag pals out at the clubs, were distributing the shit to schoolkids, some as young as ten or eleven. Feodor was taking it personally, because of his children.

"I'll get somebody on it first thing," Kampov promised.

"Me," Bokarev said. "I'm done malingering."

NINE

•

It was the end of another day in a string of undistinguished days that stretched back more years than Everett Greenwalt wanted to count. He closed and locked his wall safe and shut down his computer. As FBI assistant director in charge of counterintelligence, he rated a secretary and a corner office on the fourth floor of the J. Edgar Hoover Building, but that's all he'd ever get. His career was at a dead end.

His secretary, Mrs. Tuttle, came to the door. "Will there be anything else before I go, Mr. Greenwalt?"

"No, I'm just locking up. Do you have tomorrow's itinerary?"

"It's in your computer, Sir."

Greenwalt didn't let his momentary irritation show. Control was everything; it's what separated man from the beasts, he was fond of reminding his subordinates. He was fifty-three years old, husky, somewhat barrel-chested, but self-assured and well-groomed—handsome in a Washington insider sort of way. He wore British-tailored three-piece suits winter or summer, made in a small shop on Saville Row—he'd been stationed in London as an FBI liaison officer to the embassy, and had picked up some British mannerisms. His haircuts cost $200, his shoes were handmade in Italy, and he drove a new Mercedes Benz E class every year. He and his wife Margaret and their three teenage girls lived comfortably in Alexandria, but they had no savings, no stocks or bonds, just a good life while it lasted.

"While it lasted," he muttered to himself.

"Sir?" his secretary, still at the door, asked.

"Print me a hard copy, would you please?"

Mrs. Tuttle was an older woman, but she had embraced the computer age, while her boss apparently had not. It gave him a sense of amusement to know how she felt, and to know that she had no real idea who or what he was, just how connected he was with all the new technologies that the FBI employed.

"Yes, sir," she said, and she went back to her desk in the outer office to reboot her computer.

Greenwalt snugged up his tie, and got his dove gray worsted wool suit coat, which had a tastefully subtle pinstripe, from the closet and put it on. He'd been accused behind his back of being incapable of thinking out of the box. It's why, it was said, that he would never rise any farther, though in the early days he had pictured himself as deputy director of the agency. The number one man was a political appointee, while his deputy director was the top cop. With a criminal justice degree from Harvard plus advanced studies in criminal psychology and law enforcement administration, Greenwalt knew that he was well qualified for the job.

Except for a long string of rotten luck, or actually ten years of bland luck, nothing had ever gone wrong for him, nor had anything ever gone spectacularly right. His misfortune, he thought, was that no big case had ever landed on his desk. At no time during his twenty-year career with the Agency had the need to think out of the box come his way.

Not even during 9/11 and the aftermath. He'd been stationed as SAC (Special Agent in Charge) of all Bureau operations in the Western District—California to Colorado—while SACs from Minneapolis east had been on the firing line where careers could be made.

After the post-9/11 fallout, a lot of heads rolled, but Greenwalt, considered to be a steady hand, had been promoted and brought to Washington.

He made sure that his desk was clear, got his attaché case, and went out to Mrs. Tuttle's desk where his schedule for tomorrow was coming out of the printer. He was speaking at a Rotary Club downtown for breakfast, and then having an informal lunch on the Hill with Senators Brown and Tomlansin, both on the Intelligence Oversight Committee. In the afternoon he had several appointments, including one out at the CIA around three. His schedule would be tight, but manageable.

The telephone rang as Mrs. Tuttle was retrieving the schedule from the printer tray. She handed it to Greenwalt and answered the phone.

"Mr. Greenwalt's office," she said. "One moment, I'll see if he's left for the day." She pressed the mute button. "It's Mr. Donagle, downstairs on the Russian desk. He's been trying to reach you all day."

"About what?" Greenwalt asked, his interest piqued.

"He didn't say. Shall I have him call tomorrow?"

"I'll take it now," Greenwalt said, and he took the phone from her. With the way Putin had been acting these days, and with an increased Russian presence up at the UN and down here at their embassy, he'd been taking a particular interest in what the Russian desk was producing. He vaguely knew Bob Donagle as a newly minted Yale grad with a lot of ambition. The Bureau was interested in kids like Donagle, who were the next generation of up and comers.

"Bob, Ev Greenwalt. I was just on my way out. Do you have something for me?"

"Not exactly, Sir," Donagle said. "It's about Dick Ligget." Ligget was the Bureau's liaison to the U.S. embassy in Moscow. The post had been set up in the nineties when an Australian woman and her husband had been kidnapped and held for ransom. They had friends in the U.S. who'd contacted the FBI as soon as the woman and her husband had gone missing, and the Bureau had been dragged into cooperating with Russian law enforcement to find them. The case had turned out with a happy ending, and the Bureau had a special agent stationed over there ever since. Curiously, the one-man operation had fallen under the office of counterintelligence.

"Something going on over there that I should know about?"

"No, Sir. Mr. Ligget is due to rotate in two months, and I was just wondering if a replacement had been named."

"I'm not following you," Greenwalt said.

"I'd like the job, Sir."

Greenwalt's spirits fell. He wanted to snap at the

kid, but he held his disappointment and anger in check. It was about control, after all. "That'll be up to the director of personnel."

"Yes, Sir, I know. I just thought that since we'd worked together for the past year, that you might put in a good word for me."

"Sure," Greenwalt said after a beat. "I'll see what I can do."

THE THIRD DAY

January 4th

TEN

•

It was very early when Patti awoke, with a start, not understanding where she was or what exactly had happened to her, except that she was in pain. Her breasts hurt beyond anything she'd ever imagined, and her lungs and throat were raw, as if she had inhaled fire.

She was fully clothed, lying on the filthy mattress, the thin blanket covering her. She turned her head a few inches to the left so that she could see the window. The sky was turning a dull gray with the coming dawn, but not enough light filtered through for her to make out much detail in the bedroom, except for the outlines of the door and the dark blanket covering it.

Someone just outside in the sitting room shuffled their feet, and Patti was instantly alert. The slight noise had awoken her from a horrible nightmare in which she had been suffocating. Strong hands were holding her shoulders, and then gentler hands were doing something at her neck; tearing something away from her skin, blinding flashes of light popping off in her head, screams trapped in her throat.

It was the most horrible dream Patti could ever remember, and the worst part was that she was beginning to think it hadn't been a dream after all.

A woman had been there, and the gross, hairy man

from the sitting room had been holding her arms behind her back.

Everything came back to her in a terrible rush: the plastic bag, the tape, the struggle to breathe, the feeling of utter helplessness. She'd had the nightmare because she knew she was dying and there wasn't a thing she could do to save herself. The woman hadn't even given her the chance to plead for her life.

It also came to her in stages that she had a foul taste in her mouth, that she was terribly thirsty, that she was hungry, and that she had to use the toilet.

The blanket was pushed aside and the gross man who'd taped her wrists behind her back loomed in the doorway. He had a terrifically foul body odor that she could smell all the way across the room.

"What do you want?" Patti asked. She thought she'd said it loudly, but her voice was only a hoarse whisper in her ear.

"You know," the man said in Russian. He staggered the rest of the way into the bedroom, letting the blanket fall back behind him. He was drunk and swayed on his feet.

"Go away, or I'll call for help."

He laughed, and Patti could smell the raw odors of vodka combined with the sickening stench of rotten teeth and bad sinuses mixed with onion and garlic.

She managed to sit up, every movement extremely painful. Her face hurt, and she vaguely remembered falling to the floor as she passed out. But that seemed like days ago.

The man came around to the side of the bed. He was much larger than David, thicker in the chest and broader across the shoulders. His dark hair was long and matted, as was his beard. Several of his front teeth were missing and the few that remained were black. He was the grossest man Patti had ever seen.

She held out a hand to ward him off, but he batted it away, and shoved her back down, her head banging against the wall.

This is not happening, she thought. Yet she knew that it was. But she was slow to respond. Her arms and legs were mired in glue, her brain shrouded in fog.

"You bastard," she croaked hoarsely.

"They're going to kill you," the man said. He yanked the blanket away, then pulled her legs apart and braced a knee between them.

Patti scratched at his eyes but he turned his head and her slender fingers got tangled in his thick beard.

He pulled her hand away, and with his other pawed her breasts, the incredible pain nearly causing her to pass out. She saw spots in front of her eyes, and her stomach flopped over, causing her to wretch up bitter bile in the back of her throat.

Then he was pulling at her jeans, trying to undo the button at the waist. The bastard was going to rape her and she couldn't do a thing to stop him. He was huge, and incredibly strong, and she had no strength.

She tried to back away, but he grabbed her legs, roughly pulled her body toward him, and ripped at her jeans. She could feel his gross erection pressing against her thigh.

"No," she screamed. "You son of a bitch, no!"

She got both hands free and shoved against his chest, but it was like trying to move a brick wall, and his hands were all over her, pulling her closer, pawing at her breasts, tearing at the waistband of her jeans.

He grabbed a handful of her hair, forced her head back, and tried to kiss her, while grabbing at her crotch. She bit his lower lip, grinding her teeth against his soft flesh with all of her strength.

Suddenly she was gagging on a mouthful of blood.

The man reared back with a howl, blood gushing down his chin. He pulled his right fist back and was about to smash it into her face, when the old babushka was there with a long, thick rope, whipping it into his back and his head, the end of the rope snapping with a crack like a bullwhip around his neck and into his face, raising instant welts.

He pushed himself away from Patti, and protecting himself as best he could with upraised arms, scrambled away from the bed, past the grandmother and out the door.

Patti could hear him screaming and swearing down the hall and crashing down the stairs.

The babushka stood at the doorway. The rope she had used to beat off Patti's attacker was tied into a hangman's noose, and it hung loosely now from her left hand, dangling as if it were ready to be placed around someone's neck.

"Soon," the grandmother said in English.

Patti could do nothing more than stare at the old woman. Everything here in the dacha—the place, the people, the circumstances—was surreal. Nothing made any sense. If they meant to kill her, how did they expect to collect money from her?

She pulled the blanket up around her neck and closed her eyes for what she thought would be just a moment.

ELEVEN

•

When she woke up the sky was considerably lighter, and Lana was perched on the edge of the bed looking down at her.

"Easy," the Russian woman said, laying a hand on Patti's shoulders. "He won't try again."

Patti tried to breathe shallowly through her mouth. The horrible stench was still in the room, and all over her clothes, in her hair, and in her skin. "Who is he?"

"He is Boris. My husband."

"My God."

"He's done it before, to others, and to me. But not with you again. Sergey will kill him if he tries, and he knows it."

Patti tried to digest what she was being told. Voronin thought that she was rich because of the house in Baltimore and probably because he'd done some research and found out about her parents. They'd murdered David because he had no money, but they evidently didn't know that her father had cut her off.

They were demanding something from her that she didn't have, but she didn't think they would believe her if she tried to tell them. It was up to her to survive, and somehow escape, as impossible as that seemed.

"I'm hungry," she said. "Could I have something to eat? At least some water?"

Lana glanced over her shoulder at the doorway. She was frightened and it showed on her face. "Later this morning. I think they're all going into the city."

"I have to go to the bathroom."

"The pipes are frozen last night."

"But I have to use the toilet, for God's sake," Patti whispered urgently.

"It'll have to be outside, like everyone else," Lana said. "But we must hurry. They won't like it if you leave this room."

Patti wanted to object, but she could no longer hold it. She threw the blanket aside and Lana helped her to her feet. For a moment or two Patti couldn't get her balance; the room was tilting at odd angles and she wanted to throw up.

Lana waited patiently, until Patti nodded and said, "I'm okay now," and led her around the bed, through the blanket covering the door, and down the hall to the stairs.

People were talking in the kitchen, and it sounded like they were arguing, but Patti couldn't make out the words, only the tone.

She had to take it one step at a time. Her breasts hurt so badly that each movement sent waves of pain shooting from her chest through her shoulders and all the way down to her hips and her thighs. She knew that she would have to take off her shirt and her bra to see what damage had been done to her body, but she was afraid of what she was going to find. A friend in college had developed cancer from what she figured were injuries she'd suffered on the woman's basketball team. Within three months of the diagnosis she'd had a double mastectomy and six weeks later she was dead.

Patti didn't think she'd ever been so frightened as she was at this moment.

She wanted someone to love her. She wanted children. She wanted someone to be there for her just as she would be there for him, not like her parents who'd treated her practically as a zero. She'd been little more than an irritant to them, a thing they had to tolerate until it matured enough to move out on its own.

She wanted more than that.

But here and now she was on her own, and her survival depended on how strong she could be.

In the kitchen, the grandmother was stirring something in a large pot on the stove, but whoever she'd been talking to was gone.

At the outside door in the chilly back hall, Patti realized that she was barefoot, but she couldn't wait any longer. She tore open the door and stepped outside onto the icy concrete step, and reared back with the incredible cold. It was well below zero and her feet began to ache almost instantly.

"You must hurry," Lana said behind her.

Patti turned to her. "Could I have some toilet paper?"

"There is none, but I'll bring you something to wash up with later. Please, you must hurry, Mrs. Monroe. It's important."

Patti turned away. "You fucking people are animals," she muttered, and she stepped down to the snow-covered frozen ground and walked a couple of meters to the right.

The three pit bulls huddled in their doghouses looked out at her. Somewhere in the far distance she thought she could hear a train whistle, but she wasn't sure. There was no smell out here, only the incredible cold that bit at her nostrils and made her eyes tear up. She had no feeling in her feet.

She no longer had any choice. Undoing her jeans she pulled them and her panties down around her ankles, squatted down and relieved herself in a rush. She wanted it to be over with as quickly as possible, but she had a bout of strong cramps that made her sick to her stomach again.

It seemed forever to her before she was finished and was able to pull up her panties and jeans, acutely conscious that she was dirty, and was soiling her clothes.

She stepped away from the mess and looked back at the house. Raya, the woman who had taped the plastic bag around her head, stood at an upstairs window watching her.

"Come in the house now," Lana called from the back door.

Patti raised her right hand toward Raya and extended her middle finger. "Fuck you, bitch," she mouthed the words.

Raya laughed, then was gone.

TWELVE

•

Patti slept for what seemed like a couple of hours, but when she awoke the sky in the window was nearly dark. She vaguely remembered coming inside the house and climbing the stairs, but with the memory she felt filthy, as if she would never be clean again.

Someone brushed aside the blanket at the doorway, and Patti sat up as Lana came into the bedroom. She was carrying a steaming bucket of hot water and a couple of rags, which she put down at the foot of the bed.

"They're back, so be very quiet," she said. "I think there are still some clean clothes in your suitcase."

Before Patti could say anything, Lana turned and left the room.

It was a struggle for her to get out of bed and hobble to her suitcase, which was lying partially open on the floor. Her feet felt like slabs of raw meat, and she was frightened by how weak she felt.

She had to get down on her hands and knees to rummage through her suitcase. But she finally found one clean pair of panties, the old fleece warm-up pants she used for exercises, and a pair of socks. But her dress shoes, her leather boots, and her Nikes were gone.

David's suitcase was in the corner, and it, too, had been rifled, but she had no desire to look through it. She couldn't accept that he was dead, even though a clear picture of his body lying beside the road was burned deeply into her head.

She stripped off her jeans and filthy panties, rolled them in a bundle, zippered them into a pocket in her suitcase, and slowly washed herself with one of the thick rags, saving the other to dry off with. The water was very hot and she had to be careful not to burn herself, but when she was finished and dressed she felt an almost overwhelming sense of well-being, no matter how crazy it seemed in her mind.

She had overcome the first major hurdle; she had survived for three days.

Lana came back about fifteen minutes later with a greasy dish towel, in which something was wrapped, and a large glass of scalding hot black tea. She laid the bundle on the end of the bed, set the mug on the floor, and without a word picked up the bucket and rags and slipped out of the room.

She had brought a small chunk of stale black bread, a piece of white hard cheese, and a piece of cold, greasy kielbasa.

Patti ate the first food she'd had since the flight from

Frankfurt, and although she wanted to throw up afterwards, she nursed the tea for a long time until her stomach settled down and she was able to crawl back in bed, pull the blanket up over her shoulders, and fall into a sleep in which she repeatedly saw the bullet entering the back of David's head, and his body pitching forward into the snow in a spray of blood.

That dream morphed into one in which she was telling her instuctor that she was through with karate. He kept screaming that she was throwing away an opportunity to go to the Olympics, that she was turning her back on him and all the hard work and time he'd invested in her.

Two failures, she'd thought, waking in a cold sweat: David, because she felt that it was her fault he had been murdered, and her martial arts instructor, because she had let him down in more ways than one.

THE FOURTH DAY

January 5th

THIRTEEN

•

Sergeant Bokarev was driving the department's beat-up Lada, Kampov riding shotgun, as they pulled up behind a Moscow District Militia Evidence van and parked at the side of the snow-covered highway outside of Moscow. A half-dozen Militia radio units, and one unmarked car, plus an ambulance lined either side of the road. A dozen officers, forensics technicians, a photographer, and one plainclothes officer stood around something lying in the woods about thirty meters off the road surface.

It was a little after nine-thirty in the morning, and when Kampov got out of the car an arctic blast of cold air caught him full in the face, taking his breath away.

"Bracing," Bokarev said, coming around the car. "Makes me feel almost human."

Kampov just looked at him.

"I still have a fever. I need to cool off."

They headed down the line of vans and cars, then off the road where the other cops were gathered. Bokarev had made a couple of calls this morning to see what he could dig up about the pair of Americans, when one of his contacts suggested he might give Militia a call. Apparently the body of a foreigner had been found on a narrow highway that followed the railroad line and paralleled the main M7 motorway to the east toward Noginsk, Petushki, and Vladimir.

"Maybe it's this American guy you're looking for," Nikolai Maksimov had told him. Maksimov was a small-time errand boy for a number of clubs west of town out around the Dynamo Stadium. He kept his eyes and ears open and sometimes heard things that were worthwhile. He and Bokarev had a long-term understanding.

"It's worth a try anyway," Bokarev had suggested when Kampov had shown up at the office. "Looks like you can use the fresh air."

"Would you recognize him from the airport?" Kampov had asked.

"I won't know until I see the body."

Kampov smiled indulgently. Sometimes his sergeant could be a little obtuse. "Well then, let's take a look." Bagging Voronin was worth a trip into the cold.

They trudged over to the officers, who were standing around a body lying face down in the cold. When the officer in civilian clothes looked up his face fell. He was tall, with blond hair, blue eyes, and a pretty-boy face. His name was Ivan Zamyatin, and he was a chief investigator with Moscow Militia.

"Well, what brings Captain Kampov and Sergeant Bokarev out to my crime scene this morning?" he asked caustically.

"We were just passing by and saw the disturbance," Kampov said pleasantly. He'd had a couple of run-ins with the Militia cop and there was no love lost between them. "Who is he?"

"An American, I'm guessing, from his clothing," Zamyatin said. "Shot once in the back of the head, as you can see. No ID, but we found this in his coat pocket." He held up a clear plastic bag of white powder. "I'm betting it's cocaine."

Bokarev took the bag from him, opened it, dipped a finger in the powder and brought it to his lips. He nodded. "Some good shit. High class." He gave the bag back.

"Worth ten thousand Euros," Zamyatin said. "Is MVD interested in drug smugglers? Do you want to take this case off my hands?"

"Why should I?" Kampov asked. "Is there something else that I should know?"

"You tell me. I'm just a humble Militia lieutenant colonel, while you're an MVD captain."

Kampov felt like shit. He'd drunk too much cognac last night and had not slept worth a damn. Zamyatin was holding something back and he didn't like it. He wanted to take the man's head off, but he held himself in check. "Curious work in the morning in the snow, like this, for a humble Militia lieutenant colonel."

"We all have our jobs to do."

"Yes. In a spirit of cooperation—"

Zamyatin laughed. He stepped closer. "When the fuck did MVD ever cooperate with Militia?" he demanded. A couple of his men looked over, curious how the situation would turn out. "Do you want this case? It's yours."

Bokarev was watching, too, a slight smile at the corners of his lips.

"Have the body turned over please," Kampov said reasonably.

"Are you taking over this investigation?" Zamyatin pressed.

"If you please, Colonel," Kampov said. He could feel his self-control slipping.

Zamyatin wanted to argue, but he motioned for his men to go ahead.

Two of them took hold of the dead man's shoulders and outstretched arm and pulled the corpse over on its back. It was stiff and unyielding, and when it had been turned over its arm pointed toward the ruins of an abandoned factory on the hill in the distance. Much of the face around the bridge of the nose had been destroyed when the bullet had exited the skull.

Bokarev sucked his breath and moved back a step.

"Do you know this man?" Zamyatin asked.

Bokarev took a moment, but then he shook his head. "Never saw him before in my life, Sir."

"You do know him. I saw your reaction."

"No, Sir. I don't like blood, that's all."

But Bokarev had recognized the dead man; Kampov had seen it on his face. The American meeting Voronin at Sheremetyevo? The wind suddenly didn't seem so cold. If this was the same man, they had a real shot at putting a serious dent in the Mafia's heroin pipeline, and that had value.

The American had been handsome, but his open eyes had turned milky, and that, with his ivory white complexion, made him look like a Greek statue. Blood from the massive wound had created a big stain in the snow, some of which had frozen to the sides of his head like a halo. He'd lived long enough to bleed out. Probably unconscious and without pain from the moment the bullet had crashed into his brain, but not dead. Kampov had the morbid curiosity to wonder if the man had dreamed while he lay dying. And he also wondered if his wife, the woman Bokarev had seen with him at the airport, had witnessed her husband's execution.

Zamyatin was watching him and Bokarev, waiting for some reaction.

"MVD is taking over this case as of now," Kampov said, looking up. "This man is obviously part of a heroin-cocaine smuggling ring we've been investigating for eighteen months. If he's who we think he is, he's an American mercenary working out of Afghanistan."

"Then you do know him."

"No," Kampov said. "We know his Mafia associates here in Moscow, and we've been expecting someone like him to show up sooner or later. And he has, and so the case is ours."

Zamyatin wanted to argue, but Kampov cut him off.

"MVD thanks Moscow Militia for its timely response and professional processing of the crime scene."

"Yeah," Zamyatin said. "And fuck you, too, Captain." He turned back to his men and raised his voice. "This case belongs to MVD. You may all leave, thank you."

"Any evidence you have uncovered will be sent to my office without delay," Kampov told Zamyatin.

"Of course," the Militia lieutenant colonel said as he stalked off.

"Where do you want him taken?" Bokarev asked.

"N4," Kampov said. "I think they're best at handling dead bodies."

FOURTEEN

•

Moscow's Municipal Hospital N4, on Pavlovskaya Ulitsa, was housed in a dreary yellow brick pile of a building that had been constructed shortly after World War One. Nina had died here, and returning with the body of an American shot in the head, execution style, brought back a lot of horrible feelings for Kampov.

Bokarev had dropped him off at the emergency room entrance just behind the ambulance. "It's the same guy with the woman I saw meeting Voronin at Sheremetyevo," he'd said. "I know damn well it is. Same build, same coat."

"I'll stay here. Soon as you find out who they were, come back for me."

Bokarev had driven off and Kampov had escorted the dead man downstairs to the morgue and pathology labs.

The body had lain at the side of the road for at least a night, a full day, and a second night, with temperatures that had never gotten above zero Fahrenheit, and had frozen solid to the core.

The chief pathologist, Dr. Nikolai Travin, breezed in a few minutes before noon, all out of breath and flustered. He was a narrow-shouldered little man, with movements like a ferret's, dark eyes, and thick black hair that was combed straight back. "Why is State Security in such a rush?" he demanded. "The poor man is dead, he can wait."

Kampov held out his red identification booklet. "But State Security cannot wait."

Travin had been the doctor who'd performed the autopsy on Nina, declaring that her death on the operating table had been inevitable, given her circumstances. According to him, no doctor on earth could have saved her. He'd been covering for one of his own, of course, and at the time Kampov had still been in too much shock to do anything to the man.

Coming back now like this was not only a necessary bit of police work—the body had to be identified—but was also a test of his own self-control.

If Travin recognized the name, he gave no indication. "The body is frozen, Captain. It'll be at least forty-eight hours, probably longer, before we can begin." He started to turn away.

"A bullet to the back of the head killed the man," Kampov said. "I don't need an autopsy to learn that."

"Then why did you bring it here? What do you want?"

"The victim's body had been stripped of its identification. I need to know if he was a Russian, or perhaps a foreigner. It would give our investigation a head start."

The pathology room was large, all white tile on the floor and walls, with three stainless steel tables lined up side-by-side, rollabout carts with drawers holding surgical instruments beside each. A white sheet had been draped over the body, after its clothing had been cut away and laid out on a larger cart that had been wheeled over.

Dr. Travin picked up the sodden sport coat and studied the label. "Nice goods," he said. "Durkin's on Saville Row. Your man's British. Well off."

"His clothing is British; I don't think he was."

"Then you already know."

"I have a guess. I would like you to confirm it."

Dr. Travin wanted to argue. But he thought better of it and shook his head. He pulled the sheet off the body with a flourish, then reached up and turned on the overhead operating theater light. He pulled a microphone dangling from a ceiling fixture a little closer and flipped the switch.

"Concerning Caucasian male cadaver, no identification, delivered five January for initial evaluation and autopsy as soon as feasible. Pathologist N. Travin, M.D. Initial findings."

He reached up, switched the mike off, and turned back to Kampov. "Who killed him? KGB?"

"There is no KGB," Kampov said.

Dr. Travin waited.

"We think it was Mafia. A drug deal gone bad."

"They should be allowed to kill each other. Save us the trouble."

"I agree. But I need to know about this man."

Dr. Travin looked again at the body. "He's circumcised, so he's probably Jewish or North American or both. Nice appendix scar, maybe German, but not Japanese, and definitely not one of ours."

The body's jaw had gone slack in death, and it was frozen open. Dr. Travin got a large magnifying glass from the surgical cart and examined the cadaver's mouth. "First class dental work. Not European."

He spotted something in the body's nostrils then examined the insides of the ears and the hairline at the forehead and at the sideburns, before he straightened up and put the magnifying glass down.

"Yes?" Kampov asked. He was becoming aware of a faintly unpleasant odor, and he tried to ignore it. When he'd kissed Nina's body good-bye before her cremation, she'd been dead for three days. It was the same smell.

"He's an American."

"Can you be sure?"

"No," Dr. Travin said. "But the hairs in his nostrils and ears have been trimmed, and he recently got what I would guess is an expensive haircut. The only men I know who are that vain are Americans. Do you cut your nose hairs, Captain?"

"No," Kampov said. "I want a complete autopsy report as soon as possible."

"You said you knew what killed him."

"As soon as possible," Kampov repeated.

"Seventy-two hours, Captain," Dr. Travin said. He covered the body, switched off the overhead light, and left the room.

Kampov stood rooted to his spot for a minute or two. He was aware of the normal hospital sounds outside the swinging doors: machinery, telephones, people talking, a siren approaching the emergency room driveway. But nobody was making noises in this room, and he was brought back two years. He'd become intimate with death since Nina, and he didn't care for it.

· · ·

As Kampov was getting off the elevator from pathology, Sergeant Bokarev was coming through the emergency room door from the driveway, a big grin on his face. He was flushed with fever, but he had the bit in his teeth and wasn't about to back down.

"You look like shit," Kampov told him.

"That's probably why I feel like shit. So ask me what I found out."

"You got a name?"

"You're damned right. David and Patricia Monroe. Americans from Baltimore—that's in the States."

"Maryland," Kampov said.

Bokarev got a funny look on his face. "How did you know?"

"Lucky guess," Kampov said. "What else?"

"They came here on business. The customs agent remembered them because the guy was a major prick, but the woman seemed reasonable. Militia faxed me copies of their customs declarations, visa stamps, and the front pages of their passports. Same faces. It's them!"

Outside, they got in the car, Bokarev behind the wheel, and he handed Kampov the faxes.

The passport photo of David Monroe was a good match with the body Militia had found lying beside the road, at least as much of the face as was still recognizable. And the other passport photo, presumably of his wife, showed a good-looking woman with fine features. She was staring at the camera with a hint of amusement at the corners of her lips, as if everything was a joke to her. In that, at least, she reminded him of Nina.

"Well, we know what became of David Monroe," Bokarev said as he pulled away from the hospital, merged with traffic, and headed back to the office.

"*Da*," Kampov said. "So where is Mrs. Monroe?"

FIFTEEN

•

The U.S. Embassy is housed in a new ultramodern glass and concrete building on Novinskiy Boulevard, and as always the building was guarded from without by Militia troops in uniform and from within by U.S. Marines, also in uniform.

Traffic was heavy when Kampov parked his car and, carrying a plain manila envelope, dodged his way across the street. He held up his identification booklet for the Militia boys, and for the FSB men waiting in a parked Volga, and approached the Marine sentries at Post One—the main gate.

A young Marine sergeant stiffened. "Yes, Sir," he said.

"I want to see Dick Ligget."

"Yes, Sir, do you have an appointment?"

"No."

"I'll let him know that you're here, Sir," the young man whose nametag read JOHNSON said. He stepped into the glass booth and used the telephone, while the other Marine, whose nametag read ALVAREZ, stood his ground.

Russians who wanted visa applications, or who came to the embassy for a tour, entered through a different door. This post was for embassy staff or Russian officials with business here.

Johnson came back out. "Mr. Ligget is on the way down, Sir. You may wait inside."

Kampov pocketed his ID and went inside. He'd not been to this building, which had opened in 2000, and just through the doors he was faced with a lot of glass walls, a soaring ceiling, and an ultramodern arching staircase. American art, including blown glass figures, decorated the lobby that just now wasn't very busy. A young woman seated behind the receptionist desk gave him a smile. The place was too modern for him.

FBI Special Agent Richard Ligget, the Bureau's liaison to the U.S. Embassy, bounded down the stairs two at a time. He was a youthful-looking man, in a dark suit, crisp white shirt, correctly knotted club tie, his hair cropped short. He was all false smiles.

Kampov recognized him from file photographs. "Mr. Ligget, I thought it was time we met. I'm Chief Investigator Alexander Kampov, MVD."

"Yes, of course," Ligget said, shaking hands. "High time."

"May we go to your office?"

"Is this a business call? Official business?"

"I'm afraid it is," Kampov said. "It's about an American couple, and I'm bringing bad news for which I need your help."

Ligget looked like he wanted to bolt back up the stairs. Kampov had never met the man, but the brief file he'd seen didn't give the FBI's Moscow operation very high marks. Ligget had been here nearly three years and was due to rotate home in a few months. During that time he'd done nothing. In fact, the only notation in the file was about his wife, who'd returned to the states after less than three months here. En clair telephone intercepts had picked up only a few calls from her in all that time. Not a very happy marriage, Kampov thought.

"You'd better tell me everything," Ligget said, and he motioned Kampov to follow him upstairs.

Ligget's small office was on the second floor at the back of the embassy. He had no secretary, though there was a desk for one, nor was there much of anything on the walls except for framed photographs of the president, the secretary of state, the ambassador, and the director of the FBI. Besides the desk and a couple of chairs, the only other furniture was a file cabinet equipped with a steel bar and a combination lock.

Kampov sat down across from him and laid the manila envelope on the edge of the desk. Ligget made no move to reach for it.

"Is what you've brought me serious enough to involve the Bureau?"

"Yes," Kampov said. "Their names are David and Patricia Monroe, from Baltimore, apparently here to do some business. At least that's what they told our customs and immigration officers at Sheremetyevo four days ago."

"I see. Are they in trouble? Have they been arrested?"

"Mr. Monroe's body was found this morning beside a highway out in the country a few kilometers east of here," Kampov said. "He'd been shot once in the back of the head, execution style, and his body stripped of any identification, though money in his pocket had not been taken, so it wasn't a robbery."

Ligget glanced at the envelope. "How did you identify the body?"

"My sergeant happened to be at the airport and spotted the Monroes coming through customs, and when he got a look at the body he recognized it. We got copies of their passports and customs declarations."

"Do you have a suspect?"

"No," Kampov said. Either the man was an idiot or he was dancing around the central question for some reason. "But we think that whoever killed him was involved with his business dealings. It's where we'd like your help."

"I see," Ligget said. "What did you have in mind?"

"We'd like you to request your headquarters in Washington to do background checks on the Monroes. It would help our investigation to know exactly what sort of business they were involved in."

Ligget had placed both hands on the desk as if he expected it to fly away and was holding it down, or he was holding himself from falling over. His fingernails were perfectly manicured, and Kampov thought that they might even have been coated with a clear nail polish.

"We couldn't share such files with a foreign government," he said. "You can understand this."

"You're here as a liaison, aren't you?"

"Technically, yes. If you'll just give me Mr. Monroe's file, I'll look it over, and—" Ligget stopped in midsentence. "You didn't say anything about Mrs. Monroe."

"You didn't ask. But her husband's body was the only one the Militia found. It's possible she was also murdered and her body dumped elsewhere for some reason. But it's also possible that she is being held for ransom."

"By whom?"

"That's why I've come for your help," Kampov said. "We need to know what business they were involved with."

"Surely you know something. You must have some idea."

"We couldn't share files on one of our citizens with a foreign government; you understand how it is," Kampov said. He shoved the manila envelope across the desk. "Here are copies of their arrival paperwork along with photographs of the body and the preliminary Militia and autopsy reports. I'll have more for you in a couple of days. Mr. Monroe's body was frozen solid. It has to be thawed out before a proper autopsy can be performed."

"I want the body transferred here today," Ligget said.

"When my investigation is completed," Kampov said, and he got to his feet. "If the Bureau will cooperate with me—if you will liaise—that will be sooner rather than later." He took a business card out of his pocket and laid it on the desk. "I'll wait for your call, Mr. Ligget."

SIXTEEN

•

Back at his office, Kampov found Bokarev hunched over a steaming glass of tea from the commissary, a towel draped over his head so he could inhale the fumes. The room smelled strongly of alcohol.

"Why don't you go home," Kampov said, hanging up his coat. "You're not doing any good here. And if Yana thinks that I've ordered you to keep working she'll come after me with your pistol, and rightly so."

Bokarev looked up bleary-eyed. "If I stay home, the kids will stay home. And if they stay home their grades will suffer, and it will be on my shoulders. No matter what, neither of us can win. Anyway, I have Yana's Cuban cold remedy and I feel better already."

"Which is?"

"Tea with dark rum and a piece of lemon," Bokarev said.

"You don't sound better. Maybe you should drink it."

"Good idea," Bokarev said, throwing off the towel.

"What sort of a reception did you get from the Americans? Will we get some help?"

"Not likely," Kampov said. "But then it's our crime, committed by Russians on Russian soil. Who better to understand than us?"

Bokarev tentatively sipped the rum-laced tea. "Good," he said. "You'd better explain it to me, then."

"Really only two possibilities," Kampov said, pacing the small office. "Either it was a business deal gone bad and Voronin and his associates want their money back, or it's a kidnapping for ransom."

"Most Russians think most Americans are rich," Bokarev said.

"A dangerous misperception," Kampov countered. "Voronin is connected with the Mafia here in Moscow, but it's possible he's also connected with Chechen loyalists. Muslims."

"Al-Quaeda?" Bokarev asked.

"They've been shopping for hard currencies. We've seen our station Riyadh bulletins. The royal family has backed off."

"Uncle Osama is feeling the pinch?"

"Something like that," Kampov said. "We need the Monroes' background."

Bokarev looked up hopefully. "The department could send me to Baltimore to sniff around. It has to be warmer there."

"You're staying here," Kampov said. "I want you to find our old friend Voronin."

"Well, we've been trying that for the past year and a half without much luck."

"This time I want you to go to your Mafia friends and lean on them."

Bokarev smiled. "Ah, that's the rub then, isn't it?

They provide me information, and I provide them protection. But if I pit Mafia against al-Quaeda I can't offer them much insulation and they'll know it. Might get a bit dicey."

"It's for the *Rodina*."

"Right," Bokarev said sourly. "They'll go for that Motherland crap in a big way, won't they?"

"They don't have to grab him, just give us a hint where we might find him. What he's been up to lately. Who he's been hanging around with."

"I'll have to burn some assets. The well is going to be dry for a long time. Is it worth it?"

Kampov had asked himself that very question since this morning, and he still didn't have an answer that was satisfactory. All he could see in his mind's eye was Nina's broken, lifeless body in the hospital, but he nodded. "We won't know until we find out."

Bokarev nodded, resigned. "Right then, I might as well get to it." He downed the rum-laced tea, got up, and grabbed his coat.

"Watch yourself, Feodor."

"Those pricks wouldn't dare touch me. They don't have the balls."

Kampov got the Monroes' file, a copy of which he'd given to Ligget, and brought it downstairs to the computer/archives center, where the duty officer came to the counter. His nametag read YAKOVLEV and he looked like he was still in his teens. Last year he'd helped Kampov bust a drug trafficking/money laundering ring with tendrils that reached from Afghanistan to Columbia, and from Mexico City to Amsterdam, Berlin, Paris, London, and New York. The case had been a boring one, because in the end no arrests were made; the Russians behind the deals were too rich and too well connected to bring to justice. But Yakovlev had loved every minute of the investigation because he'd been able to use his skills as a computer expert. He'd been in his element for the six months they'd worked together, and now he had an expectant look on his pale, round face.

"Good afternoon Captain, what brings you down to the dungeon?"

"I need your help, Viktor."

The boy's face lit up. *"Da?"*

"This one might be too easy for you, but it's more important than the last case," Kampov said. He laid the file on the counter. "It's about an American couple, here to do some business. Maybe with the Mafia, and maybe they got themselves involved with Chechen Muslims. The husband was shot in the back of the head just outside of the city, his body left in the snow in the woods. His wife is missing. She might be dead, or they could be holding her for ransom."

"If she's rich," Yakovlev said. He was like a hunting dog shivering in anticipation at the edge of the field.

"Not all Americans are rich."

"I want to know everything about them. Their families, their medical, police, and voting records, real estate holdings, bank accounts, friends. Anything that you can find."

"Do you suppose they have FBI or CIA files?"

"I don't know. Could you find out?"

"Exactly how important is this, Captain?" Yakovlev asked earnestly.

It was the same question again. A couple of American entrepreneurs, a couple of opportunists who'd run afoul of a Mafia or Chechen business deal and got burned. Who cared?

"It's important to me," he said.

"Then I'll find out for you," Yakovlev said, and he scooped up the file.

Kampov stood for a moment.

"I'll let you know as soon as I find something."

"That's the one problem," Kampov said. "I don't think we have much time. I don't think Mrs. Monroe has much time."

SEVENTEEN

•

Lana came late in the afternoon, pushing back the curtain at the doorway. Patti had been sitting on the window ledge, looking out across the backyard and over the wall to the narrow street. Her knees were hunched up to her chest, which seemed to relieve some of the pain. They were at the edge of a birch forest, and she could see the rooftops of several houses in the distance down the hill. She'd heard several trains going by in the night but she couldn't see the tracks. This place was unimaginably lonely.

"They want to talk to you downstairs," Lana said.

Patti was startled out of her thoughts and she turned around. "What time is it?" she asked, her voice weak, which concerned her. If she was going to somehow get out of here on her own two feet she would need her strength.

"I think it's three o'clock. I'm not sure. Can you walk?"

"I don't know."

Lana had brought a large glass of water, which Patti drank, nearly choking and spilling some of it down her front. "I'm terribly hungry. Couldn't I have a little something to eat?"

"That's up to Sergey, but if you don't make him mad I'll try to get you something," Lana said. Her face was mottled red, her lip was split, and it looked as if she was developing a black eye. She was wearing a filthy housedress, a scarf, and rubber farm boots.

Patti straightened her legs and stood up, holding the wall for balance. The room tilted and went fuzzy for a moment, but then slowly came back into focus.

Lana took Patti's arm. "I'll help you downstairs, but then you'll have to walk on your own. Do you understand this, Mrs. Monroe? If they see any weakness they'll exploit it."

Patti motioned to the woman's face. "Did your husband hit you?"

Lana was embarrassed, but she nodded. "He wants to fuck you. Everyone does. But I told him if he tried again I'd tell Sergey."

"Are there other men here?"

"No, just my husband, Aleksei, and Sergey. But the woman wants to have sex with you, too, before she kills you. I heard her talking with Sergey last night. He promised you to her. It's all a big game to them. They're Chechen Muslims and crazy."

Patti felt terrible. She was a zoo animal caught in a cage with no escape possible. "I don't have any money."

"Don't let them know that or they'll kill you for sure."

"I'm more valuable to them alive than dead. There're deals still on the table worth several millions."

"What about your husband?"

Patti drew an involuntary breath. David was in Moscow waiting for her at the hotel. David was a jerk but he'd always been there for her. He'd be impatient and angry, wanting to know what the hell had taken her so goddamned long. But he was her Rock of Gibraltar, despite their troubles. Somehow in her delirium last night she had convinced herself that he was still alive. But it came back to her now in a mind-numbing rush. The sight of his body lying face down in the blood-soaked snow was etched in her brain.

"He's dead," she said, reaching deep inside for the anger that she knew she should feel.

"*Da,* and they'll kill you if you don't cooperate."

Patti looked into the woman's defeated face. "They'll kill me anyway."

Lana's lips tightened. "They're waiting," she said, and she helped Patti out of the bedroom and into the television room, where two young boys were playing a video game.

A girl of about seven or eight was watching them. She looked up and gave Patti a tentative smile, but then went back to watching the game.

The situation was crazy; it was the only thing that Patti could think. She was in *The Twilight Zone,* some other dimension where normal rules of human behavior didn't apply. Or maybe she was in a lunatic asylum.

Patti had to lean heavily on Lana as they made their way down the stairs, but at the bottom she was on her own.

"They're in the kitchen. Don't show that you're afraid of them."

The floor was freezing cold and Patti's bare feet were numb, but she nodded, and shuffled down the corridor to the kitchen.

Raya and Voronin stood at a counter by the sink drinking vodka and eating pickles and frozen salt pork sliced into thin strips. Their fingers glistened with grease. The old babushka was at the stove stirring something in a large pot, and Lysenko was at the big round table drinking a beer. He looked up.

"Come in and sit down, Mrs. Monroe; we have work to do this morning."

The musky odor of cooked cabbage, the sight of the salt pork, and the terrifically overheated room turned Patti's stomach and she thought she might be sick again. But she managed to control herself. She tottered to the table and sat down across from him.

The babushka brought a plate with a few slices of black bread and butter and set it down in front of Lysenko. She glanced at Patti, then went back to the stove, where she ladled what looked to Patti like borscht and brought it and a big spoon to the table.

"I thought Muslims didn't drink alcohol," Patti said, careful to keep her voice even.

A brief look of irritation came into Lysenko's eyes, but then was gone. "We have to talk about money," he said and he started on the soup.

"May I have something to eat?" Patti asked politely.

"We know about your bank accounts in Baltimore and Sydney where you do business that you wish the American and Australian tax authorities to monitor. There is practically no money in either of them. In that you were telling the truth." He looked over to the old woman. "This is very good, Grandmother."

"I'm hungry. May I have something to eat? Please?"

"But we also found out about your secret bank account in Hong Kong. The one that the authorities apparently know nothing about. It's there where you keep your real money." He continued on the soup as he talked, his motions slow, deliberate. It was a show for

Patti's benefit. "You Americans are very smart, I'll give you that much."

"There's no money in that account either. We're broke."

"I'll try to be reasonable with you, Mrs. Monroe. I want to help you, but we need twenty million dollars, U.S., and you will give it to us, after which we'll drive you to your hotel in Moscow and you can get on with your life."

"I told you that I don't have any money. It's the truth."

"You're rich, of course. Or at least your family is wealthy. Aleksei established that for us when he visited your new home in Baltimore."

Vononin looked up and smiled. "It was a lovely time, Patti. I admired your taste. I don't think it was David's; you have to be born to it to appreciate such luxuries."

"Mortgaged to the hilt," Patti said. "We were on the verge of losing it all. That's why we came to Moscow to straighten out the business."

"It's too late for that," Lysenko told her. "Now it's just a matter of finding out where you and David have hidden your money." He took a counter check and ballpoint pen out of his pocket and wrote a bank routing number and account number from memory at the bottom. "I believe these numbers are the correct ones for Hong Kong."

"There's maybe three or four hundred dollars there. At most."

Lysenko shoved the check and pen across the table to her. It had been made out for twenty million, payable to SovTech Trading, LLC, dated today. The company belonged to Voronin and was the Russian partner company to SovAustralTech, which he also managed, but which belonged to David and Patti.

"I'd like you to check the account number, and then sign it and we'll be finished," Lysenko said.

"There's no money," Patti shouted, her voice hoarse.

"Your signature, please, Mrs. Monroe. And there's no need for hysterics. We're merely conducting business."

She was going to die here, Patti thought, and no one back home would ever know what had happened. She and David flew to Moscow and dropped off the face of the earth. She'd never been close to her father, but she wanted to talk to him now, ask his advice. He was a brilliant man who, so far as Patti knew, had never made a bad decision.

"Okay," she said. She signed the check, and slid it back across the table.

Lysenko was vexed. "Do we have the correct account number?"

"It looks like it," Patti said. She'd slept all night and most of the day, but she was exhausted, and her thirst was raging. "But now I want something to eat and drink."

Raya snapped her vodka glass on the counter and in three strides was across the room. She grabbed Patti by the hair and lifted her bodily off the chair. "You will learn respect," she said, conversationally.

Patti staggered backward off her feet and landed on her back, her head bouncing off the cold floor. For an instant she saw stars, but then something incredibly painful slammed into her side, taking her breath away.

She looked up in time to see Raya's booted foot coming at her again, and she rolled into it, grabbing the woman's ankle and twisting it sharply upward and to the left.

Raya staggered off balance, giving Patti time to scramble to her feet, back away, and drop into a defensive pose.

For the longest moment no one in the kitchen moved. Lysenko and Voronin were surprised, and the babushka suddenly looked fearful, but the expression on Raya's face was a mixture of surprise and interest, not anger.

"If you're going to kill me, go ahead and get it over with," Patti told them. "Put a bullet in the back of my head like you did my husband. But don't screw with me, I won't take any more of it. I'll kill the next one who tries."

"I think taking you apart will be more interesting than I first thought it would be," Raya said. "Apparently you're more than a spoiled American bitch." She started toward Patti, but Lysenko warned her off.

"*Nyet,*" he said softly.

Patti felt as if she were on the verge of passing out. She was sure that a couple of her ribs were either broken or badly bruised, and she couldn't remember how long she'd been here. It seemed like months to her.

"We'll attempt to cash the check," Lysenko told her.

"It'll bounce," Patti croaked.

Raya was looking at her like a cat looks at a wounded mouse before it pounces. She wanted to play.

"We'll give you a little more time to reconsider," Lysenko said. "One way or the other we will get our money, Mrs. Monroe. Twenty million. It's up to you how that's accomplished, and how you will survive this ordeal. Your fate is in your own hands."

"We have all the time in the world," Raya said, her voice soft, her accent exotic to Patti's ears. "Do you, Patricia?"

．　．　．

Lana met Patti in the corridor and helped her upstairs. The television had been switched off and the children were gone. Just now the house was quiet.

"I told you not to make them angry," Lana said. "It's a wonder they didn't kill you. It's that woman Sergey brought with him; she's the most dangerous of them all."

"They're crazy."

"Not the way you think. Not Sergey, he's a professional, and Aleksei is afraid of him. It's just the woman."

A clean rag and a small piece of soap were laid out on the window seat, next to a bucket of steaming water. A pair of jeans, a white T-shirt, panties, and socks were laid out on the bed. They had been stolen from Patti's suitcase on the first day.

"Clean yourself and get dressed. I'll see if I can get you something to eat," Lana said, and she left.

For a minute or so Patti was afraid of getting undressed. She went to the doorway and peeked out into the television room, but no one was there.

She went back to the window and looked outside. Already it was starting to get dark. Night came early at this time of the year here, and the birch forest on the other side of the wall looked cold and forbidding. Alien.

Quickly peeling off her filthy clothes, she took a quick sponge bath, the warm water wonderful. She wished that she could wash her hair, but she didn't think Lana would be able to get more water. The only compliment she remembered her father ever giving her was about her hair. It was long and dark, and shone like silk when it was clean.

She suddenly wanted to cry, but thinking about her father stopped her.

"Be strong, Patti," he used to tell her. *"Don't let them see you cry. Don't let them know your weaknesses. Always remember to look for theirs, because everyone*

has a soft underbelly. You find it and hit them there. Be a winner!"

Lana came back after Patti was finished dressing. She'd brought a glass of water, but nothing more. "It's all they'd let me bring you. I'm sorry."

Patti drank it straight down. "Can I have more?"

"I'll try later."

"Do they mean to starve me?"

Lana nodded. "At least until you begin to cooperate with them. Sergey wanted to send up some bread and cheese, but Raya talked him out of it. If you get hungry enough, you'll do what they want." She took the empty glass and sat down next to Patti on the bed.

"Why are you doing this for me?" Patti asked.

"They want money."

"No, you. Why are you doing this for me? Won't you get in trouble if they find out?"

Lana nodded, a sad expression on her careworn face. "*Da.*"

"This is nuts. Your husband tried to rape me and the others want to kill me. That makes you part of it. Why don't you just walk out the door and take a train away from here?"

"Where would I go?"

"Home. To your parents. Relatives. There has to be someplace where you could go. To be safe."

Lana shook her head. "We are from Grozny. Do you know this place in Chechnya? Always there is fighting and dying. My father and brothers were killed five years ago when a Russian artillery shell landed on our house. Before that my mother and sister died of typhus. My grandmother is dead, and I don't know where my aunts and uncles are." She looked away. "All dead in the war. Or starved, sick."

"Who is the old woman downstairs?"

"Boris's mother," Lana said. "There is no place for me to go, Mrs. Monroe. Here is my home, and Boris is my husband. I am a woman. What choice do I have?"

"It's different in America."

"Then why did you come here with your husband? You didn't love him, I think."

It felt to Patti like a slap in the face. "What are you talking about?" she snapped angrily.

"He's dead, and yet you are not grieving."

Patti wanted to say something, deny what Lana was telling her, yet deep inside she understood that it was true. She'd loved David in the beginning, but looking back to when they got married she couldn't remember how she'd felt. She wasn't sure that she hadn't married him only because her father was opposed to it. She wanted to show him that she didn't need his money. She and David could manage on their own. In the last year, and especially in the past few months, she'd remained at David's side mostly out of habit, and like Lana perhaps because she had nowhere to go. She certainly could never go back to her father and admit that he was right and she was wrong.

"This is why I am helping you," Lana said. "Because you are a woman just like me. We have to help each other. There is nothing else for us. Nothing."

"We have to survive," Patti said.

"Tomorrow you will have to make a decision about the money," Lana said, getting up. "Grandmother wants to hang you, and nobody disagrees."

"I was telling the truth. I don't have any money."

"Then you better come up with the name of someone who can help," Lana said, and she left the bedroom.

Patti went to the window and looked outside. It was

fully dark now, and the crystal-clear sky was studded with more stars than she'd ever seen. But they were nothing but cold pinpricks of light, just as far away and untouchable as her freedom.

She had been used all of her life, even by the men she had turned to for love and help. David, who'd changed into a man she didn't know, one she was almost fright-ened of. And before him, her martial arts instructor, who'd tried to seduce her after a private lesson.

"We can go places, Patricia," he'd told her, touch-ing her breasts.

They were alone in the main salle at the dojo. She was seventeen and he was thirty-six. She had studied with him for nearly five years and what he was doing to her came as the biggest blow and disappointment in her life to that point.

"I trusted you," she'd told him, backing up a few paces.

He'd been relentless, his hands all over her. "Please," he whispered in her ear. "I know I'm the first and I want to make it good for you."

"No."

"We'll be fabulous together."

Patti had smashed the side of her calloused hand into his neck, rocking him backward, momentarily stunning him, giving her time to get out.

Thinking about him at this moment, she realized that she could not dredge up his name. It had been erased from her memory.

THE FIFTH DAY

January 6th

EIGHTEEN

•

Tobias Anderson got to his Georgetown office a few minutes before eight, as he did most weekday mornings. It gave him a couple of hours before the other attorneys, law clerks, interns, and secretaries showed up and the day began.

His chauffeur opened the rear door of the black Bentley for Anderson, attaché case in his left hand, *The Washington Post* tucked under his arm.

"Thank you, Carl," Anderson said. "I'll be a couple hours later than usual this evening. I'll call when I need you."

"Yes, Sir."

It was a bitter cold morning by Washington standards and not many pedestrians were out and about, though morning traffic on the Beltway coming in had already started to build.

Anderson was a tall, patrician-looking man. A stern East Coast Presbyterian, he had been raised by his wealthy parents to be a gentleman at all times, refined in his manner, in his dress, and in the way he treated people less fortunate than himself. It was an ethical code of conduct he'd learned from his father, and one that he had perfected at Harvard Law School, and one that through shrewd investments had parlayed the five million he'd inherited into a fortune of nearly seventy-five million dollars.

At sixty he was still young enough to do just about anything he wanted to do, and practicing high profile criminal defense work was exactly what he wanted. His philosophy wasn't much different from other attorneys like him: the Constitution had been written not to protect the masses from the government; it had been written to protect the individual from the masses.

Law enforcement agencies, including the FBI, didn't like him because he'd busted any number of airtight cases. But he was universally respected for his sharp mind and gentlemanly behavior in and out of court.

Anderson, Wilcox, Ryan & Sewell was housed in an upscale three-story brownstone just down the hill from Georgetown University. Anderson's richly paneled and furnished office occupied the corner of the second and third floors. The upper level, which was actually a broad balcony, contained his private law library of expensively leather-bound books, plus an area where he could do work or hold meetings with his senior partners.

He set his attaché case beside his desk, got a cup of tea from the automatic maker in the small wet bar between the main room and his bathroom, and took it and *The Post* up the circular stairs to the library, where he powered up his computer.

Along the opposite wall, a two story floor-to-ceiling and nearly priceless Tiffany window looked across Dumbarton Oaks Park and beyond to the grounds of the U.S. Naval Observatory and the vice president's mansion. Downstairs, he met with clients, up here he did his real work, and sipping his first cup of tea of the morning and gazing out the window he felt a great sense of satisfaction. All was right in his world.

Once his computer had booted up he went on-line to check his e-mails. His inbox held a dozen messages since last evening, when he'd checked before leaving for home. During a normal weekday he usually got three times as many, most of which he forwarded either to his secretary or one of his three law clerks.

Scrolling through this morning's usual batch from other law firms, and several that had been sent to him internally from his partners, he came across one from Valeri Runkov that had been sent a few minutes after eight last evening. Runkov, who worked on the Russian desk at the Justice Department, had emigrated to the U.S. from Moscow eight years ago. He'd had a brilliant four years at Harvard Law School, from where he did his last two summers as an intern at the firm, after which Anderson had hired him without reservation.

In the three years Runkov worked at the office, he and Anderson had become close, more like father and son than employer-employee. When Runkov made the decision to go over to Justice, Anderson had been saddened to see him go, but just as proud as any father would be of a son stepping out into the world on his own.

Runkov's occasional e-mails were always brief and to the point. This one was no exception, and Anderson put down his tea.

TOBIAS,
FBI GOT NOTICE LAST NIGHT FROM ITS MOSCOW
LIAISON THAT DAVID MONROE WAS FOUND SHOT
TO DEATH OUTSIDE THE CITY.
COULD THIS BE YOUR FRIEND DAVID?
VALERI

Patti had called earlier last week to say that she and David had to make a trip to Moscow to straighten up some deal that had apparently gone bad. Anderson got the impression that it was another of David's foul-ups. Patti's father, whom Anderson had known since law school, nearly forty years ago, was of the opinion that David Monroe was little more than a con artist who'd married Patti simply for her money. Not only that, he wasn't a particularly good con artist nor, from Anderson's perspective, was he a very good businessman.

Anderson, who'd watched Patti grow up, was very fond of her. He and his wife had never had children, so they'd practically adopted Patti, and had stood up for her at the civil wedding when Patti's parents refused to attend. He'd tried to talk her out of going through with it, but she was in love, her eyes filled with stars.

He didn't want to believe it could be the same David Monroe shot to death in Moscow, but he also didn't believe in coincidences. There had been no mention of a Mrs. Monroe, and that worried him.

Anderson called her home phone in Baltimore, but got their answering machine. Next he called her cell phone, but after four rings the operator apologized that the person being called was not available. Finally, he pulled up the number of SovAustralTech, their business office in Moscow. It was four in the afternoon over there so someone should have been answering the phone. But after ten rings he hung up.

Anderson stared at Valeri's message on his screen for a long time, until finally he hit REPLY.

VALERI,
I CAN'T REACH PATTI OR DAVID AT ANY OF THEIR NUMBERS.

THEY WERE SCHEDULED TO FLY TO MOSCOW
FOR BUSINESS EARLY LAST WEEK.
I'M WORRIED. FIND OUT AS MUCH AS YOU CAN
FROM YOUR CONTACTS AT THE BUREAU AND LET
ME KNOW SOONEST.
TOBIAS

NINETEEN

•

Bokarev had spent most of the day poking around
some of the bars and clubs that catered to the Mafia
organizations that operated in the Moscow area. He
was known to most of them as the kind of cop who
couldn't be bribed, but the kind of a cop who would be
willing to look the other way in exchange for information. He had the reputation of being tough but fair, and
even the criminals respected that trait in a modern
Russian. So far as he was aware, no one here in Moscow
knew about his father's death; if they had they might
not have been so willing to work with him.

It was nearly five when he pulled up in front of the
Club Grand Dynamo on Moscow's northeast side, and
left the car with a valet parker who was dressed in
American Marine camouflage battle dress.

"Are you a member, Sir?" the valet demanded.

"Piss off," Bokarev said, and pushed past him into
the club.

The valet started after him, but stopped in mid-stride,
his right hand going up to an earpiece. After a moment
he nodded and turned back.

The Grand Dynamo was one of the more exclusive

hangouts for top Mafia brass anywhere in the city, but nothing usually started here until later in the evening. Some American easy-listening music played from ceiling speakers, but none of the tables in the main room were occupied and only a couple of men were at the bar. The stage was empty.

A pretty young woman in a Playboy Bunny costume came across from the reception desk to where Bokarev stood waiting.

"May I help you, Sir?" she asked.

Bokarev held up his MVD identification booklet. "Has Nikolai shown up yet?" he asked. Nikolai Smikov was the club manager.

"I couldn't say," the girl replied. "But if you care to wait outside I'll see if he can be contacted."

"That's okay, love, I'll wait for him in his office."

"You can't do that, Sir," the girl said, blocking his way.

"Oh?" Bokarev said, smiling. He moved her gently aside, patted her bunny tail, and headed across the dance floor to a leather-covered padded door that opened to a corridor back to several small apartments and saunas and chambers where members brought their girlfriends.

Smikov, a huge bear of a Great Russian in his late sixties, had been a made man in the Mafia since he was a teenager, in part because of his ruthlessness—it was rumored, but never proven, that he had killed twelve men, most of them with his bare hands—and because of his intelligence. He'd got his start dodging the KGB during the Soviet regime, and in today's open Russia he felt that he was nearly untouchable. He had no respect whatsoever for the Moscow Militia, and only a grudging respect for Bokarev, who came to him from time to time for information. In exchange the MVD stayed out of his way.

His large, lavishly furnished office was at the end of the corridor. Bokarev went in without knocking.

Smikov was sitting back on a snow white leather couch, his trousers open, one of the young club women in a bunny suit on her knees in front of him, giving him fellatio while he sipped champagne. He looked up, irritated for just a second, but then smiled.

"Your sense of timing is shit, Feodor," he said. The girl looked up but he shoved her head back between his legs. "What are you doing out here?"

"I need a little bird to whisper something in my ear," Bokarev said. He went over to the bar, got a flute, and poured a glass of champagne. It was a nice Krug, not sweet like Russian champagnes.

"Let me guess, you're looking for the guys who whacked the American and dumped his body."

"It looked like a revenge hit. Nine millimeters to the back of the head. Very efficient."

"It wasn't us," Smikov said. He reached down and tousled the girl's blond hair, then pushed her head even closer. "I swear it."

Bokarev shrugged. "I'm looking for an old friend who's disappeared, maybe you've heard of him. Aleksei Voronin."

"The name's not familiar."

"But you can find out where he's gone to ground. I'm told that he's connected."

"A lot of guys are connected. It's the only way to stay in the game these days."

Bokarev drank his champagne and put the glass back on the bar. "This is a big one for me, Nikolai. Important.

Understand?" He looked around the office. "Maybe I'll just close this place down for a week or two."

Smikov gave him a shrewd, appraising look. "One of these days you will go too far, my young friend," he said. "But I'll put the word out on the street."

"Soon."

Smikov nodded. "Now get out of here, unless you want sloppy seconds."

"She's not my type," Bokarev said heading for the door.

Smikov laughed out loud. "Not her. I meant me."

TWENTY

•

It was nearly six o'clock and Kampov was tired and irascible. He wanted to go back to his apartment, take a long hot shower, and drink himself to oblivion so that he could forget. It was something he'd been doing for a long time now, and he was feeling the effects that so much alcohol was having on his body and mind.

Bokarev had phoned to say that he felt like hell and he was going home so that Yana and the girls could take care of him. "Smikov's going to put out the word for me. So we'll see. It's something."

"Be careful of that prick," Kampov warned. "I don't trust him."

"I don't trust anybody. That's something you taught me."

"We'll talk in the morning," Kampov had told him. "Get some rest tonight."

"*Da*."

Kampov's telephone rang as he was putting on his coat to leave. Everyone else was gone, and he debated for a moment ignoring the call, but he thought that it might be Bokarev again, so he picked it up. "Kampov."

"General Granov wishes to see you first thing in the morning," the general's secretary said. "In uniform. He's expecting your report on the Monroe case."

"I can come up to his office now," Kampov suggested. General Anatoli Granov was in charge of what was the old KGB's Second Chief Directorate, now called Section II, which was responsible for interior intelligence operations, primarily involving foreigners.

"In the morning," the general's secretary said sternly.

"Of course," Kampov said, but the line was dead, and he put the phone down. Granov was in love with the Militia. He wanted to fold the entire national police force into his section. Kampov had an idea that a little bird had complained about yesterday, and the general was going to order him to turn the case back to Zamyatin.

The evening was already dark and bitterly cold, and Kampov's car had trouble starting. Traffic was heavy downtown, and it took him nearly twenty minutes to reach his apartment, a deep depression settling over him, as it did most evenings.

He hated going home alone to his empty apartment, with all its memories of Nina. But he couldn't bear the thought of moving, because of those memories. Two years and he couldn't forget, and didn't want to put her out of his mind and, as Bokarev's wife told him, "Get on with your life. Find a nice woman and settle down again."

The doorman had brought the elevator down, and he smiled pleasantly. "Chilly evening, Sir."

Kampov nodded. "But then it's Russia and it's winter."

Upstairs he went to the bar and poured a large cognac, knocked it back, then went into his bedroom, where he got undressed and got in the shower, letting the water pound on the back of his neck.

The apartment was large, by Moscow standards, five rooms including two bedrooms, one of them still furnished the way Nina wanted seventeen years ago for children they'd never been able to have. It had something to do with her ovaries, and she'd been devastated when the doctor told them that she would never be able to conceive. She didn't want to adopt, so instead she'd devoted all of her energies to making sure that her husband was a happy man.

Which he was, until the same doctor who told her that she couldn't have children killed her on the operating table.

He closed his eyes so that he could bring up an image of her face, but it wouldn't come for a long time, and when it did it wasn't clear, as if he were seeing her through a dark veil.

"*Pizdec,*" he swore softly. He didn't know how much longer he could continue like this. Twice in the past six months, he had put his pistol in his mouth and cocked the hammer. Forty-five caliber into the brain cured all ills. It was called Russian insurance.

David Monroe was in a place now where nothing could bother him ever again. He would never have nightmares, never feel pain, never feel hopelessness, loneliness, despair, and at this moment Kampov could almost envy the man.

He got out of the shower, dried himself off, put on a robe, and poured another cognac. He went to the Monroe file he'd brought home with him and took out the enlarged copy of Mrs. Monroe's passport photo, and brought it with him into the living room, where he sat down. The picture was grainy because of the enlargement, but it showed a woman who appeared to be on the verge of smiling, as if she had just thought of something funny.

It was the same look Nina had walked around with. It was one of the things he'd always loved about his wife. Even after the news that she couldn't bear children, she'd been the first to recover, the first to laugh out loud, the first to smile in the morning.

Sometimes he would wake up before she did, but instead of disturbing her by getting out of bed he would watch her sleep, the corners of her mouth slightly turned up as if she were having a wonderful dream.

He never got tired of looking at her, and now that she was gone and he couldn't know her mood, he hoped that he had been a good husband to her.

"Patricia Monroe," he muttered. He wondered if her husband had been good to her and how she was taking his murder.

He took a drink, but the cognac didn't taste good to him, so he put the glass down. Maybe it was time for him to get on with it. He hadn't been able to save Nina, and he had been beating himself up because of it for the last two years. But just maybe he could save this woman, send her back to her parents, or sisters or brothers, back to her friends. Back to a life in which she could smile at a secret joke like she had for her passport picture.

TWENTY-ONE

•

Sometime around noon Lana had brought up a glass of tea laced with sugar, and later in the afternoon she had taken Patti outside to relieve herself in the backyard. But she'd not been able to bring any food, and no one had come to ask about money.

It was dark again, and lying in bed Patti felt as if she were swimming, or floating a few inches above the mattress. She was still thirsty, and her mouth was gummy and tasted of blood, but she was no longer hungry.

In an odd way, she almost felt good. As if her body had been cleansed. She couldn't remember how many days she'd been here without food, and for the first time it didn't seem to matter. David was dead and she was alive.

She had lost weight, and she was weak. Even moving her legs beneath the blanket seemed to take more effort than it should have, but it didn't frighten her. Nor was she worried about her future. When someone called for her, she would deal with whatever they said or did. In the meantime she wouldn't think about it.

Curiously, her breasts and her ribs no longer caused her pain.

She was lying on her left side, staring at the cracked plaster wall, when she thought she smelled something. Food. Maybe onions, and something else, which caused her to salivate.

With a great deal of effort she managed to turn over and her heart suddenly lurched in her chest. Raya Kiselnikova stood in the darkness, next to the bed, only the starlight illuminating her round face. The sleeves of her khaki military shirt were rolled up above the elbows, and she was holding a large bath towel that was sopping wet. But for some reason the worst part in Patti's mind were the skintight black leather gloves the woman was wearing.

"Your sleep is troubled," Raya said with no inflection whatsoever. "You called out for someone, but I couldn't understand."

"What do you want?" Patti asked. She was afraid of everyone here, except for Lana. But Patti was sure that this woman was crazy and that frightened her the most.

"Your Hong Kong check was no good."

"I told all of you that."

"Yes, but that brings us back to the matter of the money we need from you," Raya said. "Aleksei and I had pleasant talk about Baltimore. He has a great deal of affection for you, though none for your husband, and he told me that he admired your lifestyle. You have class, he says."

"But no money," Patti said. She was struggling to keep on track, keep her head in focus, because she felt that whatever was about to happen now would be a matter of life or death. Her survival depended on her staying with it.

"*Da*, we know that now. And Sergey wanted to kill you this afternoon when we received word from Hong Kong. The grandma wants to hang you, just like they hung two of her children in Grozny. She wants to watch your eyes as you slowly strangle to death and realize that no one, not even that foolish Lana, will come to your rescue."

"You're all insane."

Raya was rolling the bath towel into a long tube,

water dripping on the edge of the bed. "Perhaps it is because of our jihad."

"People like you find reasons to kill," Patti said, and she saw the tightening in Raya's face. She didn't know why she was saying things to irritate the woman, but she'd always had a quick tongue.

"It's the pain."

"You're a sadist."

Raya seemed sad. "You're probably right," she said. "I could tell you things that have been done to me, but it would change nothing. We let you alone today so that you could think of a way to get our money. I told Sergey that you would help us."

Patti was at a loss. All of them talked in non sequiturs; nothing they said or did made any sense.

"I thought you might be willing to make amends with your father, and ask for help. Now that David is dead, we think that he might believe you've come to your senses and redeemed yourself in his eyes."

"He's cut me off, and he won't change his mind."

"Even to save his daughter's life?"

Patti held back for just an instant. Would he pay a ransom, she asked herself, but then she shook her head, even that small effort painful.

"You were raised amongst wealthy people," Raya said reasonably, as if she was on Patti's side and trying to help her. "Aleksei said you introduced some of your friends to him. Rich friends."

"No," Patti said.

"You have to think very hard now, because tomorrow is the last day for you. I bought you this day and night, but Sergey will go no further."

"I don't know anybody with that kind of money who would pay a ransom."

"It's up to me to help you," Raya said. "Sergey made me promise that much."

She gently pulled the blanket away from Patti and let it fall to the floor at the foot of the bed.

"If you kill me there'll be no money," Patti cried. "Don't you understand, you fucking moron?"

"I think that I must have damaged your ribs when I kicked you. And I'm sure that your tits must be unbelievably painful," Raya said. Almost nonchalantly she swung the rolled up wet bath towel like it was a club and hit Patti in the chest.

The pain was worse than anything Patti had ever imagined was possible, and she screamed, the sound lost as a gurgle deep in the back of her throat, as Raya slammed the towel into her bruised ribs and again into her chest.

She had trouble catching her breath and her stomach heaved. Her heart pounded in her ears.

Raya's voice came from an impossibly long distance. "This method is painful but it's not fatal and it leaves no marks." She hit Patti in the legs, again in the side, and again in the chest.

Patti slid in and out of consciousness, not even able to raise an arm to try to defend herself. Raya stood above her wringing out the towel, water falling on Patti's face.

"I've been beaten in just this way," she said. "It was an effort by the Spetsnaz pricks to teach me humility. But they should have killed me. When it was over, five of them were dead and I escaped in the mountains."

The water had revived Patti somewhat, so that when Raya laid the towel aside and began undressing her, she fought back, pushing the woman's hands away from her T-shirt.

Raya grabbed a handful of Patti's hair and shook her

head as if she were a rag doll. "Nothing you can do will stop this." She pulled Patti's T-shirt off and tossed it on the floor. "Nice tits," she said.

She softly caressed Patti's bare breasts with a gloved hand, then undid the waistband of Patti's jeans and pulled them and her panties off.

At that moment, bent over the bed, the woman was close enough to touch. Patti suddenly mustered what little strength she had left, reared up, and gouged a deep line of scratches from Raya's left eye all the way down her cheek to the side of her neck, the wounds instantly welling blood.

Raya pulled back, stumbling and nearly going down, her face contorted in a mask of surprise and rage.

"Bitch," Patti screamed. "Touch me again and I'll kill you. So help me God, I'll fucking wipe you out."

For a pregnant moment Patti thought that Raya was actually going to leave her alone. The woman wiped some of the blood away from her cheek with a gloved hand and studied it in the darkness. She looked at Patti, who was half sitting up in the bed, shrugged, turned as if to go, then spun on a heel and smashed a clenched fist into Patti's jaw.

A billion stars burst inside Patti's head, and her pain was suddenly gone. She was falling down a long tunnel, above which someone was shouting something; but it wasn't Raya, it was a man's voice. It was the last thing Patti remembered.

THE SIXTH DAY

January 7th

TWENTY-TWO

•

Kampov, in his MVD uniform—green piping, five rows of miniature medals from his service in Afghanistan and Chechnya, his tall boots gleaming, his service hat tucked under his left arm—marched across the large office to General Granov's massive desk, crashed his heels together, and saluted crisply. It was eight sharp.

"Sir, Captain Alexander Kampov, reporting as ordered!"

Someone was seated in one of the two tall-backed chairs facing the general's desk, but Kampov could only see the top of his head. And blond hair.

Granov held Kampov's salute for a long time before he returned it. "Have a seat, Captain," he said, his voice husky. He was an old man, with an old man's ambition to make his mark before his career was over. That kind of purpose was no less deadly to bystanders these days than it had been in the Soviet regime. "You, of course, know Colonel Zamyatin."

Kampov sat down in the second chair and crossed his legs. "Yes, Sir. The chief investigator's department and mine have often worked in complete harmony in our efforts to solve crimes within the city."

Zamyatin smirked, but the general nodded sagely.

"*Da,* the colonel was telling me the same thing. Did you bring your report with you?"

"There is no written report at this point, General, we are still collating the material we've gathered."

"What material is that, Captain?" Zamyatin asked mildly. He was enjoying himself.

"I assume that you've briefed the general to the point where the investigation was turned over to my department."

"Yes."

Kampov turned back to Granov. "The body of the male has been identified as David Monroe, an American citizen from Baltimore, Maryland. He and his wife conducted barter business here in Moscow, and perhaps Vladivostok, under the company name of Sov-AustralTech, which we are certain has connections with the Mafia. The office at twenty-five Chekova Street was searched, but it has been abandoned."

Zamyatin was surprised. "I know nothing about this," he said sharply. "Why wasn't I told?"

"We have learned nothing of substance to this point."

"What arc you hoping to find?" Granov demanded.

"The whereabouts of certain Mafia elements, and of Mrs. Monroe, whom we believe is still alive and is probably being held for ransom."

"She's dead," Zamyatin said flatly.

"Have you found her body?" Kampov asked.

"*Nyet,* but it's just a matter of time. I have one hundred officers and trainees searching the roadsides in a fifty-kilometer radius of the city center. Your theory of kidnapping for ransom is all wrong. This was a drug smuggling operation that went bad, and the Monroes were executed for their indiscretions."

Kampov held his temper in check. He hadn't gotten

drunk last night, but sitting here now, listening to this insufferable ass, he thought that might have been a mistake.

"You yourself told me at the primary crime scene that you were investigating a drug smuggling ring with ties to Afghanistan," Zamyatin went on.

"I was wrong," Kampov said. "We now believe that Mr. Monroe was murdered because of a business deal gone bad."

"You've already said that," the general reminded him. "Do you have any proof that Mrs. Monroe has been kidnapped and not executed?"

"Not directly," Kampov admitted. "But the FBI has agreed to help. They are sending me Mrs. Monroe's file from Washington."

Zamyatin practically came off his seat, but General Granov held him back with a gesture.

"That was inventive but ill advised, Captain."

"Sir?" Kampov asked.

"I'm turning this case over to Militia where it rightfully belongs," the general said. "Colonel Zamyatin will be in charge of the investigation from this point. You will send over all your files and any other evidence you've gathered to his office no later than noon today."

"Of course, General," Kampov said. "And I have every confidence that Militia, under the capable leadership of Chief Investigator Zamyatin's steady and inspired hand, will bring this matter to a complete and satisfactory conclusion."

· · · ·

ometime in the middle of the night Lana came up
and helped Patti get dressed and under the blanket.
She'd also brought a handful of aspirins and a glass of
water, which helped. For the first time since her captivity, Patti was able to sleep with not much pain and with
none of the dreams about David lying in the snow.

It was day when Lana came to the doorway again
and she finally awoke. She sat up, the effort agonizing
to her ribs, but not unbearable.

"You must try to get up," Lana said, coming around
to the side of the bed. She wore a clean housedress,
nylons, and leather slippers with sheepskin linings.

"Are they going to kill me now?" Patti asked.

"Raya wanted to last night until Sergey stopped her.
Your only way out now is to somehow get the money
for them."

Patti shook her head. "Even if I could do it, once
they got the money they'd kill me anyway."

"You're a bright American woman who comes from
a wealthy family. This is about saving your life." She'd
brought an extra pair of leather slippers that she put on
Patti's feet. "Last night you fought back. They respect
you for that. Even Raya does. I heard her and Sergey
talking after she'd calmed down."

It was about survival. She could almost hear her
father agreeing with Lana.

"*Stand on your own two feet, Patricia. Lift your
head and look the bastards straight in the eye. I'm
Patricia Healy and if you don't like it, tough shit!*"

The problem was, and always had been, that she never knew who Patricia Healy was. Not really. The Boston Healy name carried her through school without her ever having to reveal who she truly was, not to others, and not even to herself. She'd never had the time, or the need, to be alone with her own thoughts, or to develop a sense of self-awareness that she suspected came naturally to most people.

Sometimes, looking in a mirror, she didn't recognize her own image. The clothes, the hair, the makeup were hers, but when she tried to look into the eyes in the glass nothing was recognizable.

Instead of doing something, anything—shrugging, smiling, winking, sticking out her tongue at herself—she would turn away and an instant later have forgotten all about it. She was a Boston Healy. Nothing else mattered.

For a few years as a young girl she'd had her karate, but when that turned bad she'd had nothing.

Even when her father had walked her down the aisle the first time she got married, she hadn't leaned on his arm or even looked at him. She hadn't felt the need. And, the next day, her name Patricia Holman, she hadn't felt the need to assimilate. She was a Boston Healy, and that was all of it. She didn't have to think who she was, what she had become. The name was everything.

"Can you stand?" Lana asked.

Patti looked up at her, noticing that she had combed her hair and was wearing lipstick and a little blush. "You've dressed up. Why?"

"It's Christmas Day," Lana said. "Russian Orthodox."

"You're Muslims."

Lana nodded, the hint of a smile at the corners of her lips. "Most of us aren't fanatics. And Russians, even Chechens, like a good feast."

Patti almost laughed out loud. Not fanatics.

Lana helped her get to her feet, and for a long time she couldn't find her balance, and the effort caused the blood to rush to her head and she realized that her jaw was swollen.

"How does Raya look this morning?"

This time Lana did smile. "Like she got into a fight and lost."

"How do I look?"

"Like you got in a fight and survived," Lana said. "Let's go downstairs."

"I don't know if I'm ready to fight them."

"It's Christmas dinner. Can't you smell it?"

Patti's stomach did a slow roll, but she couldn't smell a thing. "No."

"Well, there's a lot of food. And some of the neighbors came over, and brought wine. They're friends."

Again Patti held back. "How is it possible, I mean with me going down there? What am I supposed to say?"

"Anything you want," Lana said. "They know about you."

"That I've been kidnapped and starved and beaten?" Patti asked incredulously.

"*Da*, but Aleksei has been very good to all of us, and kidnapping, especially a rich American, is the Russian way. Anyway, they've seen Raya's face, so they know that you can take care of yourself. They appreciate it."

Patti shook her head. "Mother of God, this is all so nuts."

"Yes, it is," Lana said, and she helped Patti around the bed and out into the television room.

Instead of turning left toward the stairs, they went to the right, to the bathroom, which had a huge claw foot tub, above which was a small stained glass window.

An ornate cut glass chandelier was hanging from the tall ceiling, and a towel and bar of soap were laid out on an overstuffed easy chair next to a white porcelain sink with rusty faucets.

It looked to Patti like something out of a Disney cartoon. "The plumbing isn't frozen?"

"*Nyet,* it never freezes."

"Bastards," Patti said.

"I'm sorry," Lana said. "You may use the toilet and then wash up. There's hot water."

"I've got nothing left inside," Patti said. She tottered to the sink and washed her hands and then her face and neck, using a corner of the towel as a washcloth. When she was finished, just that simple little luxury made her feel much better.

She studied her image in the mirror over the sink for just a moment. Her complexion was a little red, and her jaw slightly swollen, but it wasn't too bad, though her face was gaunt and her hair was tangled. Her shoulders seemed smaller to her, and her clothes hung loosely. The once-tight designer jeans were practically falling off her hips.

Worse than that, however, were her teeth. She leaned closer, opened her mouth, and pushed at her two front teeth with her thumb and forefinger. They were loose, and for some reason that frightened her the most about her condition.

"Are you finished?" Lana asked from the doorway.

Patti looked up, suddenly remembering that it was her birthday. She was thirty-two today, but in the mirror she looked fifty. "I'd rather stay up here and take a bath."

"You must be hungry."

"No. I don't think so. But I'm dirty."

"Clean enough," Lana said, and she came in and took

Patti's arm. "It's good food, you'll see. You'll get your strength back."

They took the stairs slowly, Patti's free hand tightly gripping the banister. She could hear the sounds of people talking and laughing, the sounds of silverware against bowls and plates, but she still couldn't smell anything.

At the bottom they stopped a moment just before the kitchen door, and a nearly overwhelming sense of unreality washed over Patti. This simply could not be happening. It was like a Stephen King horror story in which nothing was as it seemed, and everything was extremely dangerous, otherworldly.

"You must walk in under your own power, Patti," Lana said. "It's important for you, especially in front of Raya."

"She's there?"

"Yes, they all are. Even Boris, but he won't do anything."

Patti nodded. It was about survival, and her hunger was suddenly back, almost blinding in its intensity. She walked around the corner into the superheated kitchen, and Lana directed her to an empty seat at the big round table, on which had been laid a white tablecloth and a dozen or more platters and bowls of steaming dishes, most of which she couldn't identify, and baskets of breads and biscuits, and many bottles of red wine and white wine and vodka.

At least two dozen people were crammed into the kitchen, the adults seated around the big table, several teenagers and a lot of children at smaller tables. Voronin was seated at the opposite side of the table, next to Lysenko. They were busy talking to each other and didn't bother to look up when Patti came in.

Raya had gone to the counter next to the sink to get another two bottles of vodka, and when she turned around she spotted Patti and a malicious look came into her eyes. Her face was a mess from where Patti had scratched her, but not bandaged. She had merely put some salve over the wounds and they looked gross.

"Good afternoon," Patti said evenly, as she walked to the table and pulled out the chair.

Voronin looked up as she sat down, and he smiled and nodded. "I'm glad you could join us, Patti. This is Christmas, a day for forgiveness and understanding. Don't you agree?"

Raya sat down next to Lysenko and gave Patti a hard stare for a long moment, then turned away and poured a glass of vodka, which she knocked back.

Someone next to Patti poured her a glass of vodka, and then everyone around the table, even Lysenko, but not Raya or Boris, raised their glasses.

"To America!" someone cried.

Everyone knocked back their drink, and then looked at Patti, who was still holding her small glass.

The children hadn't bothered to stop what they were doing, but every adult in the kitchen was watching her.

She raised her glass. *"Nostrovia,"* she said in as big a voice as she could manage, and tossed back the vodka. Her throat instantly contracted and her eyes teared up, but she forced herself to set the glass on the table with an even hand, and not to cough or sputter.

Gradually she could breathe again, and everyone in the kitchen had gone back to their conversations in Russian, except for Lana, who was closely watching her.

Happy birthday, Patti, she said bitterly to herself.

An older woman to her right said something to her in a dialect that Patti couldn't understand, then took her plate and filled it with food from the bowls and platters. The fish, Patti recognized, along with the traditional kidney beans mixed with shredded potatoes and garlic, the parsley potatoes and the apricots, sectioned oranges, figs and dates, and the garlic biscuits. But some of the other stuff might have been rice or cous cous, and maybe beef or some other ground meat balls with cabbage in a gravy, what might have been potato pancakes, sour cream, sauerkraut, mashed peas, and something else in a pasta wrapping.

Patti had been cold all night, but now she was so hot she could hardly stand it, and she was getting sick to her stomach and dizzy. The vodka lay like molten steel in her gut and she was having a hard time keeping things in focus.

Lana was gesturing at her, but Patti couldn't understand what the woman was trying to tell her.

The man who had given her the vodka passed her a glass of red wine and clinked glasses. She took a sip, then started on her food. She was starving and it all looked good, but she had no sense of smell and everything tasted the same, only the textures were different.

She had lost a lot of weight in the past six days, and with it strength. It had been a major task just to get out of bed and come downstairs, even with Lana's help. She couldn't afford to get any weaker. She didn't want to die here. And she wanted to be able to defend herself the next time Raya came after her. She had to eat. She had to have the nourishment.

At first she was tentative, careful to take small portions so that she wouldn't choke. Her stomach had shrunk and, intellectually, she knew that she should not be eating heavy food like this. Maybe some broth, some fruit juice, maybe some bread, but not the other stuff.

But she couldn't help herself; within a minute or two she had lost all self-control, and she began shoveling it in as fast as she could.

She lost her grip on her fork and it clattered to the linoleum floor. But it no longer mattered. She needed food.

She picked up a handful of potatoes with her bare fingers and shoved them into her mouth. She pulled the fish apart with both hands and stuffed the pieces into her mouth, and then the bread, and oranges. She couldn't eat fast enough; her hunger was overwhelming, and even though she knew that she was probably doing herself damage, she couldn't stop.

The noise in the kitchen had gradually died down and everyone was looking at her; even Raya, a smirk on her face, had stopped eating and was gazing at her from across the table.

Lana got up from her chair and she was at Patti's shoulder. "You must stop this now," she said.

Patti shoved her away and grabbed a bowl of what looked like honey from the woman next to her. She shoved a large slice of bread into the bowl, but before she could bring it to her mouth her stomach suddenly convulsed and she dropped the bread on the tablecloth, knocking over her glass of red wine.

Lana helped her up, and her stomach convulsed again.

Her head was roaring, sweat rolled off her forehead, and her legs were so weak she would have crumpled to a heap on the floor without Lana's strong hands holding her up.

"Can you make it upstairs to the bathroom?" Lana asked, her voice coming from a great distance.

Patti tried to speak, but the words wouldn't form in her mouth. She shook her head. Waves of nausea struck her and her stomach convulsed again. The bitter taste of bile rose in the back of her throat.

Lana hustled her across the kitchen and out into the backyard, and everything came up in a rush, the vodka burning her throat and the inside of her nose. Her stomach continued to heave even after it was empty, and although it was below zero she was drenched in sweat and she began to shiver almost uncontrollably.

Lana was right there holding her shoulders and leading her back to the house. "It's all right now, Patti. I'll take you back to your room. Maybe later I'll bring you some tea and maybe a little something better for you to eat."

"The bastards," Patti said softly. "The dirty rotten motherfuckers."

TWENTY-FOUR

•

Even though it was four in the afternoon on Christmas day, and bitter cold, traffic in and around Red Square was as heavy as Kampov had seen it in a long time. People were walking as if it were summer. Maybe it was wishful thinking.

He had to show his identification booklet to the armed guard at Spassky Gate before he was allowed to drive inside and park in front of the four-story Senate Building. When he got out and approached the door, the two ceremonial guards snapped to attention, bringing their AK-47s up in salute.

They looked cold, and Kampov felt truly sorry for the bastards, stationed outside on Christmas. But then he was inside, his leather heels loud on the marble floor.

He had to hand over his identification at the security station, manned by a pair of guards armed with pistols, in the middle of the entry hall.

"Are you carrying a weapon, Captain?" one of them asked.

"I left it at my office," Kampov said.

"What is your purpose here today?"

"I have an appointment with Leonid Zhernov," Kampov said. He and Zhernov had been best friends and drinking buddies in the Frunze Military Academy. Now Kampov was an MVD captain while Zhernov was a senior aide on Putin's staff.

The great hall was busy this morning, and several people flashed their IDs at the guards and were waved inside. Even now in the new Russia, Christmas Day was not an official holiday, especially not here in the Kremlin.

The guard phoned upstairs to confirm the appointment. "Your identification will be returned to you when you leave."

The second guard motioned for Kampov to step through the security arch. "It's on the fourth floor. Do not get off the elevator on any other floor."

"I understand," Kampov said, and he walked across the hall to the bank of elevators.

He'd phoned for this appointment first thing this morning, but Zhernov's secretary had not been able to fit him in until now.

"Can you tell me why you would like to see Mr. Zhernov?" she'd asked.

"It's a personal matter. We're old friends."

"Yes, Captain. He'll have a few minutes for you at 1615."

It was that time when Kampov got off the elevator

and walked back to Zhernov's outer office, where his secretary was seated behind a large desk.

She was an attractive middle-aged woman with blond hair, and when she looked up she glanced at the wall clock. "Thank you for being prompt." She telephoned Zhernov to announce that the captain was here, and then nodded toward the door. "He'll see you now."

Zhernov was a tightly built man who looked even now as if he could put on a soccer uniform and play with the Frunze team, of which he had been captain. His office was very large and well furnished. Large leaded glass windows looked over the wall and across the Moscow River. He was dressed in an expensive suit, his tie loose. File folders and reports bound in leather, along with dozens of western newspapers and magazines, were piled on his desk and on a conference table. He looked harried.

He looked up when Kampov came in. "*Eb tvoiu mat,*" he said, which literally meant, fuck your mother. "This better be important, Sascha. I'm slammed here today." He got to his feet.

"I wouldn't be here if it wasn't," Kampov said. He and Zhernov embraced, and he handed his old friend the manila envelope with copies of the Monroe file.

"Do I need to check with Granov before I open this?" Zhernov asked. He motioned for Kampov to have a seat across from him.

"He's eighteen months from retirement and wants his second star and command of the Militia. He's just covering his ass, and I need your help on this one."

"Covering his ass. You should try it sometime. It's good for the soul. Maybe you wouldn't still be a captain."

"I like being a captain; I'm not cooped up in a stuffy office all day."

Zhernov sat back and gave his friend an appraising look. "You've got that bug up your ass again. I can see it a kilometer away. What gives, Sascha?"

"David and Patricia Monroe, an American couple doing business here in Moscow, maybe with the Mafia. They showed up at Sheremetyevo six days ago, where they were met by two guys; one of them, we think, has ties with the Chechens and possibly even al-Quaeda. Mr. Monroe got himself shot to death, his body stripped of identification and left on the side of a deserted highway east of here. His wife has disappeared. Most likely kidnapped, though Militia is searching for her body."

Zhernov opened the envelope and looked at the photographs of the Monroes, lingering over the wife's. "An attractive woman. Almost reminds me of Nina." He'd been Kampov's best man. "Are they raising funds for the cause?"

"I think so."

"What's your interest here? Do you know these people?"

"What I know is in that file," Kampov said. "But I have a feeling about this one, Lenya."

"I've heard that one before."

"Listen to me. If there is an al-Quaeda or Chechen connection, and they get their ransom money, you and I know that Mrs. Monroe will be murdered."

"They'd be fools not to," Zhernov agreed.

"What if that's it? And what if they get their money?"

Zhernov shrugged. "They'll be a little better funded."

"Right," Kampov said. "And what will they do with that money? Here in Moscow?"

Zhernov started to reply, but then held off. He took his time glancing through the Monroes' file. Finally he looked up. "Nothing much has happened for you since Nina died."

Kampov tightened up. "This has nothing to do with her."

"Yes, it has. You're on a mission. You couldn't save her, so now maybe you can save this one. Redeem yourself."

."Fuck you," Kampov said, rising.

"Sit down," Zhernov said. "I suspect that no one has talked to you like this until now. You'll just have to listen. I don't care what your motivation is. All I care about is that you finally do have a motivation. Maybe you've finally got your head out of your ass."

"I came here for your help, not a goddamn lecture."

"Fair enough," Zhernov said. "What do you want?"

"Granov has turned this case over to Militia. I want it back, and I'll need to have some doors opened for me, and fast. No interference. Just let me do my job and save this woman, if I can."

"If she's still alive," Zhernov said. "And then what?"

"I don't understand."

"Yes, you do," Zhernov said. "I'm your friend, remember? If you pull this off you'll be the hero of the hour. What'll be next for you? Retirement or promotion?"

Kampov hadn't asked himself that question, because he didn't think he gave a damn.

"You'd better have the answer, Sascha, because I think that some important people will want to know."

"Will you help?" Kampov asked.

"I'll see what I can do."

• • •

When Kampov got back to his office, Bokarev was half asleep, his feet propped up on his desk. The operations center was all but deserted. Only the watch officer and a radio operator were on duty, and they didn't bother to look up. The other eighteen staffers were gone.

"Where's everybody?" he asked.

Bokarev opened his eyes, and grinned. "I sent them home. It's Christmas, you know."

"What about you?"

"Yana told me to stay here until you got back, and then bring you home. The girls have a feast planned for us."

It was the last thing Kampov wanted. He was in no mood for company, especially cheerful company. "Not tonight. Anyway I don't believe in Grandfather Frost."

"Okay. So why don't we find ourselves a couple of hot broads and fly down to Helsinki for a couple of days. Or, better yet, let's just fly down there and get us a couple of young Finnish girls."

"Does Yana know you talk like this?" Kampov asked.

"God in heaven no! They believe in *Ded Moroz,* even if you don't, and they think I'm something special."

"Then go home to them."

"Not without you," Bokarev said firmly. "And on the way I'll tell you about my Mafia pals who're going to find Voronin for us."

"No."

Bokaraev grabbed the phone and held it out. "You call her and break the news. I don't have the guts."

"*Pizdec,*" Kampov said. "I don't have the guts either."

Bokarev replaced the phone. "Good," he said, and he jumped up and got his coat. "You can sleep at our place tonight. Yana won't want you driving after you're . . . afterwards."

On the way out a courier showed up with an envelope marked *The Office of the Prime Minister.* Kampov had to sign for it, and when the courier had left he opened the envelope. It was a letter from Putin himself, giving Kampov absolute authority in the investigation of the "circumstances" of the Monroes. Anything he asks for will be immediately granted. Rank or previous assignments will be disregarded at his discretion. By order of Vladimir Putin, Prime Minister, F.S.R.

"Holy Mother of God," Bokarev said softly when he'd read the letter. "I think I'll get drunk with you tonight, because tomorrow we're going to be busy."

TWENTY-FIVE

•

Patti had passed out on the bed, and when she awoke it was pitch black outside and the house was quiet. She'd been burning up before, but now huddled under the blanket she was freezing cold. She had no idea what time it was, but from somewhere in the far distance she heard a train whistle as it approached Noginsk.

She pushed the covers aside and got painfully out of the bed. Her kidneys ached, but she didn't have to use the toilet. The leather slippers Lana had brought for her were still on her feet, and she was grateful for that and the glass of sweet tea.

The train whistle was much closer now, and Patti tottered over to the window. The backyard and the empty field and woods beyond looked bleak, from another planet, an alien world. Once, when she was a teenager, she traveled with her parents on the train down to Palm Beach. It was a bit of foolish nostalgia, romantic nonsense as far as her father was concerned, but her mother had insisted.

What Patti remembered most about the trip was the incredible sense of freedom she'd felt. She'd been wrapped in a cocoon of luxury, she had her own compartment, twenty-four-hour room service, the ever-changing scenery, and no worries whatsoever. She was aboard the train, and it was the railroad's responsibility to see to her comfort and well-being.

Her freedom was just outside the window, past the wall and into the town, where she could get on the train and be warm and safe again.

The train passed through the city without stopping and gradually its whistle faded into the distance to the west, toward Moscow.

Patti touched the frosted windowpane with the tips of her fingers, tracing a pattern of little circles. A clarity was coming over her, as if she was emerging from a fog. It was the lack of food, she expected. Religious fanatics on long-term fasts sometimes claimed they had periods during which their senses were hyper-acute. They claimed it was God touching them, and was proof of His existence. Patti thought it was more likely due to the balance or maybe imbalance of chemicals in the brain that was trying whatever it could to make sure the body survived.

She turned away from the window and stared at the blanket covering the doorway. It had to be late because the television was silent, and she couldn't hear the sounds of voices from downstairs.

So far as she was able to figure it had been six days since she and David had arrived at Sheremetyevo. His body had been lying alongside the highway all that time. It would have been discovered by now, and reported to the police. Customs would have records of David arriving with his wife. By now a search would have started, but Russia was a vast country that had a habit of swallowing people. Without clues, the police might never find her.

It was up to her to survive this. She'd fought back once and they respected her for it. They'd given her a little space. This time she needed to get word back to the States that she was being held here, and she knew exactly how she was going to do it.

Straightening up a little, she went to the door, hesitated for just a moment, then pushed the blanket aside. The television room and corridor were dark.

"Hello," she called out.

Lana's head popped up from the couch where she'd apparently been asleep. "You must keep quiet," she said.

"What are you doing up here?"

Lana shrugged. "Boris is drunk."

"What time is it?"

"I don't know. Midnight maybe."

"Tell Sergey I'll get the money, but I'll need to use the telephone."

"We have to wait until morning."

"It'll be late at night in the States."

Lana pulled her blanket away and got up. She was dressed in jeans and a T-shirt, but she was still wearing her slippers. "You don't want to play games. They will kill you."

"If they want their goddamn money I'm ready to get it for them," Patti said. "I want you to go downstairs and wake them up."

"Are you sure?"

"Yes," Patti said. "I'm going to use the bathroom now, and when they're ready for me I want a cup of tea and some bread and butter."

THE SEVENTH DAY

January 8th

TWENTY-SIX

•

Tobias Anderson came out of his study shortly after ten-thirty in the evening, finally finished with the work he'd brought home from the office. It had been a long day, made longer because he was worried about Patti and David. Runkov had not e-mailed or called him with an update, so at this point Anderson felt up in the air, though finding the body of a man named David Monroe in Moscow couldn't possibly be a coincidence.

He went into the living room, where his wife Cynthia was fixing him a martini at the sideboard.

She looked up. "Still no word from Valeri?"

"No," Anderson said, sitting down on one of the wing-back chairs.

"Maybe you should call him."

"He'll let me know when he finds something."

His wife set his martini on the table beside him as the telephone rang. She answered it. "Hello."

Anderson looked at her. She suddenly had an odd expression on her face.

"Patti, is that you?" she asked.

Anderson glanced at the record light on the telephone. It was on.

Cynthia handed the phone to her husband. "Something's wrong."

"Patti, this is Tobias. Are you okay?"

"Good evening, Mr. Anderson," Patti said, formally. "David and I are just fine, but we need some help."

Anderson put his hand over the phone. "Call Valeri on the other line and have him contact the FBI." He took his hand away. "I understand, Patricia," he said, matching her formal tone. "What can Mrs. Anderson and I do for you?"

"I want you to know that my life is in absolutely no danger. Do you understand what I'm telling you?"

"Yes, I understand," Anderson said. She sounded tired, and maybe defiant. Something was wrong with her, but she was alive, and for now that was a relief.

"I'm involved in a business transaction that I have to clear up immediately. Do you know my Hong Kong account? The one you administer?"

"Yes, of course," Anderson replied, even though he knew nothing about it.

"I need you to transfer twenty million dollars into that account as soon as possible."

Anderson's grip on the telephone tightened. He could hear his wife talking on the other phone in the hall. Apparently she'd reached Runkov. "That's a lot of money," he said.

"Yes, it is. But can you help?"

"Naturally, but it'll take me a day or two to raise it."

"Thank you," Patti said, and he could hear the relief in her voice.

"If I have a question, is there a number where I can reach you?"

The line was silent for a moment or two, but then

Patti was back. "No," she said. "But may I call tomorrow at this same time?"

"Of course. I should have some encouraging news for you by then."

"Thank you, Mr. Anderson," Patti said, her relief even plainer. "And when you see Aunty Gina, say hello for me, would you?"

Anderson was taken aback for just a second, but then recovered. "I'll talk to her tonight."

"Thank you," Patti said, and the connection was broken, but Anderson had the feeling that she'd been about to say something else before she was cut off.

He put the phone down, and his wife brought him the other one.

"Valeri," he said. "I just now finished talking with Patti, and she's in trouble."

"Are you sure?" Runkov asked. "Did she say anything about David?"

"She said they were both fine, but she wants me to transfer twenty million to some account of hers in Hong Kong that I've never heard of. And then she asked me to say hello to her Aunt Gina."

"Maybe this Aunt Gina knows something."

"The woman's been dead for five years."

"I'll call the Bureau now," Runkov said. "You'd better expect some company tonight."

"They won't want to jump through any hoops for me."

"I know," Runkov said. "But they will for me, or I'll get Howard to give Phil a call." Howard Steward was the attorney general and Phillip Rosen was the FBI director.

"Thanks, Valeri," Anderson said and he hung up.

"What's happening?" his wife asked.

"Patti's in big trouble, and we're going to try to help her," Anderson said. He took a sip of his martini, then put it down. "Better make some coffee; it's going to be a long night."

TWENTY-SEVEN

•

First thing in the morning, Kampov drove out to the sprawling complex of buildings and training sites that was the headquarters for the Federal Security Service's Center of Special Operations (CSN). Just outside of the town of Balashikha-2, ten kilometers from Moscow's outer ring highway, security for the base was even tighter than at the Kremlin itself.

He pulled up at the main gate, powered down his window, and held out his MVD identification booklet for a pair of tough-looking Spetsnaz troops who had come out of the guardhouse as he approached. They were dressed in winter white camouflage and armed with AS Val assault rifles.

"I'm here to see Colonel Ivan Baturin," Kampov said. "He promised to leave a pass for me."

"Get out of the car, Captain," the sergeant said. He was a young man and looked tough as bar steel.

Kampov did as he was told, keeping his hands in plain sight at all times.

The sergeant slung his rifle over his shoulder and hurriedly patted down Kampov, while the other man stood a couple of meters to the side, his rifle at the ready.

A third Special Forces operator emerged from the

guardhouse and came over to Kampov's car. He had a large black dog that began immediately to search for odors of explosives.

No one smiled or said anything until the K9 operator nodded his all clear and went back inside.

"Do you know your way?" the sergeant asked, handing Kampov a plastic security pass.

"*Da,* and it's Captain Kampov," he said sharply.

The sergeant saluted, though he was obviously unimpressed. "Yes, Sir. Colonel Baturin is expecting you."

Kampov held his eye for a long moment, then clipped the pass to his lapel, got in his car and drove through the raised gate.

Spetsnaz, or, *Voiska **spets**ialnovo **naznacheniya,*** were Russia's special operations forces. The military unit was divided into three divisions, which included Spetsgruppa Alfa, which was the counterterrorist arm; Special Service Operations (SSO), which trained and fielded the bodyguards for Russia's top officials, and Spetsgruppa V, or Vympel, which were the best of the best, trained for counterterrorism and any other jobs that the Federal Security Service, including MVD, needed them for.

Baturin, who commanded one of the Vympel units, had gone through Frunze with Kampov and Zhernov, the three of them pals for life until they had gone their separate ways. But Baturin had come back from Chechnya to attend Kampov's wedding, miffed that Zhernov, instead of he, was the best man. He'd promised Nina that he would break Kampov's neck if ever she got tired of her husband and wanted to be rescued. And he'd come back again to attend her funeral.

Vympel had four operative units and Baturin commanded one of the special field operations sections for the Moscow unit. He was up for his first star, and when he got it he would become vice commander of all Unit Four's field operations sections. And that's as far as he ever wanted to go.

"I'm a combat field officer," he'd told Kampov a few years ago. "If the bastards try to promote me to a desk job I'll resign my commission."

The main road looped through the birch forest passing clusters of buildings, some of them quite large, that contained the various unit headquarters, along with barracks, mess halls, armories, communications centers, classrooms, and gymnasiums and pistol ranges for indoor training. One airstrip off to the east was used for antiterrorist tactics involving airplanes, another was for helicopter deployments. A mock nuclear plant, a dam, a factory, a complete cityscape with tall buildings and narrow streets perfect for ambushes, and other likely targets were used in live fire training exercises. And throughout the huge facility were several extremely tough confidence courses, firing ranges, live demolitions practice areas, parachute drop towers, and a five kilometer stretch of paved road filled with sharp curves and steep hills that was used for driver training.

Among the largest buildings on the base was the five-story hospital. The basic training program lasted for five years, and more than half of all candidates washed out at one point or another. But injuries, often serious, were common, and so was the occasional death.

As Baturin was fond of saying: "It's a tough world."

Gunfire rattled somewhere in the distance.

The colonel came out of the Vympel Headquarters Building as Kampov pulled up and parked. He was a ruggedly built, no-nonsense military officer in his mid-

forties, salt and pepper buzz cut, square face, and wide
dark eyes that were direct. He was dressed in winter
white camos, bloused boots, a 9mm Steyr GB Austrian
autoloader in a holster on his chest.

He marched across to Kampov and they embraced
warmly. "*Eb tvoiu mat,* it's good to see you Sascha."

"It's been too long," Kampov said. He'd forgotten
how much he missed his friends, who had gotten on
with their lives while he had all but stagnated.

Baturin gave him a critical look. "You came out here
to talk because you have a bug up your ass that you
don't trust to your own people."

The MVD fielded its own spetsnaz troops, the OSN,
which were Russian National Guard. But the 8th OSN
unit for Moscow, which was named VV *Rus,* was firmly
under General Granov's personal control.

"Something like that," Kampov said.

"Let's go for a walk, and you can tell me all about
it," Baturin said, and they headed down an access road
behind the headquarters building to the urban warfare
setting at the bottom of the wooded hill. "Sounds like
you've gotten yourself in a jam with Granov."

"Not yet, but it could be heading that way," Kampov
admitted.

At the bottom they came to a street that ran directly
into the mock city. A Vympel fire team of eight men
emerged from the woods to the left and entered the
city, leapfrogging by pairs, firing as they went, tossing
flash/bang grenades into doorways and taking out the
figure of a sniper on one of the rooftops with a hand-
held missile launcher.

"Looks realistic," Kampov said.

"It is," Baturin said, heading down the street right
into the middle of the exercise. "Live fire."

"You have some good-looking boys."

"They have a lot of discipline. Not like you and me at their age. We were willing to take risks in Afghanistan."

"Getting away with it by pure dumb luck."

Baturin laughed as the battle for the city swept past them and continued around the corner at the end of the block. "What brings you out here to my Elysian Fields?"

"I need some help, Ivan."

"Officially?"

Kampov handed him Putin's letter, and after he'd read it, he handed it back.

"Assuming it's not a forgery, what do you need?"

"An American woman and her husband were kidnapped seven days ago. Chechens, we think, and probably Mafia. Her husband was shot to death just outside Moscow, and it's likely that the woman is being held for ransom. I'm going to find her, with your help, and when I do I'll need some dependable muscle."

They walked in silence to the end of the block. The cityscape was deathly silent now. "You didn't need that letter," Baturin said.

"It might come in handy if you have to cover your ass."

"Fuck it."

"Are you in?"

"Hell yes," Baturin said. "We've been three months back from Grozny, and we're getting soft. But let's put it to my boys, and see what they have to say. They might not want to work for a civilian pussy like you."

•

TWENTY-EIGHT

Special Agent Brian Wilson, the swing shift duty officer in the FBI's Operations Center on Pennsylvania Avenue, had just gotten his second cup of coffee for the night from the canteen, when his hot line phone rang. FBI Director Phillip Rosen's caller ID came up, and Wilson spilled half the coffee on his desk. In his eleven years with the Bureau he'd never once spoken with any of the three directors he'd served under.

"Operations Duty Officer Special Agent Wilson, how may I help you, Mr. Director?"

"Are you familiar with Valeri Runkov, from the Russian desk, over at Justice?"

"I know of him, Sir."

"He sent you a classified e-mail on one of our secure addresses an hour ago. He's gotten no response and he wants to know why."

Wilson was at a loss. Operations got dozens, sometimes more than a hundred, e-mails and telephone calls in a typical shift. He did not personally see all of them. That's why he had a staff to sift through the nightly deluge bringing only the important sitreps from the various field offices around the world to him for action.

"Sir, I haven't seen it yet—"

"Find it, read it, and respond to it," Director Rosen said. "I don't want to hear from Runkov again."

"Yes, Sir. Will you want a report in the morning?"

"No," Rosen said sharply and he hung up.

* * *

After ten in the evening, as Greenwalt was about to head upstairs to take a shower and get ready for bed, the telephone rang. His wife, Margaret, had already gone up and was watching television in the bedroom, and the girls were in their rooms on their computers. Sometimes he felt as if he was living inside his own little sphere, while all around him his family moved in their own worlds.

It was Bob Donagle from the Russian desk. "Something's come up that I think you need to know about, Sir."

Greenwalt controlled his spike of anger. "I'm listening."

"Brian Wilson, who's the Ops OD tonight, forwarded an e-mail he got from a guy on the Russian desk over at Justice about an American couple in Moscow. The husband was found shot to death in the woods outside Moscow, and the wife is missing."

"What's that have to do with me?" Greenwalt asked.

"The woman called a friend of hers here in D.C. and asked for twenty million dollars. It's a ransom demand. They're sure of it."

"That's why we have a liaison office in Moscow," Greenwalt said, his temper rising. "Why'd you call me?"

"I e-mailed Dick Ligget to find out if he knew anything about it. The MVD contacted him a couple of days ago and wanted a backgrounder on the couple. Evidently that's exactly what he's been doing."

"I'm listening," Greenwalt said. He was just about at the end of his patience. The Bureau's liaison office in Moscow technically came under his jurisdiction, but his office was primarily counterterrorism.

"The MVD captain who made contact, name of Alexander Kampov, thinks the husband was hit by Chechen separatists who work for or with al-Quaeda," Donagle said. "Twenty million would go a long way for them. I thought you would want to know."

Greenwalt's thoughts were suddenly spinning in a dozen different directions, but primarily toward his own future with the Bureau. This situation could possibly mean his salvation, or at least the resurrection of his career.

"Good call, Bob," he said. "Do you have the Monroes' file? The one Ligget dug up?"

"Yes, Sir. Right here."

"Good. I want you to e-mail me that file, plus anything else you've come up with from Ops, from Ligget, and whatever you can find out about this Kampov character."

"I'm on it."

"What's the name of the woman's friend here in Washington?"

"Tobias Anderson; he's a high-powered criminal attorney. I have his file here as well."

"Good," Greenwalt said. "I'm taking this case as of now. But I want a forensics team out there tonight."

"Yes, Sir. I'm sending everything I've got to your home computer now."

"Listen, Bob, I want you to keep a close eye on Moscow for me. Can you do that?"

"You can count on it, Mr. Greenwalt."

TWENTY-NINE

•

In the dark of morning, Patti woke from a troubled sleep. Sitting up in bed, she held the thin blanket to her chin. A door slammed downstairs, and someone shouted something in anger. She thought it was Lysenko and she expected trouble.

After the telephone call he'd said nothing to her, but the look in his eye had changed. He'd known that something had been wrong with Patti's behavior; she'd seen it. But he'd just shaken his head, got his coat, and left the dacha.

Lana had brought Patti back up to the bedroom, and a half hour later brought up some sweet tea.

Someone came up the stairs, and moments later the blanket covering the doorway was pulled aside. Lysenko was there, still dressed in his leather coat and boots. A faint smile was on his lips, but it was impossible to gauge his mood.

"There'll be no money," he said pleasantly, as if they were discussing the weather.

"Tobias has the money," Patti said. "He'll send it to me."

"You lied to me. You've lied to all of us, from the very beginning."

Patti forgot her hunger. Raya stood behind him in the corridor, an odd expression on her face, and all the upstairs lights had been turned on.

"I don't know what you're talking about."

Lysenko stared at her for a long time, and Patti got the impression that he was trying to come to some decision.

"You have to let me call him again, then you'll see."

"Your Aunt Gina died five years ago," Lysenko said, his voice soft.

Patti's heart lurched. "That's not true."

"Yes, it is," Lysenko said. He stepped back into the corridor. "We're going back to Moscow now."

"What about the woman?" Raya asked.

Lysenko looked in at Patti. "Hang her in the shower, less of a mess that way. Afterwards Boris can dump her body next to her husband's."

Raya was grinning. "I like it."

Lysenko went away and Raya came into the bedroom.

"Too bad for you, Patricia," she said. "Actually it's too bad for me as well. I would have enjoyed teaching you some things. You would have made an interesting student, I think."

"Goddamn you to hell."

Raya seemed to consider Patti's words for a moment, and she nodded. "Maybe we're there already." She pulled the blanket away from Patti and tossed it aside. "Get undressed."

"Fuck you."

Raya backhanded Patti's swollen jaw, snapping her head back. "Get undressed."

Spots swam in front of Patti's eyes, and she was sick to her stomach and very hot. She try to push Raya away, but the woman was undressing her, pulling her T-shirt over her head, taking off the leather slippers, and then pulling her jeans and panties off.

"It's really too bad, Patricia." Raya's voice was in Patti's ear. "I would've liked to have gotten to know you better."

She got Patti out of the bed, out into the television room, and down the corridor to the bathroom. Boris and Voronin were at the end of the hall. When Patti met their eyes, Voronin turned away, but Boris smiled.

Lysenko stood at the head of the stairs, a look of indifference on his face.

The babushka had set a stool in the claw foot tub, and the noose had been tied around the rusty showerhead sticking out of the cracked plaster wall.

Patti tried hold back, but Raya drew her roughly into the bathroom and across to the tub.

"Do this and you won't get your money," Patti said. The room was rotating around her, the floor rising and falling.

"You had your chance," Raya said. She picked Patti off her feet, lifted her onto the stool, and slipped the noose around her neck.

Patti's fear spiked. She was afraid that she would lose her balance and fall off the stool. She was going to die someday, but not now, not like this.

Raya stepped away, and Patti tried to pull the noose off her neck, when the babushka suddenly turned the cold-water tap on full.

The stream of water hit Patti in the face and chest with enough force to cause her to rear backward, and her bare feet slipped off the stool. For an instant she felt as if she were floating in midair, but the rope suddenly brought her up short with such force the intense pain caused her to cry out, but she had no breath.

Her feet swung wildly, her legs pumping involuntarily, wrenching her neck, her own weight pulling the noose impossibly tight. She tried to grapple with the rope in an effort to lift herself up, but it was no use.

Her vision started to fade, a billion stars bursting inside her head, her empty stomach and bowels heaving, her strength going.

Her feet stopped twitching and her hands fell to her sides.

She knew that she was dying, and no one was there to help her. Not David, not her father, not Tobias, not even the man she'd started dreaming about three days ago. She hadn't been able to make out his face until now. He was a Russian, she was sure of it, and he was smiling at her. His eyes were the most beautiful things she'd ever seen, a deep sadness in them as if he'd lost something very precious to him, but he was coming for her.

Too late, she thought, her eyes coming to rest on Lana's.

The grandmother was there in the corridor, along with Raya, and even Lysenko and Voronin. All there to watch her die.

As her vision faded to black, the showerhead above her broke with a loud snap, and she was falling down a long, deep tunnel, water spraying everywhere.

THIRTY
•

The predawn darkness was bitterly cold when Kampov and Baturin drove down to the urban warfare cityscape, parking the Spetsnaz *GAZik* twenty meters outside of the exercise area where Special Operations Staff Sergeant Yuri Pavlenko was waiting with his five-man fire team. All of them were dressed in white camos, red armbands for the fire team, a blue armband for Kampov, and a green armband for Baturin.

"Soft-tipped rubber bullets with dye, and light loads so nobody gets seriously hurt," Baturin said. "Night vision oculars, but there'll be no hand-to-hand this time. Just shoot and scoot. If you're hit consider yourself an immediate KIA."

"The same goes for Captain Kampov?" Pavlenko asked. He was twenty-five, wiry and arrogant. He had a faint smile on his lips.

"Since it's six to one, we'll give him a little leeway," Baturin said, but Kampov shook his head.

"If I'm hit the game is over," Kampov said. "I don't want the kids to think that I took advantage of them."

Pavlenko laughed out loud. It was a challenge, and he and his people loved it.

"I'll be at the opposite end of the ops area with the good captain," Baturin said. He glanced at his watch. "Your mission is to find and defeat the sniper in a minimum time, taking as few casualties as possible."

"His job is to stay safe and take out as many of us as possible," Pavlenko said languidly. "If he can."

"The mission total will be 150 points," Baturin said. "Twenty each for your operators, and fifty for you."

"Makes me a juicy target," Pavlenko said.

"The op begins at 0730, that's eighteen minutes from now," Baturin said. "We'll be in place by then. Good hunting, gentlemen."

He and Kampov walked back to the *GAZik* and headed to the opposite side of the cityscape as the Spetsnaz fire team dispersed and melted into the narrow, twisting streets.

"I assume that you've got a plan, Sascha," Baturin said. "These boys are good."

"And arrogant," Kampov said.

Baturin had to laugh. "They've earned the right."

"Was Chechnya tough this time?"

Baturin nodded, grim-lipped. "We lost some good

men. The letters to their parents were damned hard to write."

"I'll bet they were," Kampov said. "Turn around and go back."

Baturin gave him a sharp look. "Are you giving up?"

"Just changing the rules," Kampov said.

"Yuri won't."

"Unless he learns how to adapt, he'll get himself killed one of these days," Kampov said. "And he needs to lose some of his arrogance. Switch off your headlights, please."

"*Pizdec*," Baturin swore softly, but he switched off the *GAZik*'s headlights and headed back toward the starting point.

About fifty meters from the edge of the urban warfare operations course, Kampov motioned for Baturin to pull up. "If they're sharp, they'll post someone to watch their backs."

"Not for this exercise," Baturin said. He wasn't happy.

"You and I always did," Kampov said, getting out of the vehicle. He put on his safety goggles and night vision ocular, checked the load on his AS Val, and checked the two spare magazines in a pocket of his camos. He pulled a flashlight and roll of duct tape out of another pocket and attached the torch to the stock of his assault rifle so that he could switch it on and off with his left hand.

"You're a shit, do you know that?" Baturin said.

"All's fair in love and war; isn't that what they taught us at Frunze?"

"These kids never got the message."

"Maybe it's time they did," Kampov said. He cycled

a round into the rifle's firing chamber, switched the safety to off, and started toward the street where the Spetsnaz operators were waiting to get started.

Baturin was right behind him. "The op isn't supposed to start for nine minutes."

"I know," Kampov said.

He pulled up at the corner of a building and carefully looked down the street. For just a moment he thought that he might have misjudged the operators, but then he spotted the ghostly image of one of them less than five meters away.

The night vision ocular, hanging down from his helmet in front of his left eye, cast a pale green glow. The operator leaned against the edge of a building, his back to Kampov, and a second man stepped out of an alley across the street, and motioned to the first man, who held up four fingers. Four minutes to go.

Kampov spotted a third and fourth man farther up the street, then the fifth near them, and finally the sixth, behind a parked car. It was impossible to tell which one of them was Sergeant Pavlenko, but it didn't matter. All of them were facing forward, and all of them presented clear targets.

He stepped out into the street and noiselessly headed for the first operator. One meter out he flipped his night vision ocular out of the way, switched on the flashlight and shot the man in the back.

As he swung his rifle to the right the other five operators were turning around, not knowing exactly what was happening, but trying to bring their rifles to bear.

The flashlight beam overloaded their night vision oculars, temporarily blinding them.

Methodically Kampov shot all five of them, before any return fire was directed toward him.

He lowered his rifle as the first of the operators started complaining.

"Sorry, gentlemen," he told them. "But if you're going to work with me, you'll have to do a better job of keeping on your toes. I don't want to bring anyone back in a body bag."

THIRTY-ONE
•

Tobias Anderson lived in a surprisingly modest red brick colonial in a neighborhood of similar homes on one-acre lots looking through the trees toward the Potomac, upriver from Washington.

It was nearly midnight by the time Greenwalt parked in the long driveway, behind a line of unmarked FBI cars and an electronics forensics van. The house was lit as if a party were going on inside.

Two agents in blue windbreakers with FBI stenciled in gold on the back, comms units in their ears, were stationed in front. One of them said something into his lapel mike as Greenwalt got out of his car.

FBI Special Agent Donald Nelson, thirty-something, clean cut, Ivy League, came to the door when Greenwalt walked up. He was in charge of the initial investigation.

"Good evening, Sir. I didn't expect to see you out here tonight."

"What do you have so far," Greenwalt asked, shaking hands.

"He made a tape of her call. When he figured something was wrong he contacted a friend of his over at Justice, who pulled some strings."

"Who has the tape?"

"We made two copies, one of which is in the house, the other is in the van for a quick pass, and the original is on its way downtown for analysis. She's supposed to call back in about nineteen hours and we'll need a comparison tape to judge her stress level."

"Well done, Don," Greenwalt said, and he ignored the Special Agent's momentary look of irritation. Agents in the field did not like interference from what they called suits, the people who spent their lives behind desks. "Have you conducted your initial interview?"

"I was just getting started when I was told you'd arrived."

"Let's get on with it, then," Greenwalt said. "It's late and I expect these good people would like to go to bed."

"Yes, Sir," Nelson said. "How do you want to be introduced?"

Greenwalt waved it off. "Who I am is none of their business for now."

A half-dozen FBI special agents and communications technicians were gathered in the stair hall and living room, where telephone intercept equipment had been set up. If and when Patti made a second call it would be routed to sophisticated recording and voice analysis equipment in the van outside, and sent to an unbeatable trace program downtown. Within seconds they would know if the caller was Patti, if she was in pain or in fear for her life, and her location no matter where in the world she was. They would also pick up any background noises that might give them further clues.

Tobias Anderson and his wife Cynthia were seated together on a couch in the living room. Neither of them was dressed for bed. They'd been at this since late this evening when the call had come from Russia.

They looked up when Nelson came in and sat down across from them. Greenwalt remained by the door.

"I was about to ask if you record all your telephone conversations. Or was this call special?"

"I'm an attorney," Anderson said. "I record everything."

"How long have you been acquainted with Mr. and Mrs. Monroe?"

"Since Patti was a child. We're friends of her parents."

"Why do you suppose she called you and not them?" Nelson asked.

"She had a falling out with her father when she married David," Anderson said, glancing at Greenwalt for just a moment. "Someone called me from the Bureau just before I left my office. Did that have anything to do with this?"

"I'm not at liberty to say."

Anderson shrugged. "If need be I'll telephone Phil Rosen in the morning. We belong to the same club."

"It won't be necessary to disturb the director," Greenwalt said, coming across the room before Nelson could reply. He held out his hand. "Ev Greenwalt. I'm assistant deputy director of the Bureau's counter-intelligence division."

Anderson shook hands with him. "What's your interest in this case?"

"We think it's likely that Mrs. Monroe as been kidnapped by people with connections to Chechen separatists and possibly even al-Quaeda. The twenty million is ransom, of course."

"It's possible that David was murdered," Anderson said.

"What makes you think so?"

"Someone from the Justice Department e-mailed me last night. Said a body of an American identified as David Monroe was found in the woods outside Moscow. But Patti told me that she and David are fine."

"Who was this someone at Justice?"

"Valeri Runkov. He used to work for me."

It was the same man who had made contact earlier this evening. Greenwalt glanced at Mrs. Anderson, who had a stoic look on her round, pleasant face. "I'm afraid that Mr. Monroe is dead. Our liaison officer in Moscow is working with the Russian counterinsurgency folks to find his killers and the whereabouts of Mrs. Monroe. So we're going to need all the help you can give us."

"If I pay the ransom they'll kill her anyway; is that right?" Anderson asked.

"It would be to their advantage," Greenwalt replied. "In any event we would recommend that you didn't pay anything."

"I hadn't intended to," Anderson said. "What's next?"

"Special Agent Nelson has some questions for you. We need to find out everything about her that we can. Anything that would help us learn who's done this and exactly where she's being held."

Anderson was nodding.

"If and when she phones again, we'll be able to trace her call."

"Then what?" Anderson asked.

"I'll go to Moscow and get her," Greenwalt said.

Cynthia Anderson looked up. "We warned them last time they were here," she said. "Poor David." She shook her head. "Poor Patti."

THIRTY-TWO

Sitting in the window seat looking out at the cold night, Patti absently caressed the angry red welts that encircled her neck. She was almost beyond pain. Her entire body seemed numb, incapable of feeling anything. It was the same with her mental state.

After waking up naked in the shower, ice-cold water spraying everywhere, she'd looked up into Lana's eyes. She remembered now that she'd not been angry, or frightened, or hurt, or even confused about what might happen next, only grateful for having the woman's help.

Her existence at that moment was what it was. She had no past, but her future was entirely up to her. Give in and she would die; she was convinced of it. They were playing a horrible game with her. They wanted the money, but they knew that she wouldn't help them, so they were trying to break her spirit, trying to make her give up, until in the end she would agree to anything.

Lana had said something that seemed very urgent, but Patti couldn't remember what it was, except that she had tried to answer, but her throat wouldn't work. Her vocal cords had been damaged, or bruised by the hanging.

Only one thought kept nagging around the edges of her awareness. It was small, actually, but it had bothered her all day. Lysenko had to have some connection back in the States. Someone who'd been able to dig deeply enough into her personal life to find out that Aunty Gina was dead. So why didn't he know that she and David were broke?

But that made no difference, either. All that counted was surviving. She kept that one idea as a bright point of light at the end of a dark tunnel. The bastards would not win. She wouldn't let them.

Patti didn't think it was midnight yet, but the house was silent, the television out in the corridor off, and no voices came from the kitchen. A slight sound at the doorway brought her up out of her lethargy and she turned.

Lysenko stood in the doorway, holding the blanket aside. The starlight that filtered through the small window was too dim for her to make out his expression, but she got the impression that he was looking at her like a cat looks at its prey, and she shivered.

"What do you want?" she asked, her ragged voice barely above a whisper.

"I think you know," he replied, his voice gentle, almost caressing.

"Money."

"Yes, that, too."

Whatever else he wanted wasn't important.

Lysenko stepped the rest of the way into the bedroom and let the blanket fall back. "How do you feel?"

Patti shook her head slightly. "You tried to kill me, but I'm still alive." Talking was painful for her. Water would help, but she couldn't bring herself to ask for it.

"It was the grandmother," Lysenko said gently. "She and the others are mad at Americans."

"You ordered it."

Lysenko brushed her accusation aside. "Tell me about your life as an American," he said.

"Why?"

"I want to understand you."

Patti felt a stirring in her gut and in her chest. For a

moment she didn't know what it was, until she realized she was feeling warmth. Lysenko hadn't come to kill her. He would never do it, not even in the end. He was the only person in this situation who had any strength, any real purpose.

She wanted to find an inner peace, something she'd never had in her life, and she thought that in a strange way being here like this with him might show her the way. Because of her capture and David's death she would finally find out who Patti really was. And she was ready to embrace the knowledge.

"I want to be loved," she whispered, and for the first time in her life she didn't feel like a fraud saying it.

THIRTY-THREE

•

A few minutes before midnight, Kampov was back out at the CSN barracks with Baturin and Sergeant Pavlenko's fire team from that morning. Bokarev had been gone most of the day, making the rounds at some of the other Mafia hangouts in town, but Smikov was still their best lead.

Baturin had brought over a few bottles of good vodka and passed them around. "No hard feelings, I hope," he said to Kampov. "They're a tough lot."

"They need to look over their shoulders, because if we're dealing with al-Quaeda they'll have their bases covered from every angle."

"You're talking about this hard case your people spotted with Voronin and the American couple. Any progress figuring out who he is, Sascha?"

"Feodor thought he was military or ex-military. He had the look. But if his picture is in our files we haven't found it yet."

"What makes you think he's al-Quaeda?" Pavlenko asked.

"Voronin's worked with them in the past, and Feodor said the guy didn't look Russian."

"A rag head?"

Kampov shook his head. "Probably not."

"What, are we going on a hunch, then?" Pavlenko asked. "I think we'd like something a little more substantial, especially if we're going to put our arses on the line."

Baturin started to answer, but Kampov held him off.

"I agree with you. But I don't think we have much time. They killed the husband and they're not going to risk holding onto the woman much longer. Anything could go wrong."

"Maybe it already has," Baturin said. "If I were in their shoes I would have killed her by now."

"Unless they're waiting for a ransom."

"Have you gotten any word from the Americans?"

"No, so we'll do this my way for now," Kampov said. "We know that Voronin has Mafia connections, and he's the key to finding the hard case and then Mrs. Monroe. But Voronin has disappeared. We've put out word to most of the Mafia clubs in town that we're looking for him, but no one wants to talk to us. So we're going to lean on them, which is where you guys come in."

"Kampov's private army?" Pavlenko asked. He shook his head. "Colonel?"

"Show them your letter," Baturin said.

Kampov took out the letter from Putin.

Pavlenko read it, looked up in surprise, then read it

again before he gave it to his fire team operators. "We can still say no, Captain, but frankly I'm impressed. You run with some big dogs."

"Sascha and I went to school with a guy on Putin's staff," Baturin said. "He owes us a few favors."

Kampov had to smile. Zhernov always had the worst grades, so his friends had to help him cheat on just about every exam. He was a big drinker and a late riser, so more often than they cared to count one or the other of them had to stand in for him. And after he'd gotten two girls pregnant, and ducked out of the marriages, they'd threatened to stop taking tests for him, stop standing in for him, and if need be they would cut off his dick.

Now he was their boss. It was the Russian way.

"Do we get to shoot someone?" one of the fire team operators asked. He looked as if he was still in high school, except for his eyes, which were old and very hard.

"Dead people won't be much help."

"These Mafia guys are *pizdahs*," the kid said. "They don't understand the way things really are. We'll teach them."

"Gennadi trained in Kazakhstan," Pavlenko said. "The hard way."

"I've heard the stories," Kampov said. Training for some Spetsnaz troops was brutal, depending on the division.

"They dropped him off at Gulag 27 as a political dissident. No ID, no special privileges. If he survived, he graduated; if not—" Pavlenko shrugged. "That was in the Ryn Pesk in the southwest. Nothing but desert. A hundred and forty in the summer, and forty below in the winter.

"His job was to escape and make it to Atyrau on the Caspian. It's a couple hundred kilometers, maybe a little more. A man alone couldn't carry enough food and especially water to make it, so he did the next best thing. He took one of the other prisoners with him. A man who'd been convicted of raping and killing children."

Kampov had never heard this story. "To help carry water?"

"*Nyet*," Pavlenko said. "Halfway across the desert, when they were both dying of dehydration, Gennadi slit the man's throat, drank his blood, and ate his liver."

"It was the only way to survive," Gennadi said, distantly.

"Mr. Putin says that we must help you, and Colonel Baturin agrees," Pavlenko said. "And so we shall." He sat forward. "But be careful what you wish for, Captain, you just may well get it."

THIRTY-FOUR

•

Lysenko moved like a cobra across the bedroom to where Patti was seated on the window ledge. She thought his eyes were handsome. They were expressive, unlike David's, which always seemed hooded, as if he were hiding something.

"Your husband never loved you," he said, and Patti thought that his British accent was cultured.

"No," she said. "He wanted my family's money."

"What about you, Patricia? Right now, what do you want?"

"To live."

Lysenko gently stroked her cheek with his fingers, and she shivered. "What else? You can tell me everything. I want to understand you."

"So do I," Patti said.

"What do you mean?"

Patti shook her head. "I don't know who I am," she said.

Lysenko smiled indulgently. "Let me show you," he said. He took her hands in his, gently helped her stand up, and folded her into his arms.

She tried to resist, just for a moment, until she laid her head on his chest. His was a neutral man smell, clean with a hint of something, perhaps bay rum. It was the old-fashioned aftershave that her father used, and just now she found some comfort because of it.

She wanted to close her eyes and go to sleep, safe in his arms, yet something, some little voice deep inside, was trying to warn her with the same urgency she'd seen in Lana's face.

Lysenko eased her T-shirt over her head and let it drop to the floor. Her breasts were extremely tender, but he caressed the nipples with his fingertips, his touch gentle, and she felt no pain.

She was drifting now, in and out of a dream state, brought on in part because she'd been deprived of food for so long, and in part because of the beatings that had caused her to retreat within herself, where nothing could touch her.

Lysenko helped her lie down on the bed, and he undid the waistband of her jeans and pulled them and her panties off.

Through half-closed eyes she watched him get undressed, and when he pulled off his underwear he had an erection. The sight of his naked body meant nothing to her; it wasn't titillating or frightening. It just was.

He eased her legs apart and caressed her thighs and then her vagina before he mounted her. She felt a very sharp pain as he entered her, which suddenly cleared her head.

Now her breasts hurt, her rib cage and legs and hips were on fire. Her thirst and hunger raged throughout her body, rebounding inside her head, threatening to blow off the top of her skull.

All at once she came back to the reality of her capture and torture and starvation. He wasn't her savior, he wasn't going to show her who she was.

Lysenko was lost in the moment, his breath strong against her cheek, his narrow hips pounding painfully against her as he thrust deeply.

"No," she cried, her voice cracked. "You son of a bitch! Get off me!"

She pushed at his chest, but he was too strong and he held her by her ass so that she couldn't get away. But then something a college friend had told her about being raped and how to stop it, if only temporarily, suddenly came into her head, and she straightened out her legs and pushed her pelvis upward.

Lysenko's penis was immediately ejected, and in the brief instant when he was startled and had not recovered, Patti went wild, pushing him away, scratching at his eyes.

He leaned back to protect himself, his legs spread, and she reared up and tried to knee him in the groin, but she only hit the inside of his thigh.

"Bitch," Lysenko croaked as he tried to grab her by the hair, but she shoved him in the chest, knocking him off balance, and he fell sideways onto the floor.

In an instant Patti was off the bed and headed for the door. She had no thought what was coming next except that she had to get away.

She reached the doorway, shoved the blanket aside, and was about to leap out into the corridor when Lysenko reached her, knocking her sideways. He caught her arm and pulled her off her feet so she landed face down on the cold floor.

"Goddammit," she cried, her voice ragged in her damaged throat. This wasn't going to happen. She wasn't going to let it happen. She tried to scramble away on her hands and knees, but Lysenko was right there.

He grabbed her ankles and roughly flipped her over onto her back, her head banging against the floorboards.

She tried to get one foot free to kick him again, but he had her legs spread and he was pulling her toward him.

"You'll learn respect," he grunted.

"Not from you," Patti cried. She slammed her palm up under his out thrust chin with every ounce of her strength.

He wasn't expecting the blow. His head snapped violently backward and he lost his grip on her legs.

Patti scrambled out of his reach, got to her feet and, as he looked up at her, she slammed the side of her foot into his neck, knocking him off balance again.

Before he could recover she stepped closer and slammed her heel into his forehead, and when he went down she stood there for several seconds dancing from one foot to the other.

"Come on big man!" she tried to shout, but it only came out as a hoarse whisper. "You want to teach me something?"

A light came on in the stair hall downstairs, but Patti ignored it.

"You son of a bitch," she said.

She stood over Lysenko, whose eyes were fluttering, her fists clenched. More than anything else she wanted to kill him here and now for what he'd done to her, and she didn't give a damn about the consequences. She'd had enough, from all of them. She'd taken shit all of her life. Every man she'd ever known, especially her father, had trivialized her.

Oh, it's just Patti. You know how she is.

No more, she vowed.

Lysenko's head was thrown back, exposing the front of his neck. Stepping to one side, Patti raised her foot to crush his Adam's apple, which would cause him to suffocate. She wanted to watch the life drain out of his eyes. She wanted to wipe him out of existence.

Lysenko suddenly came to life, batting Patti's foot aside and scrambling to his feet before she could completely regain her balance. But she was able to skip backward out of his reach as he lunged for her.

He charged like an angry bull, and Patti could do little more than keep out of his way, until she came to the head of the stairs and her foot found nothing. She tried to catch the banister, but her fingers just brushed it. She was tumbling end over end down the stairs, knowing that if she was knocked unconcious or if she broke a bone she would never leave this place alive.

Her landing was surprisingly soft, and she got to her feet as Lysenko started down the stairs.

Raya was coming up the corridor from the front of the house dressed in sweats, a pistol in her hand.

Without thinking, Patti charged up the stairs toward Lysenko, meeting him halfway. Before he could react, she ducked down, grabbed his ankles, and heaved with all of her might.

He fell to the side, his shoulder bouncing off the wall, and then tumbled forward, over the top of Patti's crouched form.

Before he reached the bottom, Patti leaped up and scrambled down the stairs on top of him, smashing her fists into his face and neck and chest. He was dazed and couldn't do much to defend himself, and Patti was like a mad woman—all the demons in hell trapped behind her eyes, fighting to get out.

"*Nyet*," Raya was shouting in her ear.

But Patti couldn't stop. She wanted to hurt him with everything in her being. "Bastard!" she screamed, her throat on fire.

Someone was behind her, tugging at her arm, trying to pull her away. She looked over her shoulder expecting to see Raya, but it was Lana.

"Stop this," Lana cried. She brandished a long piece of the split birch firewood they used for the kitchen stove.

Raya was next to her, the muzzle of the pistol pointed at Patti's forehead.

"You motherfuckers!" Patti screeched, and she turned back to Lysenko as Raya's finger tightened on the trigger and Lana swung the birch log, slamming it into the side of Patti's head.

The world went gray and Patti felt herself fading. But they hadn't beaten her, not yet, the last triumphant thought staying with her until her world went black.

THE EIGHTH DAY

January 9th

THIRTY-FIVE

•

Kampov had been gone most of yesterday playing with his pals out at Balashikha-2, and this morning he'd been his old self—happy, animated, with the bone in his teeth—something Bokarev hadn't seen since Nina's death two years ago. Colonel Baturin and his Spetsnaz operators had agreed to help by pulling lightning fast raids on the Mafia clubs as soon as they were given the targets and the green light.

"Twenty-four hours," Kampov had said this morning. "It's all the time I'm giving the bastards to cooperate before we shut them down."

"There'll be hell to pay," Bokarev had warned, but he was going to love sticking it to them. For his father. "Those guys have got money, and most of them have connections."

"Starting with the Grand Dynamo and that prick Smikov."

"He might surprise you and come up with something useful just to save his own ass. A little bird told me that he might be in some financial shit. Could be he's been dealing with Voronin bringing in dope for kids, and he's looking for a way out."

"Watch your back, Feodor," Kampov had said.

"Oh, don't worry, those *pizdecs* wouldn't dare fuck

with me. They know the kind of real shit they'd be in if they tried."

Bokarev left his car with the valet parker at the Magisterium Club, which had been originally opened in the nineties by Yuri Luzhkov, who'd been Moscow's mayor. In those days it catered to high-ranking politicians, but as with most of the other clubs—the Century Club for bankers, the Moscow Commercial Club for businessmen, the Center for the Liberal Movement for the democratic faction in and out of the Kremlin, and especially the New Moscow Pride club which had been modeled after Yeltsin's Pride Club in Yekaterinburg—the Mafia had slowly taken over, and now ran most of them.

The club occupied what had been a mansion of some wealthy royalty attached to the Tsar's court, and had been restored to its original condition, including the Louis XVI furniture and thick red velvet drapes.

Yevgenni Golenko, who managed the place, even dressed in period costume, as did the floor bosses in the casino and on the main stage and dance floor. This afternoon he was decked out in a deep blue smoking jacket, ruffled shirt, and flowing tie.

Word had been gotten to him that Bokarev was on his way in, and he came out to the reception area. "The talk on the street is that you've been making trouble. What the fuck do you think you're playing at?"

Bokarev smiled. "That's not very hospitable of you, Yevgenni. I've come all this way, and you're not even going to offer me a drink?"

"You and I have ourselves a nice little agreement. You stay off my back, and I keep this operation clean. Never any trouble here. I won't allow it. This place is for gentlemen."

"How about that vodka?"

"Get the fuck out of here, little man," Golenko said.

The girl at the reception desk looked up, startled, and one of the security muscle men, who was at least six-four and 300 pounds, appeared at the doorway into the main club room.

Bokarev smiled, nodded, and started to turn away, but then swung back, pulled out his Wilson, and shoved Golenko across the room and up against the wall, the man's head banging against the ornately carved wooden paneling.

The security guy started across the reception hall, but pulled up short when Bokarev pointed his pistol directly at the man's head.

The receptionist picked up the telephone.

"Put it down, sweetheart," Bokarev told her. "It's too early in the day for me to start shooting people."

No one moved.

"Have it your way," he said to Golenko. "We'll take a little ride out to Lefortovo. I have a friend out there who's very persuasive."

Golenko nodded. "Somebody's going to kill you one of these days. It'll be too bad for Yana to become a widow and your girls fatherless."

Bokarev suddenly jammed the muzzle of his pistol into the side of Golenko's face, and pulled the hammer back, the noise loud in the quiet room. "Don't ever fucking mention my family again, you scum bastard, or I'll blow your fucking brains all over the place."

Golenko didn't move a muscle.

Bokarev jammed the pistol harder into the man's face. "Tell your man to get the fuck out of here so that we can conduct our little business and I'll get out of your hair."

Golenko's eyes went to his security officer and he nodded.

The big man glared at Bokarev, but he turned and went back into the club.

"Do we have an understanding?" Bokarev asked. "Or do I have to arrest you?"

"On what charge, you stupid prick?"

"I'll probably think of something on the way to the interrogation cell."

Golenko relaxed after a beat, and nodded. "What do you want?"

"Aleksei Voronin."

"Never heard of him."

"I'd like to know where he's gone to ground."

"I wouldn't know."

"The trouble is I need the information by tomorrow morning at the latest."

"You've got a problem. I said I can't help you."

Bokarev withdrew his weapon, de-cocked the hammer, and stuffed it in his shoulder holster.

"Actually it's your problem, Yevgenni. Because if I don't hear from you a Spetsnaz fire team will be out here to close you down."

"You don't have the authority," Golenko blustered.

"Most of them are just kids, you know," Bokarev said. "And the hell of it is, they don't like to take prisoners. Too much paperwork."

Golenko said nothing.

"Think about it," Bokarev said. "I just want to know where that fucker is hiding."

THIRTY-SIX

•

Patti awoke sometime in the early afternoon with a tremendous headache and a huge lump on the back of her head. For the longest time she lay motionless, her eyes closed, as she listened to the sounds of the house.

A woman, possibly Lana, cried out, and the babushka laughed. Children were shouting, and she could make out the murmur of at least two men talking in the TV room on the other side of the blanket.

All of it, her pain, the house noises, and in the distance the train whistle and a dog barking, meant only one thing to her at that moment. She was alive. She had been raped, she'd fought back, and she was still alive.

In some ways, it was a wonderment to her why Lysenko hadn't killed her.

She turned the thought over in her mind and tried to make some sense of it. There'd be no money. He'd already told her that much. And he'd also told her that he knew she'd sent a coded message to Tobias about her Aunty Gina.

So what was coming next? What did he know that made him think she still had some value?

The men's voices out in the corridor stopped, and Patti opened her eyes as the curtain was drawn back and Lana came in carrying a coat and boots and a bundle of clothes. Her face was red and swollen, her cheeks beneath her eyes black and blue, her lips puffed up and cracked in at least three places. Boris or someone had given her a beating, and all at once it came to Patti that

Lana had saved her life, and that's why they'd hurt her.

But Lana wasn't dead.

It meant something. It had to.

"You have to get up and get dressed now, Patti," Lana said. "They're going to drive you into Moscow."

"He said they were going to kill me and Boris was going to dump my body next to David's."

"No. They're taking you somewhere. They want you to make another call to the States."

Patti was mystified. "Call who?"

"Your friend. Mr. Anderson."

Patti pushed herself up to a sitting position, every movement bringing her excruciating pain. She thought her head was going to split wide open. "He's probably called the FBI."

"They know that. But they still think he'll send you money if you explain to him that it is a matter of life or death."

"If they get the money, they'll kill me anyway."

Lana glanced at her shoulder then came the rest of the way to Patti's side. "It's true, but think, Patricia. Every day you survive means you may be one day closer to rescue. Something could go wrong with their plans. They're all crazy. They keep talking about 9/11, and even something bigger. They need ten million dollars."

"But they're asking for twenty million."

"All I know is that you must get dressed. They're waiting outside with the car."

Patti pushed back the blanket and got unsteadily to her feet. She was naked, and her body was a mass of bruises and welts. Her ribs were prominent, and her small breasts had shrunk even smaller and they drooped. She thought that she was starting to look like the Jews in the Nazi concentration camps, with just about the same chance for survival.

Someone had to have found David's body by now and reported it. Even the Russians wouldn't allow such a crime against an American to go uninvestigated. They would have handed it over to the American embassy, and the FBI had probably become involved even before her call to Tobias.

Lana was right. Each day she survived was one day closer to her rescue. She had to hold onto that thought. That and Lana's help, plus the fact that they had not broken her spirit, were her only lifelines.

She got dressed in her underwear, jeans, and T-shirt. They had been washed and dried while she'd been unconscious. Lana had also brought felt-lined plastic boots, a long quilted orange coat, and a gray scarf.

"Who's going with me? You?"

Lana shook her head. "Raya and Aleksei. Boris will drive."

"Sergey?"

"*Da.*"

"What'd he say about last night?" Patti asked.

She shook her head again. "He just ordered Boris to hurt me."

"Christ," Patti said. "The dirty bastards."

• • •

Voronin was waiting for her when she got downstairs to the kitchen, and without a word led her outside to the car. Lysenko and Raya were in the front with Boris, so she and Voronin had the backseat to themselves.

No one said a word as Lana hurried across the yard and opened the gate and Boris drove through. They turned right on the narrow road, which ran past several blocks of dachas like the one in which she'd been held. Most of them were behind tall concrete block walls, and trash seemed to be piled everywhere. But she saw no people until they came around a curve in the street that turned left to the Moscow highway, and right to the train station and an area of shops and what might have been restaurants.

As the car swept out into the open countryside, Patti turned in her seat to get a last glimpse of the first normal thing she'd seen since her capture. Her entire body ached—not only with the pain of her beatings, but she hungered to be back among the living.

When she turned back she caught Boris's eyes in the rearview mirror. He'd been watching her. But she couldn't tell his mood.

She glanced at Voronin, but he continued to hold his silence, so she sat back in the seat and stared out the window at the passing fields and birch forests. The day was very cold and overcast and the inside of the car was overheated. But she'd been freezing now for several days so she no longer minded. She tried to swallow to ease the pain in her throat, but she couldn't produce enough spit to do it, and she closed her eyes.

• • •

Ten miles outside of Moscow they turned onto a major highway and soon after crossed the outer ring road. Tall concrete apartment buildings seemed to be everywhere, and traffic was heavy, at times slowing to a crawl.

After a while the frenetic scene was too much for her, and she had to look away. She had been deprived and isolated from the real world for so long she couldn't handle it, and she found herself almost wishing that she was back at the dacha, safe in her own room.

Moscow's skyline appeared in the distance, but Boris turned off the highway and drove directly over to a block of eight or ten tall apartment buildings. He pulled in and parked behind one of them.

A few cars and small trucks were scattered here and there across the vast parking lot, but no one was around. The buildings didn't seem to be abandoned, so Patti figured it had to be a weekday and most people were at work.

Boris got out of the car with a small leather satchel and went inside.

"What is this place?" Patti asked.

Voronin looked at her as if she were from another planet. "You will make your phone call from here."

Patti nodded. "Okay."

"Your life is in your own hands now, Patricia. I tried to warn you before, but now you must really behave yourself."

A little laugh escaped her lips. They were worse than nuts.

Voronin scowled. "This is very serious business."

"It certainly is," Patti said.

Boris came to the apartment building door and waved them in.

Lysenko and Raya got out of the car and went across to the entrance without bothering to look back.

"They looked pissed off," Patti said, getting out of the car with Voronin. "Good."

"Don't be like this Patti," he said.

She turned on him and studied his face. His nose was still red and swollen. "The next time I hit you I'm going to drive your nose right into your brain, and I'm going to enjoy seeing you twitching around while you die."

Voronin said nothing, and they went across to the

apartment building, where they took an elevator from the deserted lobby up to the fifteenth floor and down the dark corridor to an empty apartment at the end. The building smelled of a combination of plaster dust, human waste, and cabbage.

The living room and kitchen had been stripped of everything—furniture, appliances, light fixtures, and even wall sockets and switches.

Boris took a telephone and extra handset out of his satchel and had them connected to three wires sticking out of a hole above the baseboard in a couple of minutes.

"We have a dial tone," he said.

THIRTY-SEVEN
•

It was eleven in the evening in Washington when the telephone rang, and Tobias Anderson reached for it.

"Not yet," Special Agent Nelson said.

In addition to the technicians in the electronics van parked out front, Greenwalt had sent over Dr. Marvin Herschfeld, who consulted with the Bureau on hostage negotiation cases. He was a Ph.D. psychologist who specialized in reading stress patterns in the voices not only of hostages, but of their kidnappers as well.

The telephone rang a second time.

"It's a Moscow exchange," the voice of one of the technicians said into Nelson's earpiece.

"Call Mr. Greenwalt and let him know we have an incoming."

The telephone rang a third time, and Nelson motioned for Anderson to answer it.

"Good evening, who's calling?"

"Tobias, it's Patti."

"I'm glad to hear your voice. How are you?"

"Not so good," she said. "David is dead, and I'm being held for ransom."

"Yes, we know this."

The line was silent for a moment but then Patti was back. "They want to know if the FBI is listening."

Anderson glanced at Nelson, who nodded. "Yes, they're here, Patti."

Patti was silent again for a moment or two. "This is for them as well as you. I'm supposed to tell you that unless the ransom is paid I will be killed."

"I understand, and the FBI has advised that I not pay it. But I will." Anderson hesitated, and Nelson motioned for him to go on. It was the script that they had rehearsed at Greenwalt's suggestion. They were buying Patti some time.

"Thank you," Patti said.

Dr. Herschfeld was taking notes.

"You have to understand that it's going to take me a day or two to raise that kind of money."

"We understand."

"And I'll need to know where to send it."

Again there was another pause. Anderson could almost visualize Patti sitting around a table with guns pointed at her head.

"I'll call again with that information," Patti said. "I have to go now."

Nelson shook his head and motioned for Anderson to stretch it out.

"Wait a minute, Patti, Cynthia would like to talk to you—"

The line went silent, and a moment later they had a dial tone.

"Shit," Nelson said.

"Moscow's east side," the tech said in his ear. "Maybe Pervomayskiy or Sokolniki. They're still using mechanical switching."

"Can't we do better?" Nelson demanded, his voice low in his lapel mike.

"If we can convince the NRO to give us some satellite and computer time, sure." The National Reconnaissance Office sent up and operated most of the U.S. technical means assets—spy satellites—but usually for military or political high-value targets.

"She's supposed to be calling again; maybe you can narrow it down next time."

"If she's calling from the same number," the tech said. "But if they're pros there's not much chance of that happening."

"Yeah," Nelson said.

The others were staring at him.

"East side of Moscow, it's the best we could do," he said.

"The woman is very brave," Dr. Herschfeld said. He was tall and slender, with an Ichabod Crane Adam's apple. He looked the part of a college professor, which he was.

Nelson sighed. "Tell us something we don't know."

"She's on the verge of collapse. They're starving her, and certainly they've assaulted her, repeatedly."

"Sexually?" Anderson asked, before Nelson could stop him.

"That goes without saying. It's a preferred method."

Dr. Herschfeld paused a second. "I'm picking up some traces of Stockholm Syndrome, but not at as deep a level as I should have thought, given the length of her captivity. It's another reason I feel that she's is a brave, determined woman." He shook his head. "But she cannot last forever. She will break. And I believe that will come sooner than later."

"Can you give me a time line?" Nelson asked.

"Could be hours, perhaps even days. But not an entire week." Dr. Herschfeld pursed his lips. "I would very much like to talk with one of her captors."

"You think there's more than one of them?" Anderson asked.

Nelson nodded. "She said *they* wanted to know if the FBI was listening."

"I have Mr. Greenwalt standing by for you, Sir," one of the technicians said into Nelson's earpiece.

"Did you manage to get a trace?" Greenwalt demanded.

"Just a partial, somewhere on Moscow's east side," Nelson said into his lapel mike. "They're still using mechanical switching systems, and we didn't have the time. But she promised to call again tomorrow."

"Send me everything you have, including the tape of her call. I'll try to get us some satellite time."

"My people will stick it out here in case she calls back sooner."

"Good. In the meantime I'm flying over to Moscow tonight to see if I can't speed things up."

"Good idea, Sir," Nelson said. "Dr. Herschfeld doesn't think she'll last much longer."

"Bastards," Greenwalt said, and he was gone.

THIRTY-EIGHT

Dick Ligget was getting ready to leave early for the day when his direct line rang. He walked back to his desk and answered the call.

"Ligget. Who's calling?"

"Ev Greenwalt. I'm flying to Moscow tonight. Have you heard anything from the Russians about the Monroes?"

"No, Sir," Ligget said, a little flustered. "If you can let me know when you'll be arriving, I'll come out to the airport to get you."

"I'll call you once we're in the air. We've heard from Mrs. Monroe. She's being held for twenty million in ransom, and you can pass that along to your MVD captain."

"Kampov."

"Yes. Tell him that she phoned from somewhere on Moscow's east side. We could only get a partial trace, but she's going to call again."

"I managed to come up with some information," Ligget said. "Apparently they've been involved with several business deals over here. Possibly with the Russian Mafia and most likely with people who have ties to Chechen terrorists and to al-Quaeda."

"I know all that," Greenwalt said impatiently. "How much of that have you shared with Kampov?"

"None of it," Ligget said. "He doesn't need that kind of information on American citizens."

The line was silent for several beats. "It's your call for now, but I want to meet with him as soon as I get

there. And arrange for a diplomatic visa and someplace for me to stay."

"Here at the embassy?"

"Naturally," Greenwalt said.

"Could you e-mail me the material that you've gathered, Sir? Especially her phone conversation? I could
get things started here."

"I'm bringing all of it with me. All I want you to do
is let Kampov know that I'm on my way, and I'll be
taking over the investigation on the ground."

"Yes, sir," Ligget said, and Greenwalt broke the
connection.

For a long minute he stood at his desk, looking out
the window at the bleak afternoon. He hated Moscow
with every fiber of his being, and had hated it almost
from the moment he and Dolores had arrived. He'd been
counting the days until he could return home and try to
patch up his failing marriage and get on with his career.

But worse than his dislike for Russia and Russians
was his frustration at being ignored and passed over by
the Bureau. The FBI's liaison office here in Moscow
had been created in the nineties after an Australian
woman and her husband had been kidnapped and held
for ransom. Friends of the couple in the States had
asked for the Bureau's help, but the operation had been
hampered because at that time there'd been no mecha-
nism for cooperation between the FBI and the KGB.

Since that time, the Bureau's Moscow liaison office
had, for the most part, been a dead end. And especially
under Putin, Moscow was no place for an American
law enforcement officer.

Until now, Ligget thought bitterly. But the case had
been taken out of his hands by an assistant deputy director. A desk jockey in a three-piece suit.

"Goddamnit," he said softly.

He found Kampov's number at the MVD in his laptop and dialed it. The man answered on the first ring.

"*Da.*"

"Captain, this is Dick Ligget at the U.S. Embassy; I have some information for you."

Kampov switched to English. "I'd given up on you, Mr. Ligget. What do you have?"

"Mrs. Monroe is alive and is being held for ransom, as you suspected."

"She made a phone call to someone in the states?"

"Yes, to a friend. She wants twenty million."

"Well," Kampov said after a slight pause. "They're serious then."

"My boss will be flying here overnight to take over the investigation."

Kampov laughed. "Perhaps he needs to be reminded whose country this is."

"Yes, Sir."

"I assume a tape was made of her telephone conversation, and a trace made of the call."

"We only managed to come up with a partial, from somewhere on Moscow's east side."

Kampov laughed again. "May I be allowed to listen to the tape, and see the file you must have gathered on the Monroes?"

"Not at this time, Sir. Assistant Deputy Director Greenwalt is bringing that material with him. He wants to meet with you, of course."

"Of course," Kampov said. "Give me Mr. Greenwalt's telephone number please."

"I'm sorry, but I'm not authorized to pass out that information."

"Then there will be no meeting between us. I'm too busy at the moment trying to save the life of one of your citizens. Good-bye."

"Wait," Ligget said. If Greenwalt wanted to tie his hands by taking over, then so be it. Let him take over. "His name is Everett Greenwalt, and he's assistant deputy director for the Bureau's counterintelligence division. Try his cell phone; he may already be on his way to the airport." He'd brought Greenwalt's contact information up on his computer, and he gave Kampov the number.

"Thank you," Kampov said, pleasantly. "Maybe we can work together after all."

THIRTY-NINE

•

The moment he hung up from his call with Ligget, Kampov telephoned Greenwalt's cell number. It was answered on the second ring. "Hello."

"Mr. Greenwalt, I'm Alexander Kampov, MVD. I just talked with your Special Agent Ligget about the Monroes."

"How did you get this number?" Greenwalt demanded.

"I'm an officer in a federal intelligence agency. We have our methods, as does the CIA and FBI. I understand that Patti Monroe called a friend in the U.S. and asked for some serious money. Ransom money."

"That's right," Greenwalt said guardedly. "In fact,

I'm taking over the investigation. I'll be in Moscow sometime tomorrow."

"We'll be working together. That's fine. Now we must share our information and resources."

"Mrs. Monroe is a citizen of the United States. This is my case."

"Mrs. Monroe is a victim of a crime in Russia. This is our case. Your victim, my country."

"What do you want?"

"I want a copy of the Monroes' FBI file, including the audio tape of her telephone call and its analysis. Perhaps my people can help identify any ambient noises. I assume that you have employed a stress analyst as well. I would like to have that report."

"I'm sure that you would, Captain," Greenwalt said. "When I get to Moscow we'll see what information I can make available to you."

"If you get to Moscow," Kampov said.

"I'm coming in on a diplomatic mission."

"But you're not a diplomat, are you?" Kampov said. "It may take some time before we can verify who you are and why you have come to Russia on such short notice. Thirty days, perhaps six weeks . . . not so uncommon a delay."

"You son of a bitch."

"No, Mr. Assistant Deputy Director Greenwalt, I'm just a cop like you, trying to save a life and keep some very bad men from coming up with the money to mount another attack on your country, or perhaps more attacks here against my people."

"When I get there."

"Now."

"Do you want to start an international incident?"

"Don't be naïve," Kampov shot back. "The only incident, even if it's noticed and anyone cares, would come if Mrs. Monroe is shot to death like her husband and her body left beside the road out in the woods. This is a very large country. Perhaps she might even disappear forever. It happens all the time."

"What's your e-mail address?" Greenwalt asked.

Kampov gave it to him. "I want the entire file. All of it."

"You won't make a move until I get there."

"I can't promise that, and neither would you in my situation. If anything should come up, if we learn something before you arrive, we'll have to proceed. You can understand that."

"Goddamnit, you be careful, Mister. I'll see you sometime tomorrow afternoon."

FORTY

•

Patti had passed out on the way back from Moscow, and when she awoke she found that Raya had gotten into the backseat and was cradling her. Sitting now at the window in her bedroom, she could still feel the deep revulsion that had swept through her body when she'd looked up into the woman's eyes.

She had pushed herself away, and for the remainder of the drive to Noginsk had stared out the window, only once catching Lysenko looking at her, with an unreadable expression on his face.

The last afternoon train blew its whistle as it approached the station she'd spotted this morning. From this room she couldn't see the train, but she heard its whistle three times during the day and twice every night. In some measure it was a comfort to her, knowing that ordinary people were going about their ordinary lives.

For this moment, she felt safe here in her room. She'd managed the trip to Moscow and the phone call to Tobias, who'd promised to send the money. It's what Lysenko and the others wanted, and she felt glad that she'd been able to come through. As long as they were satisfied they wouldn't kill her.

Someone was at the doorway, and Patti turned as Lana, wearing a bulky overcoat, came in.

"Are we going out again?" Patti asked. She hoped not. It looked cold outside, and she didn't think she was up for another trip away from here, unless it was to go home. For now she was taking her life one minute at a time.

"No, I was at the market," Lana said. "I brought you something."

"Food?"

"Yes." Lana glanced out into the TV room, then turned back and took several small bundles wrapped in waxed paper out of her coat pockets and laid them on the bed. "It's not much, just some bread and cheese and a piece of sausage. But I don't think your stomach could handle anything else." She took a vodka bottle out of a pocket and laid it with the other things. "This is water, not vodka."

Patti wasn't hungry, but she wanted the water. She stood up and on shaky legs tottered to the bed, and sat down, nauseous and dizzy. She opened the bottle and drank a little. It felt good on her throat, but her stomach immediately began to heave, and she had to lower her head and close her eyes so that she could concentrate on not throwing up.

"I'm sorry that this is happening to you," Lana said from the doorway.

When she was finally able, Patti looked up. "Thank you."

"Will you be able to manage now?"

"I think so."

"When you're done, hide everything under the bed," Lana warned.

"Why are you helping me?"

"I told you already. Because you're a woman just like me."

"But I'm not just like you," Patti said, and she felt ungrateful for saying it.

"Yes, you are. Your life is in danger, just as mine is. We're both at their mercy, and when they're done they'll kill us unless we can come up with an excuse to stay alive."

Patti took another sip of water, and this time it was better, although she had an instant case of heartburn. She made no move to reach for the waxed paper bundles.

"You'll be making another call tomorrow, so eat something. You need your strength."

What Lana was saying suddenly dawned on Patti. "You know about the apartment and the phone?"

"I know everything, Patricia," Lana said, her voice suddenly flat. "All of us do. Even the children. It's how Sergey can be sure none of us will try to run away. Even if we got to the authorities it would be too bad for us. We're all just as guilty."

"But you've helped me."

"*Da,*" Lana said. "But so has Raya. Without her you would be dead by now."

Patti shook her head. "I don't believe it."

"But it's true. You don't know what she's gone through. It's a wonder she's not in an asylum."

"What are you talking about?"

"When she was a teenager she was gang-raped by a bunch of American soldiers in Japan, but her father couldn't report it because he was working under deep cover for the KGB. So he sent her back to Moscow to live with his sister and her husband. But the uncle raped her the first night she was back and she ran away. A Mafia pimp picked her up off the streets and took her to one of the clubs, where she was supposed to work as a whore. But she gouged out the eyes of the first man who tried to have sex with her, and the Mafia sold her to the Russian army. That's when the Spetsnaz boys got ahold of her and they wouldn't take any of her shit."

"How do you know this?"

"Sergey told me," Lana said. "She was with them for three years, and she learned how to fight their way— attack and keep attacking until your enemies are all dead. Take no prisoners. When she finally managed to get out of there she went to Pakistan and joined al-Quaeda, where Sergey found her."

"She's a nutcase."

"*Da*, just like all of us," Lana said. "Grandmother, me, you. We're women; we all carry a burden." She smiled. "Eat something, Patti, you'll need your strength." She turned and left the room.

Patti stared at the blanket that covered the door, half expecting Lysenko or Raya or even Lana's husband to come in and take the food and water away from her. But after Lana's footfalls on the stairs, the house was quiet.

After a while she took another sip of water and opened one of the bundles that contained a piece of kielbasa. The grease and the smell struck her instantly, and her stomach recoiled.

Dropping the water and the sausage, Patti got off the bed, pushed through the curtain covering the door, and stumbled down the hall to the bathroom just in time to vomit still-cool water into the sink.

She didn't care who saw her. It no longer mattered.

When she was finished, she splashed some cold water on her face, and dried with a small filthy towel.

No one was in the corridor or in the television room, and she'd not heard a thing, yet when she got back to her bedroom the vodka bottle was on the floor where she'd dropped it, but the food was gone.

FORTY-ONE

•

Lysenko came into the kitchen and dumped the bundle of food from Patti's room onto the counter. Lana had taken off her coat and boots and was at the sink washing dishes from lunch. Boris was sitting at the table drinking vodka and smoking a cigarette. His pig eyes were redder than usual.

"You're to have no contact with her unless I tell you," he told Lana, his voice reasonable. "Do you understand?"

Lana lowered her head. "If she's too weak to make another telephone call, what will her value be?"

Boris slammed down his glass and started to get to his feet, but Lysenko motioned him back. "It's not necessary this time, my friend. Your wife is right. The only crime she's guilty of is kindness, and there's nothing wrong with that. But Lana, greasy sausage, moldy cheese, and stale bread won't help. When the time is right you will give her a glass of tea with milk and sugar. But not until I say so."

Lana nodded.

"She's a strong-willed woman, a fighter, but as long as we keep her in this state she won't give us much trouble."

Boris sniggered, and Lysenko turned on him.

"It should be clear to all of you what might happen if the FBI comes here."

"They're a joke," Boris growled. "A bunch of pussies."

Lysenko nearly pulled out his pistol and shot the man in the forehead just then, but he held himself in check by a supreme effort of will. In school in England he learned, among other painful things, that a gentleman never displayed his temper. It was considered bad form.

Voronin came to the door. "The FBI will never come here," he said. "Boris is right; their liaison office at the embassy is nothing but a joke."

"I agree," Lysenko said mildly. "But they may send someone from Washington. I don't want to get into a shoot-out. I came for money."

"It's only a matter of days, Sergey. Once Anderson transfers the twenty million into our account, we'll settle up and walk away. Settle up everything."

Since last night with the woman, Lysenko had been having trouble concentrating. At the oddest times he found himself thinking about England. About the public schools where, during his first year, he'd been whipped, raped, and sodomized. The British penchant for a stiff upper lip wasn't an idle boast. In school a boy had to learn resolve and resiliency in order to survive without being damaged too badly.

He'd been thinking about the hate that simmered

inside of him. And the uncertainty about his own value. He supposed he'd been on a quest all of his life to find out who he was. With bin Laden and the *jihad,* which was in no way his war, he nevertheless felt a sense of fulfillment, a sense of self-worth, a purpose, because he was fighting his own demons. When he spilled blood he was king.

He would die in the struggle. He was realist enough to understand that. But in the meantime he was alive, no matter his momentary self-doubts.

His life in Lebanon, where he'd been born to a Chechen engineer and a Jewish mother, was from another time, another planet, so far in the past that he had no real memory of his childhood. His first memories were of the school in London where, in his fifth year, a professor had awakened his Muslim roots and had taught him that sex did not have to be painful like it was when the upper classmen buggered him in the night. He'd been thinking about those days ever since he'd arrived in Moscow.

He'd also learned about the great struggle, Muslims against Christians and Hindus and especially Jews. And by his second year at Oxford, his radicalization had been complete. His hate had been focused. He didn't care for the struggle, only the means it gave him to spill blood.

He thought again about that holiday from school when he'd had a terrible row with his parents. "Your father is a Muslim and I am a Jewess, but we have a good marriage," his mother had cried just before Lysenko had slit her throat and watched her bleed out.

His father had gone to the kitchen and when he returned he'd dropped the tray with the wine and glasses, and Lysenko had slit his throat, too.

Rivers of blood. His nightmares lately had been of him swimming in rivers of his parents' blood. And the worst part of the dreams was his lack of guilt. In fact he had no feeling whatsoever about the manner of their deaths.

From there he had escaped to the university in Jeddah, Saudi Arabia, where bin Laden had studied, then with al-Quaeda to Syria, Pakistan, and Afghanistan, where he'd met Raya and where their training had been completed.

Staring at Voronin, he was seeing only his mother's face, hearing her voice pleading for mercy, telling him that she loved him, crying, why was he doing this horrible thing? Her blood had soaked into his soul. After public school and after his Oxford professor, he'd never had a choice: His mother was a woman and a Jew, both of which he hated and feared.

Before this was over, no matter how it turned out, he would kill the woman upstairs with his own hands, just as he had killed his mother, and for the same reasons.

· · ·

It was late when Raya slipped into the living room, where Lysenko had chosen to bunk on a couch for the duration. He reached for his pistol, not knowing who it was in the darkness, and pulled back the hammer, the noise loud.

"It's me," she said softly.

Aleksei and Boris had gone to one of the clubs in Noginsk to have a late supper and something to drink, and the dacha had quieted down early. Even the television set upstairs was off.

"What do you want?" Lysenko asked, de-cocking his pistol and laying it on the coffee table.

"You know."

He'd been lying on his back, thinking about what would happen once this operation was finished. If they actually got the money, and actually got the nuclear device out of Tajikistan, life would never be the same for anyone. The repercussions would be far greater than those after 9/11. No one in al-Quaeda would ever be safe again anywhere on earth. Once the nuclear genie was out of the bottle, once a nuclear bomb was exploded in an American city, no Muslim fundamentalist, person, or nation, would be safe. After the attack on the twin trade towers, Afghanistan and Iraq had fallen. Syria would be next, along with Pakistan, and very probably North Korea. The entire world would be engaged in a war—the West against Islam. It would be a struggle that even Muhammad could not win.

Yet the struggle went on, and he was a part of it.

"No, I don't know what you want," he said.

"To make love."

"I don't love you."

"You don't love that woman upstairs, but you tried to fuck her. I just want to be held. Is that so terrible for you?"

"That was different," Lysenko said, and he still didn't know how he felt about the incident, or how he would have felt had he been successful. He wasn't a homosexual, although he sometimes enjoyed sex with boys. He'd hated his father, he'd hated his mother, he'd hated the boys in public school, and he'd hated his Oxford professor, who'd taken him to bed for an entire term.

"I could have helped, if you'd just asked me."

"I didn't need your help," Lysenko said sharply.

"From where I was standing, watching her beat you unconscious, I think you did," Raya said.

Lysenko sat up, his temper spiking.

"I know what you're feeling," Raya said. "The pain, the anger. When I was fifteen I was raped in Yokuska and my father never made it right because he couldn't blow his KGB cover. And when the Spetsnaz bastards arrested me in Afghanistan one year later, they put me in one of their whorehouses." She shook her head. "It's about power, Sergey. That's all it is. Sex is never about love, it's about domination. My will over yours, or your will over mine."

"Is that what you think?"

"Sometimes it's just being close to someone," Raya said. "Someone you respect."

She stepped into the dim light filtering through the dirty windows, and pulled off her leather boots. She was dressed in a black camo jump suit, which she unzipped, then pulled off her narrow shoulders and let it fall to the floor around her ankles. She wore a black sports bra and black bikini panties.

Her pale skin fluoresced in the darkness, and when she smiled her teeth were brilliant white, her eyes wide and coal black, her oval face framed by her short dark hair. She was a pretty woman, but most of the time her expression and manner were as hard as her narrow-hipped athletic body. Except now she seemed uncertain.

"Leave me," Lysenko said. Over the past several years of knowing her he'd often considered taking her to his bed. But each time he'd backed away from what he figured would become a commitment he didn't want to make.

"*Nyet,*" she said softly.

She stepped out of her panties and came to the edge of the couch, where she reached down and brushed the tips of her fingers across Lysenko's forehead, letting them trail down from the bridge of his nose to his cheek, and then his lips.

"You've wanted me before," she said. "And I can feel it now."

She looked at him with a hungry need, like he thought his mother sometimes did, and like the woman upstairs did.

He sat up and kissed her navel, then let his tongue travel down toward her groin. She thrust her hips toward him, and when he looked up she was smiling at him.

She started to pull the sports bra over her head, but before she could finish Lysenko leaped off the couch, pulled her hands behind her, and violently shoved her back against a round table, knocking over the floor lamp next to it.

Holding her down, he kissed her neck and her shoulders and her breasts, and she did not fight back, nor did she try to take off the bra that was covering her face, until he stepped back to take off his shirt.

When she had it off, she clawed at his slacks, undoing the button as he did the zipper and helping him pull them and his underwear down. She was on her knees in front of him and she took his erect penis in her mouth, biting down with enough force to make him understand his vulnerability.

But Lysenko pulled her away by her hair, pushed her over the arm of the leather chair next to the table, shoved her legs apart, and entered her.

Through all of it she made no noise, but she looked at him, relief on her face. She had won what she needed and she was not ashamed to let him see the gratefulness in her eyes.

When he came, the expression on her face didn't change in the slightest.

"Thank you," she said throatily.

"Maybe I'll kill you now," he said. "To show you who is in charge."

Her face relaxed and she smiled. "Perhaps you should, Sergey, because there's always the chance that I'll kill you one night when you're sleeping."

Lysenko laughed softly, then pulled her close again and started making love. "This time it's for us."

For several seconds she did not respond, but then the smile left her face, she closed her eyes and wrapped her legs around his hips. Her lips parted and she moaned.

FORTY-TWO

•

It was late by the time Kampov got back to his apartment. He took a shower and pulled on a set of sweats, then poured a large cognac. He laid Patti Monroe's file on the dining room table, along with his laptop with the disk he'd burned from Greenwalt's attachment.

Feodor had lined up seven Mafia clubs for Baturin and his fire teams to drop in on, but the operation wouldn't start until sometime tomorrow during daylight hours, when there would be fewer patrons and therefore less likelihood of serious casualty numbers.

And his letter from Putin had done wonders with Colonel Zamyatin, who promised the Militia's complete cooperation, and with General Granov, who valued his second star more than saving face.

The material Greenwalt had sent was fairly extensive, as if the FBI had been investigating them before the assassination and kidnapping. Kampov had wondered about it until he came to the IRS file. The Monroes had long been suspected of tax fraud, and they'd been under investigation for the past two years. Most of the suspicion had fallen on David Monroe, who eight years ago had run afoul of the IRS, had pleaded no contest in tax court, and agreed to a $200,000 fine, which he managed to pay off within a month after he'd married Patti.

The IRS continued to keep an eye on his business dealings, along with his wife's, because it was Patti's wedding gift from her father that had paid David's fine. Nowhere in the IRS or FBI files, however, was mention ever made that Patti knew about David's past.

At one point Kampov got up to replenish his drink. David had married Patti not for love, but for the money he'd hoped to get from her father. Finally, his sleazy past had caught up with him on the highway east of Moscow, and Kampov wondered if Patti knew what her husband had really been all about.

He spread out several of her photographs, including one that showed her perched on a stool with a guitar in her lap. She was wearing a long print dress and was apparently singing into a microphone, a dreamy-eyed expression on her face.

She looked very young in that photograph, as she did in another, which was a head-and-bare-shoulders shot. It was stamped on the back ELLENE MODELLING AGENCY, LOS ANGELES, NEW YORK, PARIS.

Patti had wanted to be a singer and a fashion model; instead she'd ended up a kidnap victim somewhere in or near Moscow.

Kampov switched on the recordings of Patti's two calls to Tobias Anderson, picked up the fashion model shot, and sat back on the couch to listen.

"Patti, this is Tobias. Are you okay?"

"Good evening, Mr. Anderson. David and I are just fine, but we need some help."

But she wasn't fine. Kampov could hear the stress and fear in her voice, and staring at her photograph he wondered how Nina would have sounded in the same situation. Suddenly he was nearly overcome by a wave of fear for the woman's life, and anger for the kinds of people who were capable of acts like these.

"Hold on," he said to Patti's photograph. "We're coming."

THE NINTH DAY

January 10th

FORTY-THREE

•

Around seven in the morning Moscow time, the FBI's Gulfstream was about two hours from landing, and Greenwalt, still on Washington time, felt like hell. He'd only managed a few hours sleep on the first leg of the flight, but nothing after they'd stopped at Prestwick, Scotland to refuel.

His wife Margaret had driven him out to Andrews last night, and she'd asked for the fifth time why he was flying over to Russia.

"Don't worry about it; with any luck I should be back in a few days."

"But why you?"

"Relax, Maggie, it'll do me good. Besides, I'm a cop and this is what I get paid to do."

"You're a desk jockey thinking about retirement. And Russia just now is a dangerous place to be. I'm concerned."

Greenwalt had been standing at the driver's side door, looking at her through the open window. She was an attractive woman, with warm eyes and a pleasant smile. She'd looked a little tired at that moment, and he reached inside and gave her a kiss.

"Russia's always been a dangerous place. But I'm a

good cop, or at least I used to be. And I have a woman to find and bring home." He smiled.

She nodded, tight-lipped. "Be careful, Ev."

"Piece of cake."

But sitting now, sipping a cup of Earl Grey tea as he studied the Monroes' file, he wasn't so sure how it was going to turn out. By promising to pay the ransom demand, Anderson had merely bought Patti Monroe a little time, possibly a couple of days, no more. And if the ransom were actually paid, the woman would be murdered the moment the wire transfer was completed.

He looked up and stared out the window at the nothingness below. On the ground it would be a miserable overcast cold morning, typical weather for Eastern Europe and Russia at this time of the year. It was amazing to him how this part of the world had produced so many geniuses in the arts, in the sciences, while at the same time nurtured some truly great criminals. The Russian Mafia had learned its lessons well from the KGB, and was second to none anywhere in the world for its brutality.

If it were an alliance between the Mafia, Chechen rebels, and al-Quaeda, actually finding her and bringing her out alive would be next to impossible. But he had to try.

He looked again at Patti Monroe's passport photo. She was a good-looking woman, whose father had turned his back on her. Anderson had advised the FBI not to contact him, and in fact it was Anderson, and not her own father, to whom Patti had turned for help.

"Tom Healy is a friend. I've known him for years," Anderson had told them. "But if you involve him, he'll be on the first plane to Moscow where he'll raise so much hell they'll have to kill his daughter no matter how much money I promise to send them. He fancies himself to be another Ross Perot; lead or follow, just don't get in my way."

"He sounds like a sterling character," Greenwalt had said.

"He is, except when it comes to his daughter. He did everything he could to stop her from marrying David, and when she went ahead anyway, he wrote her off."

"Like I said, sterling character."

The Bureau did a brief background check on Healy to make sure that there weren't connections, no matter how unlikely, between him and anyone inside Russia, or any company or banking interest that could involve al-Quaeda. There weren't, and in fact the Healy name in Boston was spotless.

The two most important men in Patti's life—her father and her husband—had been lost to her. Greenwalt had to wonder what life would be like for her if he could get her out and back home. Herschfeld's preliminary report cautioned that Patti was damaged. She was on a psychological cliff and could fall over at any moment. Bringing her back to reality would take a very long time. She was going to be emotionally scarred for the rest of her life, no matter how this turned out.

The flight attendant came aft to where he was seated. She was a pretty young woman who'd started with the Bureau a couple of years ago. Her name was Gwen and she had been a Northwest Airlines attendant.

"Would you care for some breakfast, Mr. Greenwalt, or do you have plans in Moscow?"

He smiled. "How about eggs Benedict," he joked.

"Yes, Sir," she said, pleasantly. "It'll be about a half hour. Would you like something to drink while you wait?"

FORTY-FOUR

•

In Moscow, Bokarev lay awake in his bed, listening to the sounds of the apartment. The girls had left for school an hour ago, after coming into his room to feel their father's forehead to check his fever and give him a kiss good-bye, and now Yana was doing something in the kitchen, trying her best to keep quiet.

The Spetsnaz operation wouldn't start until sometime this afternoon, and Bokarev had left a message last night with the Operations Duty officer that he still felt like shit and wouldn't be in until noon.

Yana and the girls had fussed over him last night, and this morning they'd tried their best not to disturb him, but he'd awakened a few minutes before six, his usual time, anyway.

The telephone rang in the living room and Yana got to it on the second ring. Bokarev tried to hear what his wife was saying, but her voice was low and indistinct. Then she came to the bedroom door, the phone in her hand.

"Are you awake, sweetheart?" she asked softly.

Bokarev opened his eyes. "Who is it?"

"I don't know. He says he's a friend."

Bokarev held out his hand, and Yana came around to his side of the bed and handed him the phone.

"Do you want me to fix you some breakfast?" she asked.

"Just coffee," he said, and he waited until she was gone before he answered the call. "Bokarev."

"Good morning, Feodor," Smikov from Grand Dynamo said. "I hope I'm not calling too early."

"I didn't think that pricks like you got up this early."

"Actually, I haven't been to bed yet."

"What do you want?"

"That depends on you, and the inquiry you made the other day," Smikov said. "If you're still interested I might have something for you."

Bokarev pushed the covers aside and sat up in the bed. His head was so full it seemed as if it were on the verge of exploding. "What do you have?"

"First you need to tell me something."

"Fuck you. I'm not in the mood for your shit."

"Patience, my friend, is a virtue. I'm looking for a simple quid pro quo here. I do you a favor and you do me one in return. Simple."

"You tell me where I can find Voronin and I won't close you down. Is that quid pro quo enough for you?"

"You're not an easy man to deal with," Smikov said. "I just want some assurances that this time tomorrow I'll still have a fucking business to run out here."

"Where is he?" Bokarev asked. He was losing his patience, and the Grand Dynamo had just moved to the head of today's Spetsnaz list.

"My people have found him."

"Where?"

"Not over the phone," Smikov said.

"Bullshit—"

"Not over the phone, Feodor. Come out here and I'll give you what you need. I'll be waiting."

"You prick—" Bokarev shouted, but Smikov had hung up.

Yana came back to the door. "Is everything okay?"

"Just business," Bokarev said, getting out of bed. "I have to meet someone."

"Are you sure you're strong enough?"

"I'm fine," he said. He called Kampov's home number, but got no answer, and he speed dialed the office. "Has Captain Kampov come in yet?"

"No, Sir," the OD said.

"Leave a message on his desk. Tell him I'm meeting someone this morning who says he knows the location of the friend we've been looking for."

"Can he call you on your cell?"

"Not where I'm going," Bokarev said. Cell phone calls were electronically blocked in all the clubs. "I'll call when I'm finished."

Yana was still standing at the door, a worried expression on her pretty face. "Are you sure you're okay?" she asked.

"I'm going to shave and shower, then I'll have my coffee," he told her. "Now stop being such an old lady. I have to get going."

FORTY-FIVE
•

By the time Kampov reached his office he was in a rotten mood. He'd drunk too much again last night, and had awakened late. The hot water in the building was off, he was out of coffee, and nothing in his refrigerator appealed to his sour stomach. He'd taken a handful of aspirin with a glass of water and drove downtown to MVD Headquarters, the morning as dark and depressing as his mood.

Listening to Patti Monroe's calls to her millionaire friend Tobias Anderson, he had heard the extreme stress in her voice. But he'd also detected a note of defiance.

She hadn't given in, and her asking Anderson to say hello to her dead aunt proved it.

But her second call had been different. Her voice had been much weaker, at times even guttural, difficult to understand. She'd admitted that she knew her husband was dead, and that her own life was in danger if Anderson couldn't or wouldn't send the money.

The FBI's psychologist, who'd analyzed the tapes, was certain that Patti was being starved and beaten, possibly even tortured and sexually assaulted. *She's in fear for her life*, Herschfeld had written. *Yet her voice patterns indicate that she holds her captors in great contempt.*

Neither the Mafia nor the Chechens generally mistreated their women, ideologically, but al-Quaeda, with its twisted take on Islam, did.

Kampov could understand the necessity for her captors to kill her and get rid of her body once they had the ransom money, but there was no reason to mistreat her in the meantime.

Bokarev wasn't at his desk, but he'd left a note with the morning duty officer that he was meeting someone who said he knew where Voronin had gone to ground, and that he could not be reached on his cell phone, which meant he'd probably gone to one of the Mafia clubs to check on a lead.

Kampov took off his coat, draped it over the back of his chair, and telephoned Bokarev's apartment. Yana answered on the first ring.

"*Da?*"

"Good morning, Yana, this is Alexander. Has Feodor left yet?"

"Good morning, Captain. Yes, he left about a half hour ago."

"Do you have any idea where he went?"

"*Nyet.* He wouldn't tell me. And frankly the girls and I are worried about him. He has a temperature, and if he keeps this up he could get pneumonia. Are you sure you can't spare him from the office for a few days?"

A worry nagged at the back of Kampov's head. "I tried to send him home yesterday, but he wouldn't go. He's a stubborn man."

"Yes, he is," Yana said.

"As soon as he comes in I'll send him straight back to you, and you'll keep him home until he gets better. This time we won't take no for an answer."

"Thank you, Captain, but you'll have to make it a direct order, because right after his call first thing this morning he was excited."

Kampov sat up. "Who called?"

"Some man. I don't know who, but Feodor did."

"Did you hear their conversation?"

"*Nyet.*"

"Feodor didn't say anything to you about who it was or where he was going?" Kampov asked.

"Not a word. Should I be worried?" Yana asked. "Is he in danger this morning?"

Kampov forced a light note in his voice. "Only from me when he gets to the office."

"Send him home."

"I will," Kampov said. He hung up and went out onto the floor of the duty room, where at that moment a half dozen of his officers working on other cases were busy at their desks.

A couple of them looked up.

"Does anyone have any idea where Feodor went this morning?" Kampov asked.

"No, Sir," Lieutenant Nikolai Sychev, who was working the OD position, said from his desk across the room. "I talked to him around 0900; the message is on your desk."

"Did he say when he expected to be back here?"

"No, Sir. Is there trouble?"

"There's always trouble," Kampov grumbled, and he went back into his office, where he phoned Baturin's cell. The colonel answered on the second ring, and Kampov could hear a lot of small arms fire in the background.

"Sascha, are you ready for us ahead of schedule?"

"Maybe in the next hour or two," Kampov said. "Something's come up that has me a little worried."

"What is it?"

"My sergeant called the OD this morning to say he was going to see someone who had a lead. The only people he's been talking to over the past few days are Mafia. If he's gone to one of the clubs, I don't know which one it is. He's been to eight of them so far."

"Give me the word and we'll hit them all before noon."

"Not yet," Kampov said. "But put your people on standby. We might have to move out in a hurry."

"We'll be good to go inside ten minutes."

FORTY-SIX

•

The Dynamo soccer stadium was deserted when Bokarev showed up. The start of the sports season was still months away, when the vast parking lot would be full at any hour of the day or night, vendors selling everything from vodka and kvas, to sausages and black bread. Tailgating hadn't come to Russia yet, but Dynamo in season was nearly there.

Smikov's club, the Grand Dynamo, was located in the northeast corner of the vast building in a space that had once been used for the storage and maintenance of groundskeeping equipment and a mammoth electrical generating station to assure power to the field's lights during Moscow's frequent brownouts.

Under the new Russian system, maintenance was contracted out to the highest, not the lowest, bidder, in this case the Mafia. In addition, the Russian White House had assured the soccer stadium's management that power failures were a thing of the past, and the generating station was dismantled and sold for scrap. These days, military generator sets on the backs of eighteen-wheelers were brought out for the games.

It was free enterprise, and everyone was happy, especially the Mafia, which leased the empty space for one ruble per year.

Bokarev sat in his idling Lada at the far end of the parking lot, drinking the cup of coffee that Yana had sent with him, and waiting to see if there was any activity at the flashy entrance to the club. But nothing moved: no Mercedes, Land Rovers, or BMWs pulling up, no valet parkers, no heavy hitters in their Bentley and Rolls-Royce limos. Not even the cleaning crews, which usually came out to take care of the club's section of the parking lot, were here this morning.

It wasn't right.

"Fuck it," Bokarev said. He tossed out the last of his coffee, set the cup aside, and drove the rest of the way across to the club, where he parked directly under the overhang.

The main doors were locked, and peering through the windows he could see no lights inside. He pulled out his pistol, checked to make sure that the safety catch was on, and knocked at the door with the butt, the noise loud. The only sounds were from traffic on the nearby Leningradsky Prospect.

He waited for a full minute before he banged on the door again.

Smikov had called him out, which meant the bastard had to be inside. The only thing Bokarev could think of was that the man didn't want any witnesses when he talked to an MVD cop.

He went back to his car, laid the pistol on the passenger seat, and drove around the stadium to the club's delivery entrance. Smikov's black Hummer was parked at the loading dock. No other car or truck was in sight.

For a long minute or two Bokarev remained in his car. The clubs generally didn't close until dawn, and when the last patrons had finally cleared out, the janitors would come in to straighten up the place, the cooks would show up to start prepping for lunch, and food and liquor vendors would begin arriving.

Other cars and trucks should be here at this hour.

Bokarev finally got out of the car, jumped up onto the loading dock, and tried the steel door. It was unlocked.

Pistol in hand, his finger outside the trigger guard, he stepped inside the dark storeroom, immediately moving out of the doorway so that he wouldn't be silhouetted.

He swept his gun left to right, but nothing moved, and the only sounds he could hear came from the refrigerator and freezer compressors. He went out into the club's back corridor where he checked

Smikov's office. The lights were on, but the man wasn't there.

At the end of the hall he eased the door open and stepped out into the main room, the stage on the right. Only a few dim lights were on, including those on the back bar.

Smikov was sitting on a stool, and he turned around. "A punctual cop. I like that."

Bokarev crossed the dance floor. "Are we alone?"

Smikov nodded. "Are you going to shoot me in my own place?"

"The thought occurred to me," Bokarev said. He holstered his pistol and took the stool next to the Mafia boss.

Smikov was nursing what looked to be a Bloody Mary. "You want one of these?" he asked. "You look like shit; you could probably use it."

"I feel like shit, so just tell me where the fuck Voronin is hanging out these days and I'll get out of here."

Smikov took his time. "Then what?"

"Then I stay out of your hair until I need something else."

"What are you going to do when you find him? He's got a lot of friends. If it gets around that I tipped you off I could be in some serious shit here."

"What I want him for is none of your business. And unless you missed it you're already in some serious shit out here. From me."

"Don't you think I know that?" Smikov said. "Why the fuck do you think I called you out here like this? I've got a solution that'll work for both of us. Now let me get you a drink. A little French cognac to clear your head and then we'll do business."

"Don't fuck with me, I'm not in the mood."

Smikov laughed. "When are you ever in the mood, Feodor?" he asked. He went around behind the bar and poured a snifter of brandy for Bokarev and one for himself. He raised his glass. "I just want peace out here. That's all."

Bokarev picked up the glass and knocked the drink back. At the last moment he spotted a movement behind him in the mirror, but it was too late as a garrote was looped around his neck and suddenly yanked so tightly that the stainless steel wire nearly decapitated him, and he felt himself falling down a long, black hole.

His last thoughts were about his father, sorry that he hadn't been able to do more to avenge the old man's murder, and about Yana and the girls. He hoped that Kampov would look after them.

FORTY-SEVEN
·

A customs official waited in front of one of the VIP gates at Sheremetyevo Airport as the FBI's Gulfstream bizjet pulled up to a stop and its engines began to spool down. A ground crew scurried forward to chock the wheels, because a brisk wind had come up. Ligget stood in the lee of the hangar, next to a Cadillac SUV with embassy plates, his collar hunched up.

"Thanks for the lift," Greenwalt told the captain and copilot as the attendant unlatched the door and swung it open.

"Any idea how long we'll be here, Sir?" Captain Donald Miller asked. He'd been with the FBI since he'd gotten out of the Air Force five years ago.

"Hopefully just a day or two," Greenwalt said. The moment the door opened a frigid mass of arctic air filled the cabin, and he shivered.

"If it's any longer than that operations might want us back."

"I'll need you to remain here on standby. We might have to get out of Dodge in a hurry."

"Do you expect trouble?"

"Could be," Greenwalt said, gathering his hanging bag and laptop. "I'm here to fetch an American citizen who's been kidnapped by Chechen al-Quaeda and Russian Mafia. Those guys have a long reach."

"An embassy employee?" the pilot asked.

"No. A businesswoman."

The pilot's eyebrows rose. "We'll stand by, Sir."

"Good man," Greenwalt said, and he made his way off the plane and down onto the tarmac where he was met by Ligget and the Russian official.

"We'll just need to see your passport, Sir," Ligget said.

Greenwalt gave it to the Russian, who glanced at the diplomatic cover, and then at the photo before he handed it back. "Welcome to Russia," he said, glancing at Greenwalt's hanging bag and laptop.

"Right," Greenwalt said, and he followed Ligget across to the Caddy, where he tossed his bags in back and got in the passenger seat.

"Did you have a good flight, Sir?" Ligget asked as they pulled away from the VIP terminal and headed for the access road to the highway. Dirty snow was piled everywhere, and most of the buildings and cars looked shabby. It was midmorning, but a gray overcast made it almost seem like early evening.

"Depressing," Greenwalt mumbled.

Ligget was startled. "Your flight?"

"No, this place."

Ligget didn't reply, concentrating on his driving as they merged with heavy traffic.

"Have you gotten any help from Tom Morse?" Greenwalt asked. Morse was the CIA's chief of Moscow station.

"No, Sir. If some dumb American broad wants to get herself in trouble trying to do business over here it's her problem. His words."

"Figures."

"You're bunking in one of the embassy apartments, and I've arranged a small office for you down the hall from mine. The ambassador has told everyone that you're to have the utmost cooperation."

"That's good of him," Greenwalt said absently, watching out the window. It's no wonder the Russians had lost the Cold War, he mused. They couldn't even keep their highways in decent repair. He turned back to Ligget. "Can I have access to the embassy's secure communications system?"

"Yes, Sir. I've already arranged it. Once you're on the embassy's main page, click on the Personal Locator box and your password will be braveheart."

Greenwalt nodded. "Let's hope that it's Mrs. Monroe with the brave heart. What about Captain Kampov; have you had any further contact with him?"

"No, Sir. Not a word."

Traffic was picking up the nearer they got to the embassy, and Greenwalt was amazed at the number of pedestrians going about their business despite the sub-zero temperatures, but then Russians had always been a hearty people.

He took out his cell phone and speed dialed Kampov's

number at MVD Headquarters. Someone answered in Russian. "Do you speak English?" Greenwalt asked.

"Yes, who is this?" the man asked.

"Everett Greenwalt. I believe Captain Kampov is expecting me."

Ligget glanced at Greenwalt.

"One moment, please."

Kampov came on. "Are you here in Moscow?"

"Yes, I'm on the way to the embassy. Can we meet sometime today, perhaps after lunch?"

"For what reason?"

"I'd like to know what progress you've made."

"I'll call when I have something," Kampov said brusquely.

"Bullshit, Captain. I didn't fly all this way to be jerked around. I came here to find Mrs. Monroe and bring her home. It's your country, your investigation, but she's one of mine, and I want to help in any way I can."

"Come now," Kampov ordered gruffly.

Greenwalt hesitated for only a fraction of a second. "I'm on my way."

Kampov broke the connection and Greenwalt pushed the end button and pocketed his phone.

"Kampov's agreed to see me right now. You can take me to the embassy later."

"Yes, Sir," Ligget said, obviously impressed.

• • •

MVD was headquartered in what had been the KGB's main building downtown on the old Dzerzhinsky Square, a few blocks from the Kremlin. It was an ugly nine-story yellow brick building that once housed the infamous Lubyanka Prison. Everyone in Russia old

enough to remember, was afraid of it. It was said that
the concrete floors and walls in the basement interrogation rooms were still stained with the blood of tens
of thousands of political prisoners who had been tortured and then executed.

It was nearly eleven by the time Ligget turned the
corner from Teatralny Proezd past the Bolshoi Theater
onto the broad and extremely busy square.

"Did he say if someone would be waiting to escort
you?" Ligget asked.

"He just said, come now," Greenwalt replied, imitating Kampov's gruff voice.

Ligget grinned. "That sounds like him," he said.

They passed the building, and when Ligget caught a
momentary break in traffic he made a U-turn and pulled
up in front of the main entrance, which was up a few
wide stairs across a broad sidewalk. A pair of armed
Militia men flanked the big doors, through which people in uniform, as well as civilians, came and went.

"Busy place," Greenwalt said.

"The Russians take their law enforcement as seriously as we do."

"I don't know how long I'll be, so you might as well
take my bag back to the embassy and I'll call when I
get done."

"Don't you want me to stick with you, Sir?"

"It won't be necessary. I sent Kampov the Monroes'
files and talked to him before I flew over. He knows
the score. He'll work with me."

Ligget was disappointed. "Yes, Sir."

Greenwalt gathered his laptop and got out of the car.
"What's he like?"

"I think he's a good cop, but his wife was kidnapped

and killed a couple of years ago, and I'm told by people who've known him for a while that he's not the same as he used to be."

"I shouldn't doubt—" Greenwalt said, when a battered old taxi came racing up the street straight at them. He got the impression that the rear door was open and someone was perched there, ready to jump or perhaps to shoot.

"Get down," he shouted at Ligget and he ducked down below the level of the windows.

Someone was pushed out of the open door, the body hitting the curb with a horrible thump and rolling up on the sidewalk a few feet away from where Greenwalt crouched, as the cab roared off.

The man lay spread-eagle on his back, the front of his shirt drenched in blood. His throat had been cut so deeply that his head had been nearly severed from his body.

It wasn't even remotely possible that the man could still be alive, but Greenwalt was the first to react, and he scrambled over to make sure.

The guards from the front doors came down the stairs in a dead run, their rifles at the ready, aimed directly at Greenwalt, who pulled out his badge wallet, opened it, and held it in plain sight above his head.

The first guards reached him, while other armed Militiamen poured out of the building, and the crowds on the sidewalk shrank away. Traffic on the broad avenue was coming to a halt as even more armed men converged on Greenwalt and the embassy SUV, their weapons drawn, fierce expressions on their faces.

•

FORTY-EIGHT

Kampov was preparing a list of the Mafia clubs for the raids this afternoon when one of his people stuck his head in the door.

"Someone just dumped a body on our front steps. They think it's Feodor."

For a second Kampov couldn't comprehend what his officer was saying, but all of a sudden he knew it was true, because he'd been worrying about just such a thing all morning. He jumped up and raced down the corridor to the stairs, barging past a colonel and his aide.

The main hall on the ground floor was filled with people trying to get out, but the building had been locked down, which was SOP in these kinds of situations. A pair of armed Militiamen barred the doors.

Kampov pulled out his ID and flashed it at them. "If it's Sergeant Bokarev out there, he works for me."

"Yes, Sir," one of the guards said, and he let Kampov pass.

A couple dozen people, most of them armed Militiamen, were gathered on the sidewalk, some of them keeping civilian onlookers well back, others holding their weapons pointed at a man dressed in an expensive-looking topcoat, a gold shield raised over his head.

Kampov pushed his way through, and stopped short. Feodor lay on his back, his arms and legs spread out. His throat had been slashed so deeply that his spinal column was visible at the bottom of the wound. His eyes were open and bulging, and he had bitten halfway through his tongue. A wire garrote had done this; Kampov was certain of it.

He dropped down on a knee beside his friend's body and gently closed his eyes. At this point he was already beyond anger, his emotions changing to terror at what he was going to do to find the bastards who had killed Feodor and what he was going to do to them when he had them in his sights.

In the distance he could hear a siren, probably an ambulance, but it was far too late for that now.

He turned and looked at the man holding the gold shield over his head. "Greenwalt?" he asked.

"Yes," Greenwalt said. "I'd just gotten out of my car when his body was dumped out of a cab. Do you know him?"

Kampov nodded, and got to his feet. He turned to the Militia. "Lower your weapons. It's over."

Slowly they complied.

"Who saw anything?"

"I'm sorry, Captain, but it happened too fast," a Militia corporal said. He was one of the guards who'd been stationed at the front doors. "My attention was not on the street at that moment."

Kampov could feel his temper rising. "Someone must have seen something."

"It was a taxi," Greenwalt said, pocketing his shield. "Two men, one driving, the other in the backseat with the body."

Kampov looked at him. "You don't belong here. This is my city. Go home, Agent Greenwalt."

"The Monroes are my people," Greenwalt countered. "I managed to get a partial tag number. Yankee one-seven-eight, then perhaps a Sierra or Zulu."

The siren was just around the corner, and moments

later the ambulance pulled up and a pair of paramedics jumped out and hustled a gurney through the crowd. Bokarev was obviously dead, but one of the medics checked his pulse and lifted an eyelid for a response. Kampov was touched.

"Does anyone know this man?" the medic asked.

"His name is Feodor Bokarev," Kampov said. "MVD. He was a friend who worked for me."

"This was no accident."

"No," Kampov said. "I'll notify his wife. No announcement to anyone, I don't care who, without my approval. I'll call your chief right away."

"Yes, Sir," the medic said.

A crime scene investigation team with a photographer came out of the building and started doing their work, including talking to witnesses, excluding Greenwalt, who stood to one side with Kampov.

Just like that, Kampov found himself thinking. And how would he break it to Yana and the girls?

Fifteen minutes later Bokarev's body was zippered into a bag, placed aboard the ambulance, and was gone.

Kampov glanced at Greenwalt, the laptop he was carrying, and at the U.S. Embassy tag on the car. "Send your driver away, Deputy Assistant Greenwalt, and come with me."

Greenwalt motioned for Ligget to get out of there, and followed Kampov through the Militiamen.

"Get rid of these people, and clean up this mess," Kampov growled to the armed guards.

· · ·

Word had already spread to the rest of Kampov's staff, and they all looked up from what they were doing when he and Greenwalt walked in. No one said a word, and at that moment no phones were ringing, no voices from the next room, no printers spewing out paperwork. The silence was unsettling.

"All right, people, we have a murderer to find. Let's get back to work. Be professional."

"Mafia?" someone asked.

"Without a doubt," Kampov said. "Feodor was leaning on them, and they killed him. We're going to lean even harder."

"May I talk to you, first?" Greenwalt asked.

"We'll start at the Dynamo. I want a surveillance team out there right now. But keep it quiet. And send someone to the morgue to get Feodor's things, especially his cell phone. He may have made a call we can trace."

"Should we send a forensics team to collect trace evidence?"

Kampov realized that he wasn't thinking straight; he was missing things. "*Da.*"

"We'll take care of it," Lieutenant Sychev said. "What about his wife and children; should we send someone over there?"

"No, I'll do that myself."

No one said a thing.

"We're going to get the bastards who did this to him. I don't give a fuck how many toes we have to step on," Kampov said. "And fuck the Militia. This is ours top to bottom."

He glanced at Greenwalt and motioned the American into his office, where he closed the door.

"Okay, talk to me," he said.

"You called me up here," Greenwalt said.

Kampov felt as if he were in a dream. It was the only way he knew to control a black rage that threatened to consume him. He hadn't felt like this since Nina's death. "To impress on you that we are handling this case, and we neither need nor want your interference," he said. "We will find Mrs. Monroe and return her to you."

"It's been nine days, and so far you don't seem to have made much progress, except to get one of your officers killed."

Kampov was on the edge of taking the bastard apart, but he continued to hold himself in check. "He was a friend."

"I'm sorry," Greenwalt said. "In the meantime aren't you going to put a trace on the partial tag number?"

"It would take three Militiamen half a day to find a match. By now the cab has been wiped down and is parked in some deserted alley. By morning it will be completely stripped of anything useful."

"Haven't you people heard of computers?"

"Our motor vehicle records aren't in the system yet. We have other priorities for now."

"What was it that got your man killed?"

Again Kampov held his temper in check. "The Monroes were met at Sheremetyevo by two men, one of whom we identified as Aleksei Voronin, who has ties to the Mafia here. He's since disappeared. Sergeant Bokarev was putting some pressure on some of the Mafia clubs to find out where he went to ground."

"Killing a federal cop is a big deal, even for the Mafia."

"Not so big here, Assistant Deputy Greenwalt, we're at war."

"Actually it's Assistant Deputy Director," Greenwalt said. "Exactly the wrong thing to do now would be to retaliate against the clubs. Whoever is responsible is either long gone, or has a perfect alibi. In any event if you put too much pressure on them, they'll just kill the woman and you'll be left holding nothing."

"We'll find Feodor's killers."

"You can't help him now, but we can still save Mrs. Monroe if you don't lose your head."

Kampov was thinking about Yana. He could help her and the girls, and would do everything possible to make their lives as reasonable as possible over the coming months. But Patti Monroe was still out there somewhere. Her voice from the tapes played over and over in his head.

"I'm listening," he told Greenwalt.

"You mentioned the Grand Dynamo."

"It's a Mafia club. The manager promised he might be able to help find Voronin. I think Feodor went out there this morning and they killed him. Twenty million dollars is a powerful aphrodisiac."

"Then watch the club, and have your people check phone records, anything you can to prove your Sergeant was out there. Then make your raid. In the meantime Mrs. Monroe will be calling Anderson, and now that I'm here I'll be able to trace the call."

"Not with our equipment," Kampov said.

"Of course not," Greenwalt said. "But I'll be able to trace her call."

Kampov was impressed. "Are you CIA or NSA?"

"No."

"They're the only ones who can do such a thing."

"Not quite. But when Mrs. Monroe makes the call, we'll know where she is, and we can move in. If you go around shooting up Mafia clubs there won't be another telephone call. She'll be killed like her husband was and her kidnappers will get out of the country. You know that as well as I do."

Kampov was torn between wanting to lash out at

Feodor's killers, and admitting that Greenwalt could be useful. He could do nothing to bring his friend back, but it was within his power to help Yana and to find Patti Monroe before it was too late.

His way.

He nodded. "We'll wait for her call. Where can I reach you?"

Greenwalt gave his cell phone number. "I'm staying at the Embassy. As soon as she calls I'll let you know."

"Very well," Kampov said. "We'll see just how good you are, Assistant Deputy Director Greenwalt."

FORTY-NINE

•

Patti was very weak, and when she was lucid it frightened her. She'd managed to pull herself out of bed and make it down the corridor to the bathroom three times during the afternoon and evening. She'd tried the faucet in the sink but either the water had been turned off or the pipes had frozen, and the water in the toilet bowl was disgusting.

Lying now in the bed in the darkness she saw flashes of lights even when her eyes were tightly closed. The late evening train came through the town, its whistle eventually fading in the distance.

Someone came into the bedroom, and for a moment Patti didn't want to open her eyes for fear it was Lysenko come back to rape her again.

"Mrs. Monroe," Lana said from beside the bed.

Patti opened her eyes and looked up. Lana had

brought a glass of something, steam rising from it. A dim light spilled in from the corridor.

"This is tea with honey," Lana said. She sat on the edge of the bed and helped Patti sit up. "You need to get your strength back so you can make the call tomorrow."

Patti's lips were swollen and cracked and she burned her mouth on the rim of the glass and pulled back. "It's hot," she said, her voice little more than a croak.

"Can you sit by yourself?" Lana asked.

"I think so."

Lana removed her arm from Patti's back, then took a spoon from the pocket of her jeans and began feeding Patti the tea one spoonful at a time.

It had no taste to Patti, but the tea didn't upset her stomach as badly as the cold water had, and after a few minutes she began to feel a little stronger.

"Thank you," Patti said. "Maybe I'll stop having the dreams now."

Lana looked at her. "What have you been dreaming about?"

"Someone."

"Who?"

"Someone she thinks is coming to rescue her," Raya said from the doorway. "Nice fairy tale."

Patti turned her head so fast she got instantly dizzy and almost pitched over sideways onto the floor. But she recovered almost as quickly.

"Is that what's been keeping you going, Patricia?"

"He'll kill you and the others," Patti said, her voice still weak in her ears.

"He'd have to," Raya said. "Leave us now," she told Lana.

"She hasn't finished."

Raya's left eyebrow rose.

"I'm sorry," Lana said to Patti, and she got up and left the bedroom.

"It's been nine days," Raya said, coming the rest of the way in. "If someone were going to rescue you it would have happened by now."

"He'll be here."

Raya came around the bed and Patti shrank back.

"I'd been curious about sex since I was a little girl, but I was a virgin until I was raped by American sailors from Yokuska. They dragged me into an alley and beat me nearly unconscious."

She caressed Patti's cheek with her fingertips, and Patti brushed her hand away.

"Not a very good first time for a girl. How about you, Patricia, when did you lose your virginity?"

She sat down on the edge of the narrow bed and pulled the blanket away. Patti tried to move, but Raya grabbed her by the neck of her T-shirt. "I don't want to cause you pain. But if you cooperate with me I might be able to get you out of here when it's over."

"Over my dead body," Patti said. She pulled her T-shirt out of Raya's grasp. "If you want me to make the call tomorrow, keep your filthy hands off me."

For a full minute Raya remained seated on the edge of the bed, staring at Patti.

"And send Lana back with more tea and something for me to eat."

Raya finally got to her feet, looked down at Patti again, then turned and left the room.

Patti pulled the blanket up to her chin, and hunched over to hug her knees, trying to conjure up the image of her rescuer, but it was a long time coming.

THE TENTH DAY

January 11th

FIFTY

·

Kampov awoke drenched in sweat, his heart pounding. It was dark outside. He looked over at the clock on the DVD player. It was four in the morning, and he didn't remember turning off the television and falling asleep on the couch.

Yana's face and voice were still vivid to him. He'd gone over to her apartment around three in the afternoon. The moment she opened the door and looked into his eyes, she'd known that Feodor was dead, and she stepped back, her hand going to her mouth.

Kampov stepped inside, and closed the door. "Where are the girls?"

"At school," Yana said, her voice breathless. "They should be home by four-thirty."

"You need to call your sister, have her fly up right now."

Yana turned away and went to a chair in the living room and sat down. She was dressed in jeans, a St. Petersburg sweatshirt that she'd brought back from her visit, and thick red wool socks.

She clasped her hands between her knees when Kampov walked in and sat down on the couch across from her. A radio in the kitchen played classical music. "Is it true?" she asked, her voice small.

"*Da.*"

"How?"

"It was the Mafia."

"No, Captain, how did my husband die?"

Kampov couldn't meet her eyes. He looked away. "Yana, you don't want to know, believe me."

"*Eb tvoiu mat,* how?"

"They came at him from behind and cut his throat."

"Dear God in heaven," Yana had said, and she'd gone into the bedroom and closed the door.

Kampov had called his office to have one of the women from his division come over to be with her, then telephoned Yana's sister and broke the news. She'd promised to take the next flight out, and he'd waited until the matron had arrived, which was a few minutes before the girls were due to come home, and then he'd escaped back to his own apartment. Facing Yana had been the most difficult thing he'd ever done in his life, because Feodor's assassination was his fault. But facing the four girls would have been impossible for him. They would be with their mother until their aunt arrived, and slowly they would sort things out well enough so that he could come back into their lives and do what he could for them.

He'd debated with himself about going after Feodor's killers, as his feelings said he should, or listening to the American FBI agent and biding his time until Patti made another call to the states, as his instincts as a cop said he should.

The surveillance team he'd sent out to Dynamo called around nine to tell them they'd stumbled across a drunk living under the bleachers who'd sworn he'd seen two men drive a battered gray Lada four-door away from the loading dock behind the Grand Dynamo in the morning. They would have dismissed him as delusional, except that he'd described Feodor's car, right down to the dent in the left rear fender.

Sergeant Viktor Kuzin, the team leader, had been bitter on the phone. "It's business as usual out here, Captain. The bastards murdered Feodor, and now they're having a fucking party."

"We'll make it right," Kampov had promised.

"Call Colonel Baturin right now, and let's hit these bastards tonight."

"Not yet."

"Sir?" Kuzin said angrily.

"I want you on standby out there, Viktor. But keep a close watch. When we go in I want to make sure that Smikov is there."

"He's there. We saw him drive up around six."

"Let me know if he leaves."

"Yes, Sir," Kuzin had said, only slightly mollified.

Kampov got up from the couch and walked to the windows. Dawn was several hours away, but he knew that he'd never get back to sleep. Patti Monroe had been held for nine days already. In the tape of the most recent call to Anderson her voice had been weak and ragged. He had to wonder what she would sound like if she called again today, as Greenwalt expected she would.

The question in his mind was how long could she survive.

Her face had melded with the faces of Yana and of Nina, three women in his life who'd all been presented with horrible odds.

"Fuck it," he mumbled.

He turned and got his cell phone from the coffee table in front of the couch and speed dialed Baturin's number. The colonel answered on the second ring.

"*Da.*"

"It's the Grand Dynamo. We go in just after dawn."

"Is that where Feodor bought it?"

"Yes," Kampov said. "But we have to keep a sterile perimeter. No one or nothing gets out, that includes cell phone traffic."

"How long will we have to hold it?" Baturin asked.

"A few hours, maybe as long as twenty-four."

"Can do," the Spetsnaz colonel said. "The fuckers won't know what hit them, and neither will anyone else."

FIFTY-ONE

•

The sky was just beginning to lighten in the east when Patti woke up, her entire body trembling uncontrollably. She was hallucinating that she was in the dining car of a train, eating dinner, and yet at the edge of her consciousness she understood that what she was seeing and experiencing wasn't real.

The train blew its whistle as they passed through a town, and she raised a glass of champagne to her lips. She could taste the wine, feel it warm in her stomach. She couldn't quite make out what it was she was eating, but it was delicious. French, she thought, and the finest meal she'd ever had.

Gradually the shakes began to subside and Patti slowly came out of her hallucination, sorry to leave the comfort and safety of the train. It had been her father sitting across from her, and he'd been smiling and laughing, telling her how pretty her hair was, and how proud he was of her.

She began to cry, but she was so dehydrated that she

couldn't produce any tears. For as long as she could remember she'd wanted to hear those words from her father, see his smile, hear his laughter.

If he were here with her now he wouldn't be smiling. The stern look would be on his narrow, disapproving face because she was crying. *"Enough of that, Patricia,"* he would say, and she could hear his voice. *"Crying never solved a thing. Control yourself, for God's sake, and start making the right decisions for once in your life."*

It was the same look on his face, the same words from his mouth, when she'd announced that she and David were getting married. She wondered what he would say to her when he found out David was dead, his body lying in the snow in the Russian woods.

The curtain was pulled back and Lana slipped into the bedroom and came around to the side of the bed.

Patti struggled to sit up and, like before, Lana helped her.

"This is just sugar water," Lana said. "There's nothing else fit for you to eat right now." She held Patti's lips.

The water was cold and incredibly sweet. Some of it spilled down the front of Patti's T-shirt. But the effect was almost instantaneous: her head cleared, her shakes subsided and she wasn't so cold.

"More," she said, her voice ragged.

Lana fed her more of the water, and it tasted like the champagne from the train, rich, almost decadent.

"I think I can eat something now," Patti said. "Maybe some bread, and more water."

"I'll try," Lana whispered. "They're excited now. Someone from the states called and said that Anderson has arranged for a twenty million dollar transfer from his account."

"How did they find out?"

"I don't know, but it must be true because Sergey said they were getting out of here sometime today, or tomorrow at the latest."

Patti couldn't imagine Tobias actually cooperating with these bastards, yet she hoped it was true. She didn't want to die. "If they're getting what they want, they can feed me."

Lana shook her head. "Once they get the money they think you'll try to escape."

"That's exactly what I'll do, with your help."

Lana reared back.

"But I'm going to need my strength."

"It's impossible."

"Listen to me," Patti said urgently. "You told me that you had nowhere to go, but if you help me I'll get you out of here. You can come to America."

"I don't know anybody there. They wouldn't let me in. I don't even have a passport."

"My friends will take care of all that," Patti said. "You just have to help me."

Lana backed away.

"More sugar water, and then something to eat."

The blanket was pulled back and Lana turned toward the doorway. Lysenko came in, a half smile on his lips, his body backlit from the TV room.

"You were told to leave it alone, Mrs. Viltov," Lysenko said, gently.

"Starving her won't do us any good," Lana said. "You agreed last night."

Lysenko nodded. "Of course you have a point; I merely wanted you to check with me first before you came back up here. We're nearly finished."

Lana lowered her head, tears coming to her eyes. "I'm afraid."

"No need for it, my dear," Lysenko said. He came the rest of the way into the bedroom and took Lana in his arms. "Maybe all you need is a good cry. Boris won't mind."

"He doesn't care about anything," Lana said softly.

"You made a mistake," Patti said from the bed.

Lysenko and Lana looked at her.

"You're speaking English for my benefit," Patti said. "It's all an act." Whenever he or Raya were giving orders to Lana or anyone else when Patti was present, they spoke English. It struck her just now that they were putting on an elaborate stage play to frighten her into submission. The beatings, the rape, the hangings, the starvation, all of it was horrible, but none of it was actually meant to kill her. That wouldn't happen until they got their money.

"No, Mrs. Monroe," Lana said, and she seemed to be genuinely frightened. "I promise you."

Lysenko raised his hands to Lana's head and, without any emotion showing on his face, pulled sharply to the right, breaking her neck with an audible pop.

He let go and Lana's limp body slumped to the floor, her eyes open.

Patti was struck dumb. No one was here to help her, and no one was coming to rescue her. Raya had been correct last night; it had been ten days since she and David had been picked up at the airport, and if someone were coming they would have been here by now.

Her life was in her own hands.

She looked up from Lana's body. Lysenko was staring at her.

"Someday you're going to end up like that," she said, her voice even. "I hope I'm there to see it."

FIFTY-TWO

Kampov sat in the shotgun seat of the Spetsnaz strike force command *GAZik* waiting for Baturin to get word that the repeaters for the three nearest cell phone towers had been temporarily taken out of commission.

The land lines had been cut ten minutes ago, so no telephone calls would be made from anywhere inside the club, unless someone had a sat phone.

Baturin had stationed four armored personnel carriers, each with a fire team of seven operators and one non-com, just off Leningradsky Prospect to the southwest, near the Petrovsky Palace to the northwest, Ulitsa Novaya Bashilovka to the southeast, and the stadium's main driveway to the northeast.

The only other ways out of the Dynamo were either the Metro Station, where two operators on foot were waiting in the shadows, or by helicopter, but a Spetsnaz gunship was standing by one kilometer away in the parking lot of the Hippodrome to stop that from happening.

Over Sergeant Kuzin's strong objections, Kampov had thanked the MVD surveillance team for sticking it out all night, and sent them home.

"So far as we can tell the only one left inside is Smikov, and maybe some of the girls," Kuzin said bitterly. He'd wanted to take everyone down, hard, as payback for Bokarev.

"Could your people have been spotted?" Kampov asked.

Kuzin nodded. "Probably." He glanced over at the

APCs and Spetsnaz operators. "We'd like to stick around, and go in with you."

Kampov took him aside, out of the earshot of the others. "It's going to get ugly—"

"I don't give a fuck," Kuzin said.

"We're going to break some laws, Viktor, and I don't want any shit coming back on you or your team," Kampov pressed, and he didn't wait for Kuzin to object again. "You and your people are off duty right now, and that's an order, Sergeant."

The morning was gray and bitterly cold, with a light wind from the northwest, and Kampov felt like shit from last night. Too much brandy and too little untroubled sleep. When this business was at an end, however it turned out, he was going to take a vacation, something he hadn't done since Nina's death. They used to go to Odessa and sleep late, play in the water, eat at good restaurants, and stay out sometimes until dawn, dancing, but that was then and this was now.

Shit, he thought. There was no going back, and he had no clear idea how to go forward.

Baturin was dressed in daytime camos, a Steyr GB combat pistol in a holster strapped to his chest. He pressed a finger to his earpiece, and a moment later said "*Da,*" into his lapel mike.

"Are we ready?" Kampov asked.

Baturin nodded. "Units one, two, three, and four stand by, we're going in. Pavlenko, now."

Sergeant Yuri Pavlenko was in command of the fifth APC, parked next to the command *GAZik,* with a handpicked fire team of seven operators. Its engine roared into life and the personnel carrier took off across the Dynamo's vast parking lot directly toward the club entrance, where four operators would be dropped off, before heading around back where Pavlenko and the other three men would come in through the rear entrance.

Baturin was right behind them, pulling up at the front doors as the first four operators dismounted.

One of them raced to the front door, but it was locked. He took out an impressive lump of plastic explosive and had it molded to the door's hinges, an acid fuse inserted and cracked, in under ten seconds.

"Fire in the hole," he shouted as he stepped smartly back around the corner.

The plastic went off with a formidable bang, and before the operators were inside the club, a second bang came from the back entrance.

Fire alarms sounded throughout the building, but no one came out to investigate.

Barturin and Kampov brought up the rear behind the four operators, who leapfrogged two-by-two through the lobby, out onto the dance floor, and into the restrooms and back bar, their Val assault rifles at the ready position.

They were professionals, blooded in Chechnya, and they went about their work with an unhurried precision. Anything that moved was to be considered a hostile and would either immediately follow directions or would be taken down.

A corporal trotted across the dance floor to Baturin. "Clear here, Sir."

Baturin nodded. "Yuri?" He listened to something in his headset, and looked at the corporal. "They're clear in the back. Make sure this area remains secure."

"Yes, Sir."

"They've got Smikov in his office," Baturin said, and Kampov led the way across the dance floor to the door to the rear corridor.

"Anyone else?" Kampov asked.

"A young girl," Baturin said, tight-lipped. "Everyone else must have been tipped off we were on our way." He spoke into his lapel mike. "Coming in."

Two operators were at the end of the corridor and the third was at the open door to Smikov's office. They looked bored, but they acknowledged the colonel. This had been way too easy so far.

Smikov was seated behind his desk, an attractive young woman, perhaps eighteen or twenty years old, sitting on the couch. Smikov had a smirk on his face, but the girl looked frightened.

"Is this the one?" Sergeant Pavlenko asked. His rifle was pointed in Smikov's general direction. It was plain that he was hoping the Mafia boss would try to make some move.

"Captain Kampov," Smikov said.

"You shouldn't have done it," Kampov said. Now that he was here he was beyond simple anger.

"I don't know what you're talking about."

"He had a wife and four daughters. Their lives will be difficult now."

Smikov shook his head and spread his hands. "I heard about it. But he was pissing on some dangerous guys. And I warned him to take it easy. But you know Feodor; he never listened."

"All he wanted was to find out where Voronin has gone to ground," Kampov said. "Not so difficult. And he would have protected his source. Even a hint where we might find him would have done. Instead you killed my friend."

"You can't prove a thing," Smikov said. "But you didn't need all this muscle. You could have given me a call and I would have been happy to come down to your office to have a little chat."

"Where can I find Aleksei?"

"I don't know," Smikov said. "I never bothered to find out."

"Very well," Kampov said. He pulled out his pistol and put one round into the center of Smikov's forehead, driving his body and the chair backward, blood spraying on the wall behind him.

Sergeant Pavlenko was impressed.

Kampov switched aim to the girl. "Do you know this name, Aleksei Voronin?"

"Sascha," Baturin warned. His daughter was seventeen.

"Voronin," Kampov demanded. "Did you hear your boss or anyone else talking about him?"

The girl was frightened out of her skull and she was nodding. "He has an office in Moscow," she whimpered. "But I don't know anything else."

Kampov's finger tightened on the trigger, but Baturin put his hand on top of the pistol and pushed it downward.

"You can't shoot her," the colonel said. "She's just a kid."

Kampov looked at his friend, and after a beat nodded. "Feodor didn't have a chance."

"I know. But someone from one of the other clubs will know where this man you want is hiding. We'll find him, today."

Kampov gave the girl a bleak look. "Go home," he told her.

She jumped up and hurried out of the office.

"A young woman is coming your way," Baturin radioed. "Let her pass."

Kampov de-cocked his pistol and stuffed it in the holster under his jacket. "I want an engineering squad with a bulldozer out here this morning to dismantle this club."

"A lot of important people come to places like this," Baturin said. "A lot of politicians."

"I'll take responsibility," Kampov said.

"The prime minister's letter?"

"*Da*," Kampov replied. "And I'll want the word to get out, because we're going to dismantle every fucking Mafia club in the city until we find out what rock Voronin is hiding under."

FIFTY-THREE

·

Sometime after dawn, Lana's body had been removed, and a winter coat, plastic boots, and a scarf had been laid at the foot of the bed. A large glass of lukewarm tea, sweetened with honey or sugar, had been left on the window seat, and when Patti woke up she drank it straight down.

Today was the end. According to Lana, Tobias had gotten the twenty million and now nothing was left to be done except give him the account number where it was to be transferred.

In about ten minutes, enough of Patti's strength had returned so that she could get dressed to go out.

She turned and looked out the window for a moment, wondering if she would ever see this room again. If they were taking her back to the empty apartment in Moscow, she would try to make her break and get lost in one of the other buildings. Hopefully she could find someone who would be willing to call the police.

Now that Lana was gone, no one was left to help her. She was on her own, and no matter what was coming next she wasn't about to simply roll over and die. If they were going to kill her they would have to work for it.

She went to the doorway, pushed the blanket aside, and stepped out into the empty TV room.

No one was in the corridor, but at the head of the stairs she could hear someone talking downstairs, and she hesitated for a few moments to listen. Aside from recognizing Lysenko's voice, and perhaps Raya's, she couldn't make out what they were saying, though they didn't sound angry, and she started down, using the banister for support.

She was very weak, and by the time she reached the bottom, it felt as if her legs were going to give way at any moment, and she had to stop and lean against the wall.

Boris came to the kitchen doorway and spotted Patti. "She's here," he said in Russian.

Patti looked up at him and studied his nearly emotionless face. "He killed your wife," she said. "Doesn't that matter to you?"

Boris looked at her as if she were talking about tomorrow's weather. "*Nyet*," he said indifferently.

"What about your children?"

"They'll survive, or they won't."

Lysenko came to the doorway. "Your friend has got the money," he said. "We're going back to Moscow where you can call him with the instructions."

"And then?"

"We'll come back here and wait for the funds to be transferred."

"You're going to kill me after you get the money."

"There'll be no need for it," Lysenko said. "Raya and I will be leaving and you'll be on your own."

"Do you think I'm that stupid?"

Lysenko looked at her with a faint smile. "As a matter of fact I do," he said. "Otherwise you and your husband wouldn't have gotten yourselves into this situation."

"And stupid people deserve to die."

"What's your point, Mrs. Monroe?"

"You want the twenty million because—" Patti stopped, something suddenly occurring to her. "You want that exact amount because you want to buy something, and that's what it'll cost. Twenty million sure as hell won't buy you a safe retirement somewhere. But it will buy you what? An airplane, a yacht, a bunch of guns, machine guns, bombs? Stingers so you can shoot down passenger jets? Are you one of those fucking fanatics who think 9/11 was all our fault?"

Voronin came down the hall from the other way. "I think what Patti is talking about is a guarantee that when we get the money we'll let her go free."

Patti looked at him. "You may be a bastard, but at least you're not a dumb bastard."

"What do you propose?" Lysenko asked.

"I want a cell phone. I'll program the Militia's Moscow number into the speed dial, and set up a text message. Patti Monroe. Kidnapped. Aleksei Voronin. Noginsk."

"Are you crazy?" Voronin sputtered.

Patti almost laughed out loud. "Me? Crazy?" she asked. "Once you get your money, I'll keep my finger on the send button until you drop me off in front of my embassy in plain sight of the Marine Guards. Then I'll give you the phone and you can drive off."

"Agreed," Lysenko said, his voice so soft Patti wasn't sure that she'd heard him right.

"She knows our faces, our names," Voronin protested.

"It doesn't matter, we'll be gone," Lysenko said.

• • •

The weather was just as overcast and dismal and cold as yesterday, and the same traffic was on the highway into Moscow. The cars and trucks carried people who were going about their normal day-to-day business unaware of what was happening in the black Mercedes sharing the road with them.

Patti, sitting in the backseat between Raya and Voronin, thought about reaching the button for one of the windows and screaming for help when the window was down. But even if she attracted someone's attention that way, what could they do?

Closer into the city, Boris drove past the apartment building from where she'd made the call yesterday, and went the rest of the way downtown, along the river for a while, and then into the business district.

Patti sat up. She knew these streets. She and David had been here before. Many times.

When they turned onto Chekova, the building where their offices were located was at the end of the block. The staff would be there, or someone in one of the other offices in the same building would recognize her and would say hello, and they would have to realize just looking at her that something was seriously wrong.

Was it possible that the bastards were so arrogant, so sure of themselves, that they were making the blunder of the century?

She sat back, careful to keep her expression neutral. All she needed was one chance, just one little break to come her way, and she would capitalize on it. No way in hell would they open fire on innocent people downtown in broad daylight.

Boris pulled into a parking spot in front of the three-story brick building and Lysenko turned back to Patti.

"If you call out, or try to run, I'll shoot you," he said. "Do you understand?"

Patti nodded.

Lysenko handed her a cell phone. "I'll give you the battery when the money is sent." He got out of the car and opened the rear door so Patti, Raya, and Voronin could get out, and he hustled them across the sidewalk and into what had been the suite of offices for Patti and David's Moscow business.

The three rooms had been stripped of nearly everything. All the furniture and even the light switches and fixtures had been removed, leaving only a wooden stool sitting in the middle of the front room where the secretary did her work. And coming down the hall, Patti looked through the open door of what had been the Roskov Textile Exchange, and those offices were empty as well.

"You've been planning this ever since you came to the states to visit us," Patti said to Voronin. "Even killing David."

Voronin gave her an indifferent look. "You brought it on yourselves."

"One point five million for the fertilizer deal, not twenty million so your partners can buy new toys so they can kill people."

Voronin shrugged.

Boris took the phone and extra headset out of his bag and hardwired it to a baseboard telephone jack, as Raya took off Patti's coat and sat her down on the stool.

"You're bleeding," Raya said.

Patti touched a finger to the seat of her jeans and came away with blood. A spike of fear shot through her, but she held herself in check. "That should make you fucking freaks happy."

Lysenko handed her a slip of paper on which was written two sets of numbers, nine digits each. "The first is our bank and the second is our account number."

Boris dialed the Andersons' number, and handed the headset to Lysenko and the receiver to Patti. After a few moments the connection was made and the telephone began ringing outside Washington.

"Why isn't he answering?" Lysenko demanded after the fourth ring.

"It's the middle of the night over there, and he's an old man," Patti said, hoping that the FBI was stalling for time to make the trace.

"Cut it off—" Lysenko said, but then Anderson picked up on the seventh ring.

"Hello," he said. "Patti, is it you?"

"Yes," Patti said.

"I'm very glad to hear your voice. How are you doing?"

"Not so good. They're starving me."

"Are they there with you, can they hear me?"

She looked away from Lysenko, who was gesturing toward the note with the bank numbers. "Yes, they're right here," she said. "They know that you have the money. They want me to give you their bank numbers. I have them written down for you."

"How do they know I got the money?"

"They must have someone there, watching you, or maybe it's a computer hacker."

"All right, I'll take the numbers, but I need to get a paper and pen from my study."

"The FBI is recording this call," Lysenko said to Patti, keeping his voice low. "He doesn't need to write anything down."

"Tobias, wait," Patti said.

FIFTY-FOUR

•

Greenwalt left the embassy's communications center in a dead run, Patti's call coming into his earpiece from the intercept equipment. The Jupiter spy satellite that had been re-aimed for this operation had picked up the call, shunted it to Moscow, and made the trace within seconds.

"You don't need to write it down," Patti was saying. *"The FBI is recording everything I say."*

Ligget pulled up in front with the Caddy SUV, and Greenwalt climbed in the passenger seat.

"The Bureau isn't here," Anderson said. *"I sent them away. They don't want me to pay the ransom, but I disagree. I think it's the only way these people are going to release you."*

"Do you know where number twenty-five Chekova Ulitsa is?" Greenwalt demanded.

"I will in a second," Ligget said, and he programmed the address into the dash-mounted GPS receiver.

The line was silent for a moment, but then Patti was back.

"Okay, get the pen and paper."

"Just give me a minute."

"Got it," Ligget said. He glanced in the rearview mirror, waited for a moment, then floored the SUV and made a U-turn, just behind a truck.

Greenwalt speed dialed Kampov's number on his cell phone. It was answered on the second ring.

"What do you have, Mr. Greenwalt," Kampov said sharply. It sounded to Greenwalt as if the Russian cop was pissed off or in a hurry or both.

"Mrs. Monroe is talking on the telephone with Tobias Anderson. I've traced the call to twenty-five Chekova Street, and I'm on my way with Agent Ligget."

"Eb tvoiu mat," Kampov blurted. "We'll be there in two minutes. Don't do a thing without me. Do you understand that, Mister?"

"Okay, Patricia, give me the numbers now," Anderson said.

"Wait," Greenwalt shouted. "She's going to give Anderson the bank numbers."

"You're monitoring the phone call right now?" Kampov demanded.

"Stand by." He put the phone down and pulled out his notepad and pen and copied down the numbers as Patti recited them. When she was finished, Anderson repeated them back to her to make sure he hadn't made a mistake.

"This is a great deal of money, Patricia," he said. *"I don't want to send it to the wrong bank."*

"When will you send the money?" Patti asked.

"There are certain difficulties, but I will try to get it done today. Possibly very late, in which case the money won't be transmitted until tomorrow. Just hold on, dear, it won't be much longer."

"Thank you—" Patti said, and the connection was broken.

Greenwalt picked up the cell phone. "She's gone, but she gave Anderson the bank routing and account numbers."

"How did she sound?" Kampov demanded.

"Beat up," Greenwalt said, and he hit end.

Ligget was expertly weaving through traffic, ignoring red lights when he could.

"How much longer?" Greenwalt asked.

"A couple of minutes."

Greenwalt used his satphone to speed dial the Bureau's operations center in Washington, and gave the on-duty officer the bank routing code and the account number.

"Tell me what you can."

The operations officer was back in less than thirty seconds. "Riyadh," he said. "It's an affiliate of the Saudi Cairo Bank."

"Any luck with the account holder?"

"No, but we'll work on it. May I ask the CIA for some help? I know a guy over there who's a computer genius."

"Do it," Greenwalt said, without hesitation. "And let me know the second you find out anything."

FIFTY-FIVE

·

We need to get out of here right now," Lysenko said. He yanked the telephone wires out of the wall, and went to a papered-over window that looked out on the street and tore back a small corner.

"What is it, Sergey?" Voronin demanded.

Lysenko turned and stared at Patti, who managed a smile.

"It won't be long now," she said.

"The old man was lying," Lysenko said. "The FBI was there. They traced the call."

"Impossible," Voronin said.

Raya hauled Patti off the stool and helped her on with the coat. "They have some serious satellites," she said. She pulled her Makarov pistol out of her shoulder holster and concealed it in her jacket pocket where she could get at it easier.

Lysenko went to the door and sent Boris ahead to start the car.

"He'll transfer the money, just like he promised, no matter what the FBI is telling him," Patti said. "He figures it'll save my life, and you people will be caught and the money recovered. He's a man with powerful friends, and he figures he can make anything happen."

Lysenko turned back. "For your sake, I hope you're right."

They waited in the corridor until Boris got behind the wheel of the Mercedes and started the engine. A trolley bus passed in the street, and after three women walking together turned the corner Lysenko took Patti's arm, hustled her across the sidewalk, and handed her into the backseat.

Voronin got in on the other side, and Raya slid in beside Patti.

Lysenko stopped for a moment and looked up into the sky toward the northwest. Patti couldn't see his face from the backseat but it was obvious from his body language that something was wrong.

He climbed into the car and slammed the door. "Get the hell out of here," he said in Russian.

Boris slammed the car in gear and sped off down the street, merging with traffic, as a military helicopter suddenly swooped overhead and flared to a hover over the Chekova building. Rappelling lines dropped from either side and a half-dozen black-clad figures dropped down onto the roof.

Patti looked back, as the Mercedes turned the corner at the end of the block, in time to see some sort of an armored car or truck coming up the street at a high rate of speed from the opposite direction and pull to a halt in front of the office building.

They'd come to rescue her, as she knew they would. They'd traced the call and knew where to find her.

Lysenko turned in his seat and looked past Patti out the rear window to make sure that they had not been spotted and were being followed.

Patti's eyes met his for a moment, but she was careful to keep a neutral expression. Her freedom was so close, she didn't want to do or say anything to screw it up. If the Russians had traced her this far, they'd have to find her in Noginsk. Somehow.

She looked away as a Cadillac SUV coming up the street in the opposite direction passed, and she caught a brief glimpse of a man with a broad face staring at her.

He was an American. She was certain of it. His overcoat, his hairstyle, his expression, everything, said American to her.

She wanted to turn and wave to get his attention, but Raya had taken out her pistol and was watching.

"Who was that?"

"What do you mean?" Patti asked, her heart thumping.

"The car that we just passed. You knew the men."

"No, I didn't."

Raya raised the pistol.

Patti held up her hand. "I swear to God, I didn't know those people. I never saw them before in my life."

"What is it?" Lysenko asked, in Russian.

"Unless I miss my guess, I think that SUV that just passed us is an embassy car," Raya answered. "U.S. Embassy."

"Are you certain?"

"*Nyet,*" she admitted.

She said something rapid fire in a dialect Patti couldn't understand, which seemed to startle Lysenko, who glanced at Patti and shook his head.

"Not yet," he said in English.

Patti felt a little thrill in her gut. She was frightened and excited at the same time, because both Lysenko's and Raya's faces wore a look of concern. The bastards were worried, which meant they might make a mistake, but it also meant that they might kill her and dump her body out in the country.

She glanced at Voronin, who was staring at her. He had the same look on his round face.

FIFTY-SIX

•

At the corner, Ligget was stopped by a pair of Spetsnaz operators who were blocking traffic. The helicopter continued to hover ten meters above the rooftops, but there didn't seem to be any other movement in or around the building.

"Stay here," Greenwalt ordered. "No matter what happens don't let them make you leave."

"I might not have any choice, Sir," Ligget said.

"It was her in the car. I saw her."

"What?" Ligget sputtered, but Greenwalt leaped out of the SUV, holding his FBI identification over his head.

The Spetsnaz operators had their assault rifles at the ready. "*Nyet,*" one of them said forcefully.

"I need to speak to Captain Kampov," Greenwalt shouted over the noise of the helicopter. "Do you understand English? It's urgent!"

The operator shook his head.

Traffic had magically disappeared, nor was a crowd building up, as would normally happen in the states. Everything here was out of kilter, all wrong to Greenwalt's way of thinking.

He stepped back and reached for his cell phone, but both Spetsnaz operators suddenly trained their rifles on him. He slowly spread his arms. One of them said something into his lapel mike, his eyes not leaving Greenwalt.

A half-minute later Kampov emerged from the building and came down the block. He'd holstered his pistol, and he looked pissed off. He said something in Russian to the operators, who hesitated, but then lowered their weapons.

"Are you sure you had the correct address?" Kampov demanded.

"Yes," Greenwalt said.

"Well she wasn't there."

"I know. But we'll find her now."

Kampov's eyes narrowed. "What are you talking about?"

"I saw her five minutes ago. She was in the backseat of a black Mercedes, heading away."

"How do you know it was her?"

"I've studied her photographs," Greenwalt said. "She was in the backseat of a ninety-nine or 2000 E320."

"Did you get a tag number?"

"Just a partial. Yankee one-five-something-something. I didn't get the last number or the last two letters. It went too fast. But you need to post an APB."

Kampov was excited. Greenwalt could see it in the man's eyes. "Do you know how big this city is?"

"Smaller than New York."

"But we don't have the cooperation of the Militia," Kampov said. "We'll never find the car by throwing up roadblocks like in *Dragnet*."

"Christ—" Greenwalt said.

"But we'll find out who the car is registered to and where the owner lives," Kampov said. He nodded. "We'll get her this time, Mr. Assistant Deputy Director." He smiled. "Good work."

Greenwalt felt a flush of pleasure in spite of himself. "I used to be a good cop."

"I'm sure you were," Kampov said. "Wait here."

FIFTY-SEVEN

•

Boris drove fast but carefully, so as not to get into an accident, or to attract the attention of a Militia cop. Everyone was tense, but no one said a word.

Once they were safely out of the city on the country road to Noginsk, and certain that they were not being followed, Patti considered whether she'd ever see the dacha again. It was early in the afternoon, and broad daylight, but she still feared that they would pull up, march her into the woods, and shoot her in the back of the head like they had done to David.

She did not believe he had suffered, but it was afterwards that bothered her. Would his soul survive his death? The rabbis had said yes. Even so, dying was something that happened only to old, sick people.

When she was in her teens and early twenties she'd put the entire concept out of her mind. Ancient religions were just that—foolish nonsense meant to frighten little children and comfort old women. But at this moment, watching out the car window at the passing countryside, she could envision herself inside David's body as the bullet entered his brain and he pitched forward. No pain, but maybe a rush of senses, a leaving of the body, rising upward, happening so fast that nothing could be done.

And then what? Heaven? She wanted to think it would be like that—so easy, so comforting. As they passed the place where she thought David had been shot to death, however, she lowered her head and closed her eyes. God, she wanted to believe. With everything in her heart she wanted to believe in a better life.

But when she opened her eyes again, it was just the snow-covered birch woods outside, and Voronin daubing his nose.

She lay her head back and closed her eyes again. They were going to kill her unless she did something to stop them. But she didn't know if she had the strength to fight back, and she didn't want to find out what David had found out. Not yet. It was too soon.

• • •

Patti woke suddenly, and the only images she could recall were bright shards of colors and shapes, as the gate to the dacha swung open, and she thought she saw Lana in her rubber boots. But it was just the old babushka.

Boris pulled into the yard, and they all got out and went into the kitchen. Raya hustled Patti into the house and upstairs to the bedroom.

"You'll get your money," Patti said. Her legs felt like rubber, and she was so thirsty all the spit in her mouth had dried up.

"I think it's too late for you now," Raya told her. "Your call was traced, which means the FBI is involved. They won't allow Anderson to send the money outside the country."

"Goddamnit, he'll do it for me!"

Raya eyed her speculatively, but then shook her head and left the room.

Patti waited for a few seconds and then went to the doorway, pushed back the blanket, looked out into the empty TV room, and crept to the head of the stairs, her right hand trailing on the wall.

She could hear voices drifting up from the kitchen, Raya and Lysenko and Voronin and maybe Boris. They were speaking in Russian and she could pick out a lot of what they were saying, although some of the words or phrases were unclear. But it was obvious they were arguing.

"They could not have traced the call so soon," Lysenko said.

"They have satellites," Raya argued.

"That was a Spetsnaz raid."

"*Da,* but if that was an American embassy car that we passed, it would mean that the FBI is working with them."

"They had help."

"What are you talking about?"

"From here. Inside this house. There's no other way they could have gotten to the office so fast."

The kitchen was silent for a long moment, but then Voronin said something that Patti couldn't quite catch. It sounded as if he were pleading.

"You're the only one in this house with a connection to the office, besides Mrs. Monroe," Lysenko said.

"Posel na khyi," Voronin shouted. It meant "go fuck yourself."

"You and your fucking heroin," Lysenko said.

Patti began to shiver almost uncontrollably, even though she was burning up with a fever. She had to hold on to the banister to keep from tumbling down the stairs.

When the single pistol shot came, it was so loud inside Patti's head that her heart lurched and she nearly fainted.

"Put him in the root cellar," Lysenko ordered, his voice calm.

The babushka said something in reply.

"It won't matter," Lysenko said. "We're all leaving here tomorrow after one more telephone call from town."

"What about my house?" Boris demanded.

"You and your mother are going back to Grozny, and that's where you'll stay for now."

"Nyet," Boris said, sharply.

"There's plenty of room in the cellar for another body," Lysenko said.

Someone stomped across the kitchen and the outside door slammed.

Raya said something that Patti couldn't catch, but she must have asked about the phone trace.

"It was Aleksei's connection to the business office."

"At the very least, by now the FBI has your bank

numbers. Even if they allowed Anderson to send the money, the bank wouldn't release it."

"You're right," Lysenko agreed. "But tomorrow we'll send him Mrs. Monroe's numbers in Damascus."

"I didn't know that she had an account there."

"She will by morning," Lysenko said.

Raya said something else Patti couldn't understand, and then the woman laughed. "That's good, Sergey. Brilliant."

FIFTY-EIGHT

•

By two in the afternoon it was obvious to Greenwalt that finding out to whom the black Mercedes was registered was probably going to take all day and night, and he cursed himself for not getting the entire number.

On the basis of the letter from Putin, Kampov was assigned six Department of Motor Vehicle clerks—all that were available—to go through the records by hand. The files were housed in a dimly lit, cavernous room, with several million cards.

"Too bad you don't read Russian," Kampov said. "Then perhaps you could be of some use here." They were sitting in the supervisor's office while she was out in the stacks helping her clerks. Everyone had been impressed by the letter from the prime minister.

"I didn't come this far to sit on my ass," Greenwalt said. "In the states our cops can tap into the DMV records from their squad cars and have the information within seconds."

"It must be wonderful," Kampov replied dryly.

"Christ," Greenwalt said, half under his breath.

"*Da,*" Kampov said. "Tell me again, who else besides Mrs. Monroe you saw in the car."

"Two men in the front, and a man and a woman with Mrs. Monroe in the back."

"So you've already said. But was there enough time to come up with descriptions?"

"It was quick, and I was focused on Mrs. Monroe."

"I understand—" Kampov said.

"The driver was dark, heavyset, full beard; the man in the passenger seat was not as dark, short hair, slender, maybe military or ex. I got the impression that the woman in the backseat was young, slender, and maybe military; and the guy sitting on the other side of Mrs. Monroe was heavyset, round face, light hair, big square glasses."

Kampov sat up. "*Pizdec,*" he swore. "The guy with the glasses was Aleksei Voronin, and the one in the front was with him when they met the Monroes at the airport."

"Do we know who he is?"

"Not sure," Kampov said. He looked up. "One thing though, she's still alive."

"She looked bad."

"All that as they drove past?"

"Yes," Greenwalt said absently.

Kampov glanced through the windows at the clerks busy trying to find all the registration cards that matched the partial tag number and the black Mercedes.

"I'd like to borrow one of your technicians for an hour," Greenwalt said.

Kampov looked at him with interest. "What kind of technician?"

"A fingerprint man who speaks some English. I want to dust the office."

Kampov shrugged. "You'd be looking for a smaller needle in a bigger haystack."

"We have some pretty good digital records on terrorists and people suspected of having terrorist links."

"Russians?"

"Some," Greenwalt said.

Kampov nodded after a moment.

"Have him pick me up here."

"What will you do with the fingerprints, if you find any?"

"I'll send them to the Bureau's database."

"Very well," Kampov said. He made a phone call to his office and gave the order.

Ligget had returned to the embassy and Greenwalt called him. "It's going to take all day and night over here to come up with the registration. In the meantime I'm going back to the Chekova Street office with an MVD fingerprint tech. We'll send whatever we come up with back to Washington. See if they can find a match."

"Yes, Sir," Ligget said. "Dan Wilkes called from ops and left a message for you. His friend over at the CIA, Otto Rencke, said there's no name for the BLOM bank account, just the number."

"It's about what I figured. Call Dan and give him the heads up on the prints, and have him ask his friend if he can give us some help with them."

"Will do."

Greenwalt ended the call and pocketed his phone.

"The technician is Sergeant Ivan Alipov," Kampov said. "He's young, but he's one of our best men. He'll meet you out front in a few minutes."

Greenwalt glanced out at the stacks. "Call me when you come up with something."

"I expect the same from you."

"Of course," Greenwalt said. "What about your Spetsnaz friends?"

"They're standing by," Kampov said. "If we don't turn up anything by morning, they'll start hitting all the Mafia clubs in town, and keep hitting them until we find where Voronin has gone to ground."

"That wouldn't work in the states."

"Too bad."

· · ·

Kampov's fingerprint man listened to what Greenwalt was looking for, and when they got over to the Chekova office he set his kit down on the floor, while Greenwalt took a quick look in the three rooms.

Kampov had told him about the blood on the stool, and by now it had dried to a black crust. She had been starved and beaten, and most likely raped, and probably had internal injuries. It wasn't necessary to take a sample and try for a quick DNA analysis; everyone knew that it was Mrs. Monroe's. Directly across the room several wires dangled out of a hole in the baseboard where the telephone had been hard wired.

"In here," he said.

Sergeant Alipov came from the hall. "That's blood," he said.

"She sat there and made the phone call."

"Are we looking for her prints?"

Greenwalt shook his head. He couldn't take his eyes off the blood. What the hell had the bastards done to her for the past nine or ten days? "Door frames, window frames. Four people, other than Ms. Monroe, were in here. They must have touched something."

"Yes, Sir," the MVD technician said, and he quickly

got to work, starting at the door and fanning outward toward the papered-over window.

• • •

By four Sergeant Alipov had come up with prints and partials on a dozen different people, at least three of them probably women or small men, and had driven Greenwalt over to the U.S. Embassy.

"This is connected with Sergeant Bokarev's assassination, is that right?"

"Yes, it is."

"Then good luck, Mr. Greenwalt. I hope you and Captain Kampov catch the bastards."

"You can count on it," Greenwalt promised.

His name was on the list at Post One, and the Marine guards passed him through without question. Upstairs, Ligget scanned the fingerprints, which had been lifted the old fashioned way, with tape that was then affixed to cards, and e-mailed them to Washington.

"Dan called a couple hours ago, and said that his friend at Langley has agreed to help with these," Ligget said.

"Good."

"Now what?" Ligget asked.

"We wait for some answers, and hope that Mrs. Monroe survives until we can get to her."

"What about the money that Anderson is supposed to be sending?"

"It'll never happen," Greenwalt said. "It's up to us now."

"And the Russians."

"Yeah, the Russians."

FIFTY-NINE

•

Patti had tried without success to remove the bars from her window, and that effort had drained what little strength she'd had left. She'd slept fitfully for a few hours and when she woke she went to the door, but Boris was sitting in front of the television so she hadn't dared to try the bathroom window.

Whatever was going to happen was almost completely outside of her control, but when the time came she would fight back with whatever strength she had left.

Raya came into the room that evening; only a dim light spilled in from the corridor. She'd brought a glass of tea, laced with honey, and two pieces of buttered black bread.

"Take your time eating this so that it doesn't upset your stomach," she said, putting the bread and tea on the windowsill.

"Why are you doing this?" Patti croaked.

"You'll need your strength."

"Tobias is sending the money."

"No, the FBI won't allow it. But we have an idea how we can help him get the money to you."

"And then you'll kill me."

"*Da*," Raya said.

"Maybe I won't help you."

"Then we'll kill you now. Or perhaps in the middle of night, when you're sleeping, I'll sneak into this room and slit your throat. Perhaps we'll send Boris to beat you to death with his fists. I think he'd like that. Maybe he'll sodomize you with a piece of firewood to show you what real pain is all about. Or, maybe we'll strip you naked and toss you out into the backyard with the pit bulls. We've been starving them for three days now, just in case."

Patti was struck dumb by the woman's lack of emotion. Looking up into Raya's eyes, she could not see even a hint of passion or life. No one was home. The woman was dead.

"Eat and drink," Raya said. "Regain your strength. Who knows, perhaps someone will save you."

"None of you believe that."

"No," Raya said at the doorway. "Do you, Patricia?"

For a long time after Raya left, Patti remained huddled under the blankets.

Finally, she pushed aside the blanket and struggled to sit up. For several long moments her head swam and her stomach did a slow roll. She saw flashes and pinpoints of lights in her eyes, and for a few seconds sweat popped out all over her body; afterwards she shivered violently for several minutes until she managed to hug her knees to her chest, which somehow calmed her.

The leather slippers were gone, and she had no idea what had happened to them, or how long ago she had lost them.

She got out of bed, the floor freezing cold. Her bare feet seemed to be impossibly far away. It was as if she were looking through the wrong end of a telescope.

A lot of blood had stained the bare mattress, but she felt no pain or cramps like she often did during her periods, when she sometimes bled so hard that it leaked from her tampons. Nor could she figure out when her period was due. The basic arithmetic of counting the days was beyond her.

The tea was lukewarm by the time she got to it, but

it was sweet and her stomach accepted it. She forced herself to stop after it was half gone, so that she would have something to wash down the bread.

She ate slowly, taking small bites, and taking her time chewing, because she couldn't produce much spit and she didn't want to die of something so stupid as choking to death.

She had very little taste left, only for the sweetness of the tea, and the bread was just a substance, which she doggedly finished, bit-by-bit.

A long time later, when she was finally finished, her stomach was so distended that she was in pain, but a sense of well-being came over her.

Raya might slit her throat tonight, or Boris might beat her to death, but she wasn't going to starve.

She lay down on the bed, the blood cold on her bottom, and went immediately to sleep.

THE ELEVENTH DAY

January 12th

SIXTY

•

In the bedroom, Patti woke again, a very dim light coming through the barred window. It took her a long time before she realized that she had slept through the night and that it was nearly dawn.

She didn't feel as bad as she had yesterday; the sweet tea and bread had been a tremendous help.

Lysenko stood just within the doorway, and when she spotted him her heart gave a lurch. He was here to kill her now, but he had an odd, pensive, almost dreamy expression on his interesting face, not that of a killer's, which gave her a shred of hope.

"What do you want?" she asked.

"We're going to send a fax to your friend. In your handwriting."

"Aren't you taking a big risk?"

"No."

"They were Spetsnaz troops in town," Patti baited him. "Those guys don't screw around. If you send a fax, they'll know about it."

"We'll be gone from here before they can react."

"And I'll be dead."

"That depends on you," Lysenko said. He came around to the side of the bed. He was holding something behind his back, and Patti thought it might be a gun.

"Raya doesn't think that the FBI will let him send it to you."

"This time he'll send it to your bank in Damascus."

"I don't have an account there."

Lysenko laughed quietly. "No. But a woman who looks very much like you showed up at the bank and opened the account. She'll come back when the funds have been transferred."

"I'm frightened," Patti said.

"You should be."

"You don't understand." Patti tossed the blanket aside and got unsteadily to her feet. "If I get a chance to kill you, I'll do it. And I'm afraid of myself because I know I'll enjoy it."

This time Lysenko laughed out loud.

"You're a coward!" Patti screeched, her voice ragged. "You're a fanatic. A fucking bomb maker. You and everyone like you stand in line to kiss bin Laden's ass. I'm sure your mother must be proud of her little boy."

Lysenko visibly reacted, a look of intense anger, even rage, on his face, but before he could say or do anything, Patti was on him.

"I speak enough Russian to understand what you and Aleksei and that bitch were talking about after we came back from town. The money's for the cause. The jihad. You people are good at killing women and children, or sending kids to blow themselves up. Collect your money and pass Go, straight to paradise. The twelve-year-old boys will magically turn fifteen so they can fuck the virgins waiting for them without violating the Koran. Isn't that how it's supposed to go?

"But you're not a Muslim. You're a Brit, with culture and education. I can hear it in your voice, which makes you a pitiful bastard. I did you a favor shoving you away and knocking you down the stairs so that you wouldn't embarrass yourself. It's a wonder you even got it up in the first place.

"You and Boris are quite the pair. Neither of you can get a woman without raping her."

Lysenko reached out and caressed her cheek with his fingertips before she could bat his hand away. His touch had been soft, the most obscene thing that had happened to her so far. She wanted to spit in his face, but she couldn't.

"Sit down, Patricia," he said, his voice as gentle as his touch had been.

She did as she was told, the small bit of strength she had left suddenly gone. The threats and the beatings and the pain had been bad, but this was worse. He had the look of Hannibal Lecter from *The Silence of the Lambs*, pleasant, understanding, intellectual. The insane psychiatrist had been in absolute control of himself and the situation, especially at the end. It had been the scariest movie she'd ever seen.

Lysenko had been holding a clipboard behind his back, on which was a fax transmittal form. He handed it and a pen to her.

The pen felt clumsy in her hand, her fingers shrunken, her joints painful. "What should I write?" she asked.

"To Tobias Anderson."

She wrote the name, her penmanship, reduced to a childish scrawl, just barely legible. "I don't know if he has a fax machine at home."

"We'll send it to his office," Lysenko said, and he dictated Anderson's fax number in Georgetown, along with a brief message to send the money to the new account number in Damascus.

Patti was having trouble concentrating and focusing. She had to have every number and every word repeated several times before she got it right, but he didn't seem upset.

"The password for the account is *Aunty Gina Lives*."

Patti's breath caught in her throat.

"I think he'll appreciate the little joke," Lysenko said.

She wrote the three words.

"Sign it, please."

She did it and he took the clipboard and pen from her.

"Get dressed for outside. We're leaving in a few hours."

"For where?" Patti asked.

"Does it really matter?" Lysenko asked. "Everyone else here, except for Raya, will be dead. It'll just be the three of us."

"What about the children?"

"What about them?" Lysenko asked, without expression.

"You can't murder them," Patti said.

"Oh?"

SIXTY-ONE

•

At the Motor Vehicle Registration Department, Kampov stared at the card for the last Mercedes in the series. All the others had been legitimate names and addresses. MVD clerks had spent the evening and into the morning hours running down each match, until this one, which was bogus.

"The address does not exist, Captain," Marina Peshkov told him. She was the supervisor of records.

"Mafia?"

"Probably," she replied tiredly. No one had gotten any sleep last night. "We see this sort of thing from time to time. But what can we do? A registration that does not match the vehicle, or the owner, or the address?"

Kampov handed back the card and got his coat from the back of a chair. "Thank your people for me. I'm just sorry that it was a dead end."

"We're happy to be of assistance to the MVD," the woman said. She was a big buxom blonde with three kids, no husband, and a lot of ambition, who'd been a great help once Kampov had shown her Putin's letter. "Call me any time that you need something."

"Sure," Kampov said and he left the office, took the stairs up to the ground floor, and outside where he was surprised to see that it was light out. He debated calling Greenwalt, but it was only a little after eight and he wanted to go home, take a quick shower, and change clothes before he went back to his office.

Unless something new had come overnight, he would call Baturin back into action and they would begin raids on the other Mafia clubs around town. Sooner or later they would find Voronin.

When they found him they would find the woman, and he would personally shoot the sons of bitches who'd taken her.

The morning was bitterly cold, and traffic was heavy as usual. By the time he got to his apartment he was pissed off because of the wasted effort. After his shower he took a quick cognac, got dressed in a fresh white shirt, jeans, and a dark sport coat.

Before he went out he went through the Monroes'

files spread out on the coffee table in the living room and picked out his favorite photograph of Mrs. Monroe. It was the one of her sitting on a stool wearing a long dress and holding a guitar on her lap. She looked earnest and vulnerable, like Nina had sometimes when she was caught unawares. It was this image that had most affected him.

He'd hidden the photo in the bottom of the pile because every time he looked at it his gorge rose. Ever since he had compared Mrs. Monroe's fate with his wife's he'd been skirting around the edges of his self-control, and Feodor was no longer here to give him balance.

"Bastards," he muttered darkly as he left his apartment.

SIXTY-TWO

•

Ever since this business with Patti had begun, Anderson had posted a couple of interns at the office after hours in case she called there instead of the house.

His bedside telephone rang, bringing him instantly awake from a light sleep. It was a few minutes after two in the morning. The caller ID was from Georgetown. He picked up on the second ring.

"Yes?"

"This is Josh Taylor from the office. We just received a fax message from Mrs. Monroe." He sounded excited. "Shall I read it to you?"

"No, bring it here, please," Anderson said, pushing the covers back and sitting up. The FBI outside in the driveway would intercept it, and he wanted to see what it was about before he shared it.

"I'll be there in under twenty minutes," the intern said.

Anderson's wife woke up. "Is it another call from Patti?" she asked.

"She sent a fax to the office," Anderson told her. "One of the kids is bringing it over. Go back to sleep."

"I want to see it."

"I'll wake you if there's anything new," Anderson promised, but she'd pushed the covers back and gotten out of bed.

"We'll need some coffee," she said, putting on her robe and slippers. "How about the FBI?"

"We'll wait until we see what she's sent us."

"Do you think that's wise?"

"They haven't done much for her so far," Anderson said.

"No," she said, frowning, and she went downstairs.

Anderson splashed some cold water on his face, then got dressed in his robe and slippers. When he got downstairs the doorbell rang. It was one of the FBI technicians, in a dark blue windbreaker.

"We'd like to see the fax when it gets here, Sir," the young man said.

"I'll take a look at it first," Anderson said.

"Sir, I have to insist, or else I have to report it to my boss."

"Go right ahead, son. Because first thing in the morning I'm going to call the White House and talk to Stan Berkholtz, the president's chief of staff. He's an old friend of mine. Perhaps he can light a fire under the Bureau, before the bastards in Russia kill her."

"Understood, Sir," the FBI tech said and went back to the van.

• • •

The doorbell rang again fifteen minutes later. It was the young intern from the office. He handed Anderson a manila envelope with the firm's return address. The FBI technician had gotten out of the van and snapped a photo of the intern's license plate.

"You made good time, Josh," Anderson said.

"Thank you, Sir."

"Would you care to come in for some coffee?"

"I'd better get back, in case something else happens."

"Good man," Anderson said.

"What about them?" the intern asked, nodding over his shoulder.

"If you're stopped and they want to ask you some questions, tell them that I'm your lawyer."

The intern grinned. "Yes, Sir." He went back to his car and drove off.

The technician gave Anderson a bleak look, but then climbed back inside the van.

Anderson relocked the door and set the alarm, but opened the envelope and took out the fax before he went into the kitchen to share it with his wife. Nothing he'd ever seen or heard in his entire life shocked him so badly.

The account number and password phrase were terrible enough, but it was Patti's nearly illegible handwriting that was so frightening. He could see her in a shabby room somewhere, guns pointed at her head as she was ordered to write the message. Her captors guessed that the FBI was stalling for time, and in all likelihood they would never get the ransom money he'd promised.

According to the Bureau they would kill her even if they got their money. "It's to their advantage not to release her, especially not after all this time," Special Agent Nelson had told him after Patti's first call.

"What can we do?" Anderson asked.

"Stall for as long as possible. Let our people on the ground find her."

Anderson went into his study and booted up his computer. Once he was on-line, he entered the bank routing code Patti had sent. It came up for the BLOM Bank in Damascus, a telephone number and a fax number.

Next he got onto the bank's site and entered the account number. When it came up a password box dropped down.

Anderson's wife came into the study. "What is it?"

"Patti's fax," Anderson said. He entered *auntyginalives,* and hit the login tab. Patricia Monroe's name came up, along with an account balance of five thousand dollars U.S. that had been deposited yesterday, but with no other activity.

Anderson's wife read the fax and looked at the monitor. "My God, is she in Syria now?"

"It looks like it," Anderson said, at a complete loss for the first time in his life that he could remember.

"Maybe if you send her the money, she'll be okay."

Anderson couldn't take his eyes off the screen. It would only take a few keystrokes to send the twenty million he'd dumped into a special account to Damascus.

According to the FBI he would be signing her death warrant.

"What are you going to do, Tobias?"

He looked up at his wife and shook his head. "I don't know."

SIXTY-THREE

•

The fax has been sent to your friend," Lysenko said at the doorway.

Patti was sitting at the window, looking out at the bleak morning. She didn't turn around. "I want the battery for the cell phone."

Lysenko stared at her for a long time before he stepped back and let the blanket fall over the doorway. He stayed there for a full minute, listening, waiting for something, anything, sobbing. All along he'd wanted her to plead for mercy, just like his mother had pleaded for her life before he'd slit her throat.

But the bedroom was silent and it irritated him. He was going to kill her sooner or later no matter whatever else happened, but first he wanted that one little thing from her. It would even be enough if she showed him her fear. That's all.

He went downstairs where the babushka was making something for the childrens' school lunches. Raya was seated at the counter, her booted feet up on the rung of the stool next to her. She'd packed her leather bag and put it by the door. She was wearing a shoulder holster.

"Where's Boris?" Lysenko asked.

"He went to get gas in the car," the babushka said. "When are we leaving?"

"Later this morning," Lysenko said. "And never mind about the lunches. I want the children ready to travel as soon as Boris gets back."

Raya had watched the exchange with an amused smirk on her lips. No one was leaving this house alive except for her and Lysenko. They'd discussed the end game before they'd ever left Pakistan.

"Are you packed?"

The old woman dried her hands on a towel. "There's nothing for Boris and me in Grozny. The children will be a nuisance."

"You can't stay here."

The woman nodded. "We can be a help in Pakistan. The children can go to school with the Taliban. They could be useful when the time comes."

"We'll see," he said.

"Good," the babushka said, and she scurried out of the kitchen.

"Like mother like son," Raya said with a smirk.

"Where's Lana's body?" Lysenko asked.

Raya nodded toward the root cellar. "Down there with Aleksei."

"Do the children know?"

"If they do, they don't seem to be broken up about it."

Lysenko went to the sideboard, poured a glass of red wine, and drank it down.

"Do you think he'll send the money?" Raya asked.

"I don't know," Lysenko replied absently. "Maybe."

He could see the damage and terror that detonating a nuclear weapon in the states would cause, but he didn't care.

Ten million U.S. would buy bin Laden his suitcase nuke from the old Soviet depot inside Tajikistan. The other ten million, plus what he'd already put away in offshore banks, would buy personal security for himself to disappear permanently.

It would not be enough money for three people, not even two.

Raya read something of this from his expression. "Maybe we should keep it all, and simply run away."

"I've thought about it."

"I know you have."

"Where would you like to go?" Lysenko asked.

Raya shrugged. "Someplace far, someplace warm. But not the desert."

Lysenko smiled. "How long before we became bored?"

Raya glanced toward the door to the stair hall. "Have you found this . . . stimulating?"

Lysenko followed her gaze. "Interesting," he said. "Surprising."

"But not as interesting as seeing it through. All the way."

He said nothing.

"You and I will never be martyrs to the cause, Sergey."

"Perhaps."

"What else is there for us—except *mokrie dela*? Wet work. Spilling blood." Raya smiled almost shyly.

"I don't know," Lysenko said after a moment. Nothing.

SIXTY-FOUR

•

In the U.S. Embassy, Greenwalt tried reaching Kampov on the Russian's cell phone, but the call was automatically transferred to the MVD. A man answered in Russian, and all he caught was Nikolai Sychev's name. It was a few minutes after two in the afternoon, and Greenwalt felt that time was slipping away from them.

"Mr. Sychev, do you speak English?"

"It's Senior Lieutenant. Yes, I do," the OD said. "You must be Assistant Deputy Director Greenwalt. What can the MVD do for the FBI?"

"I'm trying to reach Captain Kampov. He doesn't answer his cell phone."

"He sometimes does that. Is there a message for him?"

"Yes, goddamnit," Greenwalt shouted. He was frustrated with the fucking dim Russians. "I've got two fingerprint matches from the Chekova Street addresses."

"Give me the names—"

"Tell Kampov that I'm coming over to his office," Greenwalt interrupted. "I'll meet him there in fifteen minutes." He slammed down the phone.

Ligget was looking at him. "Welcome to Moscow, Sir."

"You mean to tell me that it's always this bad?"

"No, Sir. You've caught them on a good day."

"Christ," Greenwalt said. He looked at the e-mail printout. Two names, two brief files. But if Kampov would get his head out of his ass, they might just reach Patti Monroe sometime today.

"I'll drive you over there," Ligget said, and he grabbed his coat.

When they stepped outside, the sharp wind took Greenwalt's breath away. He'd never experienced weather this cold in his life, and he swore that each hour here would be his last. No power on earth could ever make him return to this godforsaken country. What had fascinated Patti and her husband to do business here was completely beyond him.

"The fingerprints nail the al-Quaeda connection," Ligget said on the way over to the MVD. "The sixty-four-thousand-dollar question is whether or not the money's supposed to stay here."

"I don't think so."

"Another 9/11?"

"That's what has me bothered. With twenty million dollars they could hurt us a lot worse than bringing down a couple of buildings."

"If they get the money."

"Yeah," Greenwalt said. "Let's see that they don't."

One block from MVD Headquarters, Kampov called Greenwalt's cell phone. "You have something for me?"

"Two names, so far, but we're still working on it."

"Russians?"

"One of them's a Chechen, the other's a British citizen," Greenwalt said. "MI6 has promised to jump in if we need their help. I'll meet you at your office; maybe we can clear this thing up today."

"I'll be there in ten minutes," Kampov shouted over the noise of what sounded like a bulldozer, and he broke the connection.

"Fucking Russians," Greenwalt muttered.

"Is he going to see us?" Ligget asked.

"Ten minutes. We'll wait out front."

"Someone over there might get a little nervous if they see us showing up again and just parking out front."

"I don't give a shit. Circle the block if you want."

• • •

Lubyanka Square was extremely busy despite the bone-numbing weather, and they'd made it around twice when they spotted Kampov getting out of a dark blue Mercedes in front of the building.

Ligget pulled over and stopped behind him, and he and Greenwalt jumped out.

"Give me the names," Kampov growled.

"It's too cold out here, let's go inside," Greenwalt said.

"The names," Kampov demanded.

Greenwalt handed over a copy of the e-mail. "The first one is Sergey Lysenko, who we suspect has ties with al-Quaeda. He's a Brit, but he was born in Lebanon to a Muslim father and a Jewish mother. We don't have any current photographs of him, except for the two they sent us."

Kampov studied Lysenko's photograph. "Was he one of the men in the car with Mrs. Monroe?"

"He might have been," Greenwalt said. "But I couldn't testify to it for a warrant."

"That's not necessary here," Kampov said. He flipped to the second photo and identification, and he suddenly looked up, startled. "I know this man."

"Boris Viltov," Greenwalt said. "We found his name along with some information on a laptop that was captured in Afghanistan. Apparently he was being trained to take the war back to Chechnya. There's a Grozny address, but that won't do us any good."

"Yes, Viltov. We took a look at him about eight months ago on a tip from one of our informants. But we didn't come up with anything, and dropped it."

"You know where he is?"

"He lives in a dacha in Noginsk with his wife and three children, about fifty kilometers from here."

"That's it, then," Greenwalt said, excited.

"Good work," Kampov said, pulling out his cell phone. "Now return to your embassy and I'll let you know when we have her."

Greenwalt laughed. "Not a chance in hell."

Kampov speed dialed a number and turned away. He said something in rapid-fire Russian.

"He's talking to a man named Ivan," Ligget said at Greeenwalt's shoulder. "We have a new target in Noginsk. Get mounted."

"Get mounted?" Greenwalt said, amazed. The Russian cop was a cowboy.

Kampov said something else, when Greenwalt's cell phone rang. It was Nelson from Washington.

"Mrs. Monroe sent a fax to Anderson early this morning, but the call didn't originate from Moscow this time, and we only got a partial trace, but we're still working on it."

"Let me guess, Noginsk?"

"Jesus H. Christ, how'd you know?"

"One of the guys whose fingerprints we pulled from the Monroes' downtown office lives out there," Greenwalt explained. "What was the message on the fax?"

"Anderson wouldn't share it with us, and in fact he threatened to call one of his buddies in the White House to put some pressure on us. On you."

"Have you heard anything from upstairs yet?"

"Not a word."

"Well if someone wants you to reach me, take your time, will you, Don? I think this will be a done deal within a few hours."

"Can do, Sir," Nelson promised.

"Good work." He broke the connection and pocketed the phone.

"Go back to your embassy," Kampov told him. "If we find Mrs. Monroe out there, I'll call you."

"She sent a fax from Noginsk this morning."

"*Pizdec*," Kampov said. "You're riding with me."

"Go back to the embassy, Dick," Greenwalt said. "Nelson might try to reach me there. Stall him."

Ligget was obviously disappointed, but he nodded. "Yes, Sir. I hope it works for you."

"I hope it works for Mrs. Monroe."

SIXTY-FIVE

•

Although it was early afternoon when Kampov and Greenwalt reached the staging area that the Spetsnaz had used for the raids on the Mafia clubs, the sun was already low in the sky.

Colonel Baturin had picked an open soccer field in Sokolniki Park, well within the outer ring highway, where fifty of his support troops had formed a perimeter, though it was unlikely that any Russian would wander over to ask questions.

Kampov had called ahead and he and Greenwalt were allowed to pass the checkpoint, the earnest young operators obviously pissed off that they weren't on either of the fire teams going in.

A pair of armored personnel carriers was parked in the middle of the field. A sergeant and seven operators, all dressed in camos and night vision glasses, waited near the vehicles.

As Kampov drove onto the field, a heavily modified super-silent Kamov extended series Ka-32 helicopter appeared out of the darkness from the southwest, with no running lights, and touched down twenty-five meters from the APCs.

Baturin, Sergeant Pavlenko, and six operators jumped out of the open hatch and strode across to the other troops as Kampov pulled up and he and Greenwalt joined them.

"Who is this?" Baturin asked in Russian.

"Everett Greenwalt, FBI, here to help with the investigation," Kampov said in English. "Without his expert help we'd still be raiding the clubs."

"Very well," Baturin said.

Sergeant Pavlenko pulled out a map of Noginsk and the immediate surroundings and opened it on the floor just inside the hatch of one of the APCs.

Kampov studied it for a couple of seconds before he stabbed a finger on a street at the edge of town, a couple of blocks from the train station. "It's a dacha belonging to Boris Viltov and his wife. Three children and a grandmother could be inside."

"Anyone else out there?" Baturin asked, still speaking in English for Greenwalt's benefit.

"At least two," Greenwalt said. "A Brit with ties to al-Quaeda and a woman who I'm guessing is paramilitary as well."

"You saw these people?"

"Yes," Greenwalt said, and he explained the circumstances.

"He identified fingerprints from inside the office," Kampov said. "It's the only reason we're here now."

"May we assume that anyone inside the dacha is a perp?" Sergeant Pavlenko asked.

"Except for the children," Greenwalt said.

Sergeant Pavlenko gave him a dreamy look. "Have you ever been to Grozny?"

"No."

"Baghdad?"

Greenwalt shook his head.

"I suggest you stay away from those places, or else your pretty notions about children will get you killed."

"We'll do this by the numbers, and only the perps go down," Baturin said after a beat. "One: Captain Kampov and his FBI guest will take the lead car to Noginsk. Two: Sergeant Pavlenko will be in command of APC units one and two that will follow the lead car. When they arrive on scene a perimeter will be established around the dacha."

"Maybe someone should go in on foot to try to negotiate," Greenwalt suggested.

Everyone ignored him.

"Three: I'll be in the chopper with Unit Alpha. We'll touch down half a klick east of the town, where we'll hold up until Sergeant Pavlenko is in position and evaluates the tactical situation."

He looked up. "Someone get Captain Kampov and his guest SQ-70s," he said. They were subcompact communications units that included a combination microphone-earpiece that was attached by adhesive to the bone behind an ear.

One of the operators came over with the units.

"You're not a field operator, Sascha, so don't get

yourself killed," Baturin said. "Mr. Greenwalt is your responsibility."

"It's your show," Kampov said. "I just want the woman out in one piece. But one thing. She may be hurt. We found some blood at the Chekova Street office."

"Yes, I know," Baturin said. "I saw it, and we'll take her possible condition into consideration." He glanced again at the map. "Four: When I give the green light, we hit at once. Unit one from the south, two from the north, and Alpha from the air." He looked up at his operators. "Watch your crossfire, report your positions and body count. Any questions?"

There were none.

"You've seen photographs of the woman we're here to save. There are no other considerations."

All of that was in English, which meant every Spetsnaz operator was fluent. Greenwalt was impressed despite himself, but he was still freezing his ass off.

"You heard the man," Sergeant Pavlenko shouted. "Move it out." He turned to Kampov as the men smartly mounted the APCs and helicopter. "After you, Captain."

SIXTY-SIX

•

It was getting dark as Lysenko hurried down a back alley two blocks from the dacha. The last day train had come through town a half hour ago, its whistle blowing, and the only sounds now were a dog barking somewhere in the distance and very faint music.

The sky had cleared, the wind had picked up, and the temperature had plunged. He was going to be glad to get out of this shit hole of a country. If they got the money, he was going to take Raya's suggestion and go to ground somewhere warm.

But at this moment he was spooked. He ducked into the deeper shadows beneath the overhang of a ramshackle storage shed and looked back the way he had come. Nothing moved, and after a half a minute he continued to the end of the block where he held up again to make sure that the street was clear.

If anyone had been following him he was prepared to kill them. For as long as he could remember he had been angry at the world, but standing here now in the cold he couldn't say why. Maybe he never knew.

The narrow street was mostly two- and three-story apartment buildings that had been constructed before World War One. Many of them had small courtyards with stalls that had once held farm animals and circular areas lined with stone where manure was saved until spring, when the farmers living here would go out into the fields that had been hacked out of the birch forests.

But, except for kitchen gardens, those days were done. Noginsk had become a factory town.

Lights were on in most of the apartments, but for now the street was empty; it was dinnertime.

Lysenko made his way down the block to a lean-to attached to one of the apartment buildings. A battered Toyota van was parked inside. He unlocked the side door and slid it open. A large nylon duffle bag was where he had left it twelve days ago. He had begun to worry that someone might have broken into the van and stolen it, which would have been too bad because the bag contained the means for his escape should he be traced this far.

He'd also worried that Raya might have come to the van to take a look and realize that he'd lied to her. She was staying here with the others. From now on he traveled alone.

It was easier that way.

Relocking the van, he let himself into the apartment building and went upstairs to the second floor. No one else lived in the building. Six months ago he'd rented all four of the apartments for enough money that the owner didn't bother asking any questions.

He stood just outside the door and pulled out his pistol. The hairs at the nape of his neck stood on end. Something was wrong, he could feel it in the air, smell it, taste it.

The door was unlocked. He eased it open with the toe of his boot, and slipped inside, his weapon swinging left to right. But no one was here; the sparsely furnished two room efficiency was silent.

Holstering his pistol, Lysenko switched on a small table lamp and went to the fax machine, but the in-tray was empty. Anderson had not sent a confirmation yet.

He disconnected the telephone and plugged in the Toshiba laptop he'd been using for this operation. When the machine was booted up, he went on-line to check the bank balance in Damascus. It remained at $5,000 U.S.

Sitting back, his coat unbuttoned, a scowl crossed his features. The business with Patti's Aunt Gina at the very beginning had queered the deal. Had the bitch not sent that message the money might have been sent. Anderson would not have known that she'd been kidnapped, and he might not have contacted the FBI.

Over the past eleven years he had accumulated

some money in a numbered account on the island of Guernsey, but not enough for him to go to ground, to disappear so completely that no one would ever find him.

He had to do more than eliminate potential witnesses then silently slip away. He needed real money.

Still, he felt something else. The only time he was alive was when he was in the middle of a life-and-death operation—a mission in which he struck back at the bastards who had made him what he was, was an important, even necessary part of his life.

He understood, on an intellectual level, how twisted that way of thinking was, but it was how his environment had made him.

A number of years ago, before 9/11, he and bin Laden had walked along a rocky track high in the Hindu Kush of Afghanistan so that they could talk, away from the suspicious looks of the mujahideen.

"What are you doing here among us?" bin Laden had asked him.

Lysenko had no answer that made any sense to him, so he'd countered with his own question. "What about you? You're a multimillionaire. Why did you trade that life in Saudi Arabia for living in caves?"

"My belief in Allah," bin Laden had answered without hesitation. "But you believe in nothing, do you?"

Lysenko had thought about it for a long time, until he finally turned back to bin Laden. "Killing for money. I'm a contractor. It's a job."

"What about God?"

Lysenko laughed.

"England?"

"It was never my home."

"Your family? Your blood?"

Lysenko shook his head. "There's no one."

They walked in silence for a time, bin Laden obviously troubled. Lysenko was nothing more than a tool to be used, and then put away once the task was completed. But they'd had this kind of a conversation before, bin Laden trying to find out about Lysenko, who was no Muslim fanatic, yet willing to help the jihad.

"What will you do afterwards?" bin Laden asked. "Come back here?"

"Vanish," Lysenko said. "Go to ground until the backlash is over. Could be years."

"Yes, we realize this, and we're prepared," bin Laden replied. He stopped and looked directly into Lysenko's eyes. "You must believe in something other than money."

Lysenko had shaken his head, and he and bin Laden had returned to the cave complex, the question left unanswered.

He looked up, a sudden urgent thought crystal clear in his mind. It was time to go. Right now.

Shutting down the computer, he turned off the light and went to the window in time to catch a glimpse of the silhouette of a Russian military helicopter disappearing below the tree line to the east, and his heart froze.

He knew that the telephone calls were being traced, and he knew that the Spetsnaz was coming. He hadn't, however, counted on them showing up so soon, though he had a contingency plan, as always.

Grabbing the laptop he raced downstairs, tossed it in the van, then headed down the alley back to the dacha in a dead run.

That day in the mountains, bin Laden had wondered

whether Lysenko was willing to give up his own life without hesitation.

Tonight he would find out.

SIXTY-SEVEN
•

The dacha was on the north side of the city a couple of kilometers from the edge of the birch forests and empty farm fields. The early evening was fully dark by the time Kampov and Greenwalt pulled up and parked at the end of the street, a short block from the house. Lights were on in some of the second floor windows of other houses along the street. And behind them the glow of city lights downtown southeast brightened the sky.

Baturin's helicopter had already touched down in a field half a kilometer to the east, and as Kampov got out of his car the two armored personnel carriers pulled up, their highly muffled engines nearly noiseless in the cold night air. Pavlenko and his operators jumped out.

Half of them headed down the street to the back of the dacha, while Pavlenko sent the other seven operators directly down the street, through the deeper shadows, to the front gate where they would set Semtex plastic explosives on the hinges.

No words had been spoken between any of them.

Greenwalt waited in the car, but he powered the window down.

The air smelled of a combination of wood smoke and something rotten, maybe garbage, or overflowing septic systems, which often happened in places like these in the winter where the frost could reach deeper into the ground than two meters and sewer pipes froze solid.

A minute later Fire Team leader One radioed from the back gate at the end of the block. "One in position."

Kampov heard it in the comms unit behind his ear.

"Roger," Pavlenko replied softly.

"Two in position."

"Are you clear?" Pavlenko asked.

"Two clear."

"Alpha, one and two in position," Pavlenko radioed to Baturin. "Our perimeter is clear."

"Stand by," Baturin replied.

SIXTY-EIGHT

•

Patti raced down the corridor to the bathroom as fast as she could move on wobbly legs. She grabbed a dirty bath towel from a pile on the floor, wrapped it around her arm, and smashed her elbow between the bars, breaking out the windowpane. Her heart thumped wildly against her ribs, and she was mindless of the bitter cold wind.

She had been sitting at the window seat in the bedroom in a half-daze when she'd spotted what looked to her like a helicopter disappearing in the trees toward the Moscow highway just outside of town.

At first she thought that she'd been hallucinating, but then she hadn't been so sure. It had only been a dark silhouette, and she figured that if she had been dreaming about a helicopter filled with men flying here to rescue her, she would not have imagined it running without lights. Somehow they'd come this far, and she needed to let them know that she was here, before Lysenko or one of the others saw it.

She unwrapped the towel from her arm, brushed away the loose shards of glass still sticking out of the rotten wooden frame, and stuffed the towel out the window and began waving it.

"Come on," she whispered desperately. "Over here! Goddamnit, over here!"

"Get away from the window," Raya said from the doorway.

Patti turned around, losing her grip on the towel, which hung up on the window frame, her blood freezing in her veins.

Raya was dressed for outside in a leather jacket and boots bloused into night fighter's black camos. She held a pistol in her right hand. She glanced at the window and the towel fluttering in the breeze. "They'll shoot anything that moves. In the dark, even you."

"When they get here they'll kill you," Patti said.

"Which is why you'll help us," Raya said, smiling. "We'll all survive this night. But we'll have to work together."

Patti stepped away from the window and moved toward the sink. She wasn't going to die here. Not without a fight.

Raya came the rest of the way into the bathroom. "In the end, of course, Sergey means to kill you and your husband," she said, her voice soft.

Patti looked at her own image in the mirror above the sink when she realized that what Raya just said made no sense. "What?"

"*Insha'Allah*," Raya said, and she raised her pistol,

the muzzle inches from Patti's head. "Come downstairs with me and we'll leave together. Just maybe I can save your life."

Patti smashed her elbow into the mirror, shattering it, long daggers of glass falling into the sink.

"What are you doing?"

Patti looked over her shoulder at Raya. "Shoot me and you'll never leave this place alive," she growled.

Someone was coming up the stairs in a big hurry.

Momentarily distracted, Raya turned toward the door.

Patti grabbed an eight-inch shard of broken mirror, opening a deep gash in the palm of her hand, and plunged the glass dagger into the side of Raya's throat, blood gushing in a big spout from the wound.

"Oh," Raya said, before blood flooded her windpipe and she staggered backward. She brought the pistol to bear directly at Patti's face and began to pull the trigger.

But Patti was on her, batting the weapon aside before it discharged. She slammed the side of her fist into Raya's face, and the woman's head snapped back.

Raya was drowning in her own blood, her eyes rapidly losing focus. She tried to raise her gun, but Patti slipped to one side and kicked the back of the woman's knee.

As Raya's leg collapsed under her and she went down, Patti slammed a heel in her side, breaking several ribs, and then kicked again, connecting with the woman's temple, knocking her out before she suffocated.

"Come on," Patti said, dancing from one foot to the other. She wanted Raya to get up and fight back. She wanted to inflict even more pain to repay what she had endured. She was sick and tired of being patted on the head and accepting it. She was tired of never defending herself, of a lifetime of feeling unsure, inferior.

Lysenko appeared in the doorway, pistol in hand, and took in the scene in a split second.

Patti dove for the glass shards in the sink, but he was across the room to her before she was half way. He grabbed her arm and slammed her against the wall, the muzzle of his pistol jammed into her temple.

"You don't want to die here," he whispered in her ear.

Patti suddenly understood everything with a great clarity. Mindless of the pressure of the gun barrel against her head, she turned and looked up into Lysenko's eyes.

"Without a hostage you're a dead man," she said.

SIXTY-NINE

•

Now! Now! Now!" Baturin's voice came into everyone's headsets.

"Stay behind me, Captain," Pavlenko told Kampov. He glanced over at Greenwalt, still in the car. "Don't go wandering around, Mr. Greenwalt, one of my boys might mistake you for a perp."

"Fire in the hole," one of the operators at the front gate suddenly radioed.

Two seconds later a pair of impressive bangs hammered off the walls and the heavy wooden doors blew into the courtyard. A moment later a pair of explosions came from the back gate down the street around the corner.

"One, through the gate," the team leader at the rear of the house radioed. "Backyard clear."

Pavlenko and Kampov raced down the street as team two leapfrogged through the shattered gate. Here they were most vulnerable from shooters in the dacha's upstairs window.

"Two inside the front courtyard, clear."

Baturin's helicopter rose up from behind the woods across the road and before Pavlenko and his people reached the door it was directly overhead in a hover as a backup in case Pavlenko and his people ran into trouble. The side hatch was open and two 7.65mm machine guns were manned.

Two operators mounted the porch, and on signal from one of them, the other swung a lead-filled steel battering ram, smashing the door at the bolt lock, shattering the door frame.

He discarded the tool, and swung his assault rifle into position as the first man entered the house.

"Yakolev through the front door," the operator radioed. "Clear."

The other operator entered the house, five troops right on his heels, Pavlenko and Kampov directly behind them.

Kampov got a brief glimpse of a burly man with a Kalashnikov rifle appearing in a doorway at the end of the corridor, when one of the operators fired two shots, both catching the man in the head and he went down.

"One down in the corridor," the operator radioed.

Three shots were fired from somewhere in the back of the house.

"Didenkov, one down in the kitchen," the operator radioed. "*Pizdec,* stand by," he said.

Pavlenko held up a hand for his operators to wait.

"Talk to me, Anatoli," he radioed.

"We have two bodies in a root cellar beneath the kichen. One male, one female."

"Monroe?" Pavlenko demanded.

"Negative."

"One and two, continue your sweep," Pavlenko ordered.

He and Kampov started up the stairs with two other operators.

"Command, Yakolev. I'm in a room at the front of the house with three children," he radioed.

"Armed?" Pavlenko asked.

"Negative. No explosives either," Yakolev radioed. "Sarge, these kids are young and they're scared shitless."

"Get them out of here," Pavlenko ordered.

"Yakolev coming out."

"Kitchen clear," Didenkov radioed.

"Command, we're on our way upstairs," Pavlenko said. "Stand by."

"Roger," Baturin radioed. "Your perimeter is clear. But a white towel is hanging from a broken window on the northeast side."

"Any sign of movement?" Pavlenko asked.

"Negative."

"Copy," Pavlenko responded.

"Is there any sign of Mrs. Monroe," Greenwalt radioed.

"Stay off this channel," Pavlenko said.

"No," Kampov responded.

At the top of the stairs Pavlenko and his two operators held up for just a moment. The corridor was in darkness until suddenly light spilled from a doorway at the end of the hall.

"Yuri, a light just went on in the northwest window," Baturin radioed.

"I have it," Pavlenko said. He turned to Kampov. "Someone's back there with your hostage, and they just said 'hello, we know you're here.' "

SEVENTY

•

In the bathroom, Patti's legs would have given way beneath her if Lysenko hadn't been holding her. The muzzle of the pistol was jammed painfully into her temple and it was hard to breathe with his arm around her chest. Attacking Raya had wiped out what little energy she had left, and now her head was spinning and she was sick to her stomach, her hand dripping blood on the floor.

Within less than a minute after the two explosions, soldiers or militiamen had stormed into the house and shots had been fired. Patti figured that Boris and his mother were dead. They would not have allowed themselves to be captured. She just hoped that the children hadn't been harmed.

Someone came down the corridor and stopped just outside the door. She could hear one of them murmuring something, but his words were too low for her to catch. She wanted to shout a warning, but it wouldn't make any difference. They would come to the doorway, see the situation, and do whatever it was they were going to do.

Lysenko wanted to escape with his life, but at this point she didn't think he would hesitate to pull the trigger if he believed there was no way out for him. He had to have a plan, but she couldn't see it.

A dangerous-looking man dressed all in black stepped into the open doorway. He held some sort of a rifle with a long tube attached to the end of the barrel, thick green tinted goggles pushed up on his forehead.

"I've found the woman. One of the perps has a Glock at her head," Pavlenko said in Russian, most of which Patti understood. He seemed to listen to something for a moment. "Not without collateral damage. Stand by."

"My compliments to your commanding officer for a tight operation," Lysenko said, conversationally. "Now that you have come this far, this is what you will do next."

Pavlenko was apparently relaying Lysenko's words, his voice still soft, his eyes never leaving Lysenko's. "I'm listening, Sir," he said out loud.

"Take your men and equipment away from here. That includes the helicopter flying cover for you. I will give you five minutes."

Pavlenko was relaying the message to Baturin when a man in civilian clothes, a pistol in his hand, stepped around the corner.

Patti stiffened. She knew this man.

"Captain Alexander Kampov, I presume," Lysenko said. "Aleksei has told me about you." He tightened his grip on Patti.

"It looks as if you had a little trouble up here," Kampov said, motioning to Raya's body lying in a pool of blood.

"Your Mrs. Monroe murdered her. Something quite unexpected. Ms. Kiselnikova was a well-trained fighter."

"You have two choices," Kampov said. "Either lay down your weapon and step away from Mrs. Monroe, or die."

Pavlenko continued to relay the conversation to Baturin.

"Maybe not this instant, right here in this bathroom, but before the night is out you will either be in custody or dead," Kampov said. He glanced at Pavlenko. "Frankly, Sergeant, I'd rather not deal with the paperwork if we end up having to arrest this scum, then take him to trial and hang him."

"I'm not afraid to kill this woman and die now. Are you?"

"Let's see," Kampov said. He pulled the comms unit from behind his ear and pointed his pistol at Lysenko's head.

Patti's heart skipped a beat. "Not like this!" she shouted hoarsely.

Lysenko smirked. "Mrs. Monroe is a better judge of character than you are."

Kampov held his aim for several seconds then lowered his pistol.

"What do you want, Mr. Lysenko," Pavlenko asked.

"No one else need die here tonight if you do exactly as I say," Lysenko said.

Pavlenko relayed the words.

"I want a civilian helicopter here within the hour to take us to Sheremetyevo, where you will have a foreign-registered airliner standing by, ready for take off."

"Where do you wish to go?"

"Damascus. Once we're there, Mrs. Monroe will be free to go, provided the ransom has been paid into our account."

Pavlenko nodded after a moment, then turned to Kampov. "The colonel wants us out of here now. He's calling for a chopper."

"He'll kill her," Kampov said.

"The colonel thinks not."

Kampov looked at Lysenko. "You had your chance," he said, and he backed out of the bathroom.

Lysenko dragged Patti to the window, where he kept out of the line of fire, as the helicopter suddenly peeled off to the east and disappeared behind the tree line.

He counted at least six men in black camos, plus Kampov, hustle across the courtyard to the destroyed gate. No doubt an equal number had come through the back way. There'd been two explosions.

He'd forseen this possibility, and he had devised a plan to deal with it. If the Spetsnaz operators were true to form they would block his access to the only two highways out of town and wait for him to come to them. It was unlikely that they would actually send a helicopter; instead they would stall for time. By morning they would have snipers around the house waiting for him to make a mistake and show himself in a window, and they would take their shot.

But it wasn't going to happen that way.

SEVENTY-ONE

·

Kampov followed Pavlenko out of the courtyard and down the street to the armored personnel carriers, the troops from the back of the house trotting around the corner a minute later. The first stage was over. They'd taken out all but one of the kidnappers, without any casualties of their own, and had confirmed that Mrs. Monroe was alive.

Greenwalt got out of the car. "What's going on?"

"Everyone's down except for Lysenko and Mrs. Monroe," Kampov said. He was waching Pavlenko load the operators aboard the two APCs. "He wants a helicopter to fly him back to Moscow, and in the meantime we're to move back."

"You're not going to let that happen, are you? For

Christ's sake, at least seal off the perimeter and get a hostage negotiator down here."

"I'm going to kill him."

Pavlenko walked over. "They call him the Butcher of Grozny. A real professional. If we push him he'll kill the woman. But if we give him some room he'll make a mistake sooner or later. The colonel is calling for a helicopter, but it won't get out here until first light."

"What's the plan?"

"Only two highways out of town," Pavlenko said. "We're going to pull back a few hundred meters and deny him access." He looked away. "*Da,*" he said softly into his mic. "Time to go," he told Kampov.

"Aren't you going to leave someone here?" Greenwalt asked.

Pavlenko looked at him. "I'll wait at the end of the block with two of my operators in case he comes this way on foot. You and the captain are welcome to remain with us."

"He might leave the back way, through the alley," Kampov said.

"Doesn't matter. He'd end up at one of the roads we're covering."

One of the APCs backed down the street and disappeared around the corner. The other driver was waiting for Pavlenko.

"Get your car out of here and park it around the corner," Pavlenko said, and he turned and walked back to the APC.

Kampov took out his pistol and stuffed it in his coat pocket. Now that he had found Patti he wasn't going to leave her.

"Take my car," he said.

"Where are you going?" Greenwalt demanded.

"He's on the move with her, and I'm going to catch up with them."

"How the hell do you know that?"

"He knows what the Spetsnaz are capable of," Kampov said. "He's figured out how to get away even though he's surrounded."

Pavlenko was staring at him from the APC's open hatch.

"He's got a plan; men like him always do. It's how they survive. And I'll figure it out," Kampov said. He turned and, keeping in the deeper shadows, headed back to the dacha.

"Jesus H. Christ," Greenwalt said. He glanced over at Pavlenko, who merely shrugged.

SEVENTY-TWO

·

The helicopter had flown off and the Spetsnaz troops were gone, but Lysenko remained by the open bathroom window until he heard what sounded like an APC rev up and leave.

The night and the house were suddenly silent.

"Stupid," he muttered. All to save some mindless American bitch.

He pulled Patti away from the window, hustled her out into the corridor and downstairs, where he hesitated again to listen for a sound, any sound. The house was cold. Both the front and back doors had been left open and the intensely frigid wind blew straight up the stair hall.

"You can still get the money," Patti said.

"There was no money," Lysenko said. "You and your foolish husband were nothing more than mortgaged Americans."

"But Tobias is rich. He'll send the money. I know he will."

"He's working with the FBI. It's the only way those Spetsnaz bastards found this place. It sure the hell wasn't your MVD captain on his own."

"I can make it happen," Patti said.

Lysenko gave her a long hard look. "We'll see," he said.

He hauled Patti down the hall to the kichen. Boris lay crumpled in a heap at the door, a Kalashnikov rifle on the floor beside him. He'd been shot in the head.

They had to step over him, Patti's bare feet touching the still faintly warm blood, and she recoiled so hard Lysenko almost lost his grip on her arm.

"God in heaven," she sputtered, her stomach rolling, sweat popping out all over her body.

Inside the kitchen Boris's mother had been flung backward onto the round table, the same kind of rifle on the floor beside her. She, too, had been shot in the head, and her eyes were open and filled with blood.

"Where are the children?" Patti asked, the words choking in her throat.

"Dead somewhere, probably," Lysenko said indifferently.

He led Patti to the back door, where he held up just inside the mudroom. Nothing moved outside. Even the three pit bulls had been shot to death and were lying just outside their doghouses. The back gate had been blown off its hinges.

He gave her Lana's coat and rubber boots from the

mudroom and when she'd pulled them on he hustled her outside.

He turned around and checked the roofline before he hurried across the courtyard to the gate, where he cautiously peered around the corner. The armored personnel carrier was gone, and so far as he could tell none of the Spetsnaz operators had stayed behind.

It was more than stupid, it was criminal, he thought. It was no wonder they'd lost in Afghanistan and had gotten themselves into an unwinnable situation in Chechnya. All of them were *aparachniks*, unable to think creatively.

Patti began to shiver so hard that she was barely able to stand.

"I'm not going to carry you," he warned her. "If you can't walk I'll kill you here and now."

Patti revived a little and managed a weak smile. "Whose skirts would you hide behind? Unless you expect your mother to come save you. You need me, and you know it."

Lysenko felt his control slipping. His grip on her arm tightened so hard that she cried weakly in pain.

"I can walk," she said.

The trouble was, he did need her to get free of Noginsk, and go deep in Moscow where he might have a final shot at getting the money. Ten million would have been for bin Laden's bomb, and the other ten million was for him to go to ground. But Raya's suggestion had made sense. Twenty million *was* better. And without an attack on the U.S. the only real pressure to find him would be exerted by al-Quaeda, and that he knew how to deal with.

The Spetsnaz had showed its willingness to back off when she was threatened. *Not without collateral damage,* the sergeant had advised his commander, who'd probably been in the helicopter. And the order had been to not take the shot, which would have resulted in the woman's death as Lysenko's trigger finger jerked reflexively when the bullet entered his brain.

"Very well," he said, forcing himself to calm down. "It's only a couple hundred meters from here."

"What is?"

"You'll see," he told her.

SEVENTY-THREE

•

Greenwalt had driven Kampov's Mercedes around the corner at the end of the block and parked in the shadows. Leaving the engine running, and the heater on full blast, he went around to the passenger seat, powered up his laptop, and plugged his sat phone into a serial port.

"He's got a plan, and I'll figure it out," he grumbled, imitating Kampov's guttural voice.

Sergeant Pavlenko stood in the shadows of a tall brick wall across the street from two of his operators, who were practically invisible in the dark. If Lysenko came this way from the dacha he would be caught in a deadly cross fire.

In general, from what Greenwalt had witnessed, Russians were mostly inefficient, still hidebound with bureaucracy, but these Spetsnaz troops were damned good. He found himself admiring them, despite himself, especially the kid who had led the three children out of the house, despite the risk that they might have been booby-trapped.

He speed dialed a government-secured internet provider and when it came up on the screen, he logged onto the FBI's executive website, entering his password twice when he was prompted.

When he was cleared he entered the Operations Center site, and sent an instant message to Dan Wilkes.

URGENT NEED FOR YOU TO CONTACT YOUR CIA FRIEND TO GIVE ME IMMEDIATE ACCESS TO OUR JUPITER IN INFRARED MODE.
I WANT TO TRACK THREE LIVE BODIES IN REAL TIME.

Within seconds Wilkes was on line.

STAND BY.

Greenwalt glanced over at Pavlenko, and he got cold just looking at the man standing out there. It had to be at least twenty below zero.

Less than one minute later, the National Reconaissance Office logo came up on screen, a National Assets page briefly flashed, warning that this was a Top Secret site, and asking for a password, followed by three or four other screens, also asking for passwords that came up and disappeared, until the display stopped at a page titled: TECHNICAL MEANS CONTROL CENTER, on which every spy satellite in orbit was listed.

Greenwalt's hand shook slightly. Whoever Wilkes's friend at the CIA was, he was frightening.

He scrolled down to the Jupiter 3a, and entered. A split-page screen came up showing the satellite's real time images over a section of Moscow, its orbit characteristics, and several boxes with tracking data, as well as a control bar along the bottom.

Greenwalt repositioned the bird's view slightly to the east to Noginsk, zoomed in and adjusted the view until he was seeing only a radius of three hundred meters from the dacha, and hit the infrared tab.

At first it was difficult to figure out what he was seeing from the jumble of indistinct heat blooms cluttering the screen. Most of them were ragged squares that he realized were the roofs of the dacha and other buildings nearby that were radiating heat.

It took only a few seconds to figure out how to erase those images by right clicking the mouse. As soon as that clutter was gone from the screen, he spotted the image of the car he was sitting in, which he erased, and the brighter but smaller images of a few streetlights down the road, which he removed.

The satellite's infrared image was mostly dark now, except for the images of Pavlenko and his two operators on either side of the street, all stationary. A single image was moving toward the dacha, which Greenwalt took to be Kampov. Two other images were moving slowly down the back street away from the dacha.

One of them seemed to be radiating more heat than the other, probably because of the differences in body masses.

"Gotcha," Greenwalt said. The images were of Mrs. Monroe and her captor.

He got out of the car, the intense cold taking his breath away, and hurried across the road to where Pavlenko was standing in the deeper shadows.

"Go back to the car before you freeze to death, Mr. Greenwalt," Pavlenko said.

"Mrs. Monroe and Lysenko have left the house."

"How do you know this?"

Greenwalt shook his head. "I can't tell you exactly how I know; you'll just have to take my word for it. But they're definitely heading down the street on the other side of the house. They probably got out the back way."

"I think not."

Colonel Baturin's voice came over the comms link. "Mr. Greenwalt, does your government have a satellite above us at this moment? One that tracks infrared images?"

"I'm sorry, but I'm not at liberty to say."

"All units, Command, hold your positions, this op remains as planned."

"Okay, I'll do it myself," Greenwalt said. "At least let one of your people come with me."

"Sascha, copy?" Baturin said.

"Your captain took off his SQ at the dacha," Pavlenko said. "And that's where he's headed right now, Colonel."

"*Pizdec,*" Baturin said. "One of these days he's going to get himself killed, and it will be on my conscience."

"Shall I send someone after him?"

"*Nyet.* Hold your position."

Greenwalt took the comms unit from behind his ear, handed it to Pavlenko, then turned and walked back to the Mercedes. "Fucking Russians," he said half under his breath.

Kampov's ghostly image was within the dacha's compound, and the other two continued away.

He backed out of the NRO's program all the way to the FBI's Ops Center and sent Wilkes an instant message.

GOT WHAT I NEEDED. TELL YOUR FRIEND THANKS.
THIS ISSUE WILL BE RESOLVED WITHIN THE HOUR.

Wilkes's reply came immediately.

TAKE CARE.

Greenwalt shut down his laptop, checked his pistol, and headed on foot down the street away from the dacha. Pavlenko made no move to stop him.

This section of Noginsk seemed to be in lockdown mode. Nothing moved: no traffic, no sounds, other than the wind around the eaves of the buildings. Nor were there any distinctive odors now other than a faintly sour smell on the air, though trash seemed to be piled everywhere. In the summer, he figured, this place would be a shit hole. For now it was just cold.

SEVENTY-FOUR
•

Kampov held up at the open front door of the dacha and held his breath for a long moment, every sense straining to detect the presence of someone inside. But the house was deathly still and dark.

Gripping his pistol tightly he rolled through the doorway, and keeping low darted across the stair hall.

A man's body lay where it had fallen half out of the kitchen door at the end of the hall. There were other bodies in the house, but they were not his concern.

Kampov took the stairs two at a time, as quietly as possible. At the top he held up again to listen for any sounds. But it was quiet up here, too.

The bathroom light had been switched off, and keeping close to the wall, Kampov made his way to the open door. Girding himself he brought his pistol up, stepped around the corner, and swung the muzzle left to right.

The bathroom was empty except for the woman's body.

Kampov rushed down the hall and down the stairs to the kitchen door. He started to step over the body when he saw that someone had stepped in the blood pooled around the man's head.

The small footprints led across the kitchen to the mudroom where they disappeared. They were obviously Mrs. Monroe's and she'd stepped barefoot into the blood. But at least the bastard had given her shoes or boots to protect her feet. It meant that he needed to keep her alive to make his escape.

Kampov hesitated for just a second at the open back door to make sure that Lysenko wasn't waiting for him, then rushed across the yard to the shattered gate.

He spotted traces of what might have been blood a few meters down the street to the right. She had cut her hand up in the bathroom, and within twenty or thirty meters she was leaving a trail hard to miss, even in the dark.

Keeping to the shadows as much as possible, Kampov hurried down the deserted street, a rage building in his chest that threatened to blot out all of his sanity.

He was seeing Nina's pale white face in the hospital recovery room where they had taken her after the botched operation to save her life.

When the nurse pulled back the sheet, he'd touched Nina's cheek with trembling fingers. Her skin was still soft and warm; she'd been dead for less than an hour. But her features were marble white because she had bled out on the table. No power on earth or in heaven would bring her back to him, and at that moment he had wanted to lash out at something, at anything.

But he had bent down, kissed his wife on the lips for the last time, gave the nurse a bleak look, and forced himself to walk out of the hospital before he killed somebody.

This night would be different. He was going to save Mrs. Monroe and he was going to kill Sergey Lysenko.

SEVENTY-FIVE
•

At the corner across from the apartment, Lysenko studied the street. As before, nothing moved, and only a few of the windows showed any light. It was as if this part of Noginsk was holding its collective breath.

Boris and Lana's neighbors had known what was going on from the beginning. The word had probably spread, and when the military helicopter and APCs had shown up, everyone in the vicinity locked their doors, pulled the curtains, and hunkered down to wait until morning. It was the Russian way, learned after a lot of hard years under the KGB's control.

He'd not counted on this sort of thing happening,

but he was enough of a realist to understand that mistakes might be made, leading the MVD or Spetsnaz out here. And he had enough experience to understand how the situation would unfold. A man and a woman out on the streets on this side of the city would be suspect. But in the middle of town, and on the other side, traffic would be moving normally. Two women would have no trouble. He had made a contingency plan months ago before he'd come back to Moscow.

He turned back to look at Patti. Her complexion was milk white, and she had stopped shivering. He suspected that she was in the beginning stages of hypothermia.

He let go of her arm, pulled off his coat, and put it over her shoulders.

She stumbled back and tried to turn away, but he grabbed her arm again.

"If you make a noise, or if you try to run, I'll kill you," he said.

"You've said that before," Patti mumbled. She'd come this far. She only had to survive a little longer until her rescuers realized that Lysenko never wanted the helicopter from Moscow. It was merely a ruse to buy him time. She had to slow him down as much as possible.

Lysenko looked around the corner again. The street was empty.

He propelled her out of the shadows and they started across, but Patti stumbled and nearly fell.

Once again his nearly all-consuming anger threatened to blot out his ability to think straight. He didn't need the woman after all. A bullet in her brain would end it here and now and, except for one minor task left to be done, he would be on his own again, as he had been for most of his life. He would deal with the lack of money. That problem wasn't insurmountable. And there was still another possibility of getting the funds from Anderson.

But he wasn't ready to kill her yet, and he didn't have a clear answer in his head why not. Maybe Raya had been correct, maybe he wanted to teach this woman the lessons that he'd wanted to teach his mother before he'd killed her. He'd felt unclean and unnatural ever since. Maybe he wanted nothing more than to cleanse his soul of the stains he'd been burdened with in England.

He half-dragged, half-carried Patti the rest of the way to the shed, where he shoved her aside. She fell to her hands and knees at his feet.

• • •

For a long time Patti stayed on all fours, not moving. Her head was spinnng and her stomach churning, but she wasn't in any real pain now. If she ran, she didn't think that he would risk firing his pistol and giving away his position.

Lysenko had opened the Toyota's side door and he was doing something.

She looked up as he pulled a wig and a dress out of a nylon duffle bag. For a second she was confused. Why had he brought clothes for her? It didn't make any sense, until she realized that the dress was too big for her. It was meant for him.

"Dressing like a woman so you can sneak away?" Patti said, her voice distant and hoarse in her own ears. "But then what?" All she needed was time. They would come for her.

Lysenko looked down at her. "You wouldn't understand." He raised his pistol and pointed it at her head.

"Don't do it, Sergey," a man called from across the street.

Patti knew the voice, or thought she did. But it was impossible. David was dead. She'd seen him fall, she'd seen his body. Lysenko had shot him in the back of the head.

She was hallucinating again. It was the only explanation, and yet at the dacha Raya had said that she was going to kill Patti *and* David.

"Not yet," David said, closer now.

God in heaven, it was as if a quart of adrenaline had been pumped into her system.

She looked over her shoulder as her husband hurried toward them, his right hand out. For a delicious moment she couldn't believe what she was seeing, yet sweet relief washed over her. David was alive! Somehow he'd survived being shot, and he'd come to rescue her.

All along she'd been wrong about him. He did care about her. It hadn't been about her money after all. It was about love. Finally somebody in the world actually loved her for who she was.

Ignoring the muzzle of the pistol inches away from her forehead, she managed to struggle to her feet, bracing a hand against the side of the van for balance.

"David," she said, trying to catch her breath.

David ignored her. "I didn't think that prick of a lawyer would call the feds," he told Lysenko.

Patti didn't understand. Nothing was connecting in her head.

"It's too late," Lysenko said.

"Trust me, Sergey. We can still squeeze the bastard if you can get us out of here."

Patti was struck not so much by what her husband was saying, but by his subservient tone of voice. "I thought you were dead."

David turned on her. "You saw what you wanted to see," he said, his voice harsh. "It's been your fucking trouble all along."

She staggered backward as if he had physically struck her.

Lysenko looked over his shoulder toward the alley they'd come down. "What makes you think he'll cooperate and betray the FBI?"

"I'm telling you, I know that son of a bitch Tobias. He'd walk on water to save his precious little Patti."

"Do you know what they did to me?" Patti asked. Her head was spinning out of control. It was as if she were looking through a broken window and the entire world was tilted at a crazy angle. "Do you even care?"

"He cares very much," Lysenko said. "Enough so that he told us your weak points."

"No."

"He came to us with the plan six months ago. Ten million for the cause and ten million for himself. He's an inventive man, your husband."

The sudden crushing realization of how wrong she had been came down around her head.

Patti pushed away from the van, and tottered close enough so that she could slap David's face, but he easily batted her hand away.

"Did you honestly believe that I could ever love a putz like you?"

Her father had been right about him, and so had Tobias, but she hadn't listened. She hadn't been able to listen until now, because all she'd ever wanted was for someone to love her for who she was, not what she was worth. She wanted to be loved for what was inside of her head, what was inside of her heart, and she'd been willing to give the world for it, because she needed validation. She needed to feel that she, all by herself, had worth.

She thought that she'd found it with David, but now she realized that she hadn't really learned who she was until the past eleven days in the dacha. They had done things to her, but they'd not been able to break her spirit, or cause her to retreat within herself.

She was a strong woman, a fighter. It was something no one could ever take from her. Not even David, not even now.

"Who did you kill in the woods that day?" she asked.

"A Mafia bag man from the states," Lysenko said. "A nobody." He had lowered his pistol. "There'll be no money."

"There's no need for anyone else to die here to-night," someone said in English from down the street in the opposite direction from the dacha.

A man dressed in what looked like an expensive topcoat was walking toward them. He was holding a gold badge above his head. "My name is Everett Green-walt. I'm an assistant deputy director with the FBI, and I'm here to negotiate for Mrs. Monroe's release."

Lysenko grabbed Patti's arm and pulled her close, pressing the muzzle of his pistol against the side of her head. "If anybody dies it'll be the woman."

Greenwalt ignored him. "Mr. Monroe, I presume," he said, stopping a few meters from David. "You come as something of a surprise. Was this your plan?"

"Where's your gun, you dumb bastard?" David demanded. "Do you think he won't shoot you?"

"Most of the time I've not found the need to carry a

weapon," Greenwalt said, pleasantly. "But if Mrs. Monroe is shot to death, both of you will die here on this wretched street tonight. And it will all have been for nothing. So I would suggest that you be reasonable. Release the woman; you'll never get any money for her. Put on your disguises, and leave before the Spetsnaz shows up. Maybe you'll get lucky and live to fight another day."

Lysenko pointed his pistol at Greenwalt. "Maybe I'll shoot you first."

Greenwalt nodded. "You couldn't miss at this range," he said reasonably. "But then you wouldn't be any better off than you are now. Perhaps even worse. The Bureau takes a dim view of people, such as the Butcher of Grozny, gunning down its agents, and especially upper level managers. They would take a particular interest in finding you. Some of our guys are damned good."

"Fucking hell," David shouted.

Patti looked over her shoulder as Kampov came up the street, pistol in hand.

Lysenko turned and grunted, switching aim back to Patti's head.

Patti could feel him tensing. He was going to shoot right now, just when her saviors had shown up. But it wasn't fair, goddamnit! Not like this! Not now!

She suddenly jerked her head backward and Lysenko instinctively pulled off a shot, the pistol firing with a tremendous bang right next to her head, the bullet ricocheting off the pavement.

He started to bring the pistol to bear on her, but she reared back far enough to kick his gun hand, the pistol clattering to the pavement.

Before he could recover, she spun around, smashing her left heel into his chin, rocking him on his feet. But he managed to reach into his pocket and pull out a second pistol.

Kampov sprinted forward firing three shots on the run, the first smacking into the side of the van, the second hitting Lysenko in the left shoulder, staggering him backward, and the third catching him in the chest, knocking him against the van, where he collapsed.

David fumbled in his coat pocket, but Greenwalt calmly drew a pistol and fired one shot, catching him in the face, sending him sprawling on his back.

For a seeming eternity Patti was struck dumb, rooted to her spot beside Lysenko's body, her eyes fixed on David lying motionless in the middle of the street. For the second time in eleven days she'd seen her husband shot to death.

She wanted to tell him what an incredible son of a bitch he was. She wanted to look into his eyes and see that he understood what she was saying to him. She wanted to see some guilt for what he had put her through. Maybe some remorse.

She took a step forward. "You bastard," she muttered.

"Get down! Get down!" Kampov was shouting desperately.

Patti turned, confused. She didn't know what was happening now. "What?"

"Patricia, move," Greenwalt shouted from the opposite direction.

Patti turned back in time to see that Lysenko had risen up on his damaged left arm and was bringing his pistol to bear on her, a wild look in his eyes.

He said something that to Patti sounded like *mother,* and her heart practically stopped.

Kampov fired one shot, catching Lysenko in the middle of the forehead, driving him back against the van. He slumped over, the pistol dropping from his hand.

Patti's knees began to fold and she started to slump to the ground.

Kampov reached her first, scooping her off her feet and sitting her down just inside the van. "You're safe now," he said.

"It's all right," she said.

Greenwalt was there, kicking the pistol away from Lysenko's body. He holstered his pistol.

Patti looked up at him. "I thought you said that you didn't have a gun." She was babbling and she could hear herself, but she couldn't stop.

Greenwalt smiled. "I lied."

Patti turned back to Kampov, who pulled the coat a little closer around her body.

"Our boys heard the shooting. They'll be here any minute," he told her. "The helicopter will take you to the hospital in Moscow. Just hang on."

"What took you guys so long?" she asked.

"Might never have gotten here if it hadn't been for the help of Mr. Greenwalt," Kampov said. "He's a good cop."

"My friends call me Ev," Greenwalt said.

THE PARTING

January 14th

SEVENTY-SIX

•

A stern-faced Russian nurse pushed Patti across the busy international terminal at Sheremetyevo Airport, Greenwalt walking along beside her. She looked up at him and smiled. "How did you find me?" she asked.

For the past two days her wounds had been tended to, and she had been rehydrated, given massive doses of vitamins and plain beef broth at first until she could tolerate solid food. As soon as she was able to speak and think coherently she had been debriefed by two pleasant young women from Kampov's division, but they'd not been allowed to answer any of her questions. Nor had Greenwalt, who'd stood at her side the entire time.

"The Bureau has a few tricks," he said.

Patti didn't know what she was supposed to feel about David's death. She was still numb. But she suspected it would hit her sooner or later, and when it did she was going to need a friend nearby, maybe family, maybe Tobias. Maybe her father.

They reached the customs barrier, where their passports were checked and stamped, then continued across to the VIP section, where the nurse left them. The morning was crystal clear and even colder than it had been over the past week. Through the big windows they could see steam or smoke rising straight up from vents outside. The FBI's Gulfstream was connected to a large-diameter hose that pumped warm air into the aircraft.

"What makes someone turn out the way David did?" Patti asked. She'd struggled with that question while she lay in bed at the hospital. Nothing in her life to this point had ever surprised, hurt, and disappointed her so deeply. She didn't know how she'd handled the last eleven days. She didn't even know how long it would take her to recover. Certainly her mental wounds would take longer to mend than her physical ones.

"No one knows," Kampov said, coming up from behind.

Patti turned in her chair and looked up at him.

"How are you feeling?" he asked.

"A lot better."

Kampov and Greenwalt shook hands. "Thanks for your help," Kampov said. "You're a good cop."

"You're not bad for a Bolshevik."

Kampov laughed, but Patti could see a serious sadness in his eyes.

She pushed the blanket off her lap and struggled to stand up. Her feet were heavily bandaged and she had been given thick felt boots to wear. She'd even been allowed to shower, do her hair, and put on a little makeup. The MVD had brought most of her clothes from the dacha and had them laundered. She was hurting, but she felt clean.

"Hey, take it easy," Greenwalt said. He tried to help her, but she pushed his hand away and managed to stand on her own, even though her feet were extremely tender.

Kampov stuck out his hand, but instead of reaching

for it she fell into his arms, and after an awkward moment he embraced her.

"I dreamed of you," she said softly. "Back at the dacha, during the worst of it."

"That's because you needed to find something to hope for," Kampov said tenderly.

"No, I really dreamed of *you*," she said. "I could see your face so clearly that when you showed up I actually recognized that it was you."

"Impossible. We never met before."

Patti smiled and nodded. "Yes, I know. But it's true nevertheless."

"You'll find someone, Patti," Kampov whispered in her ear.

She was startled, and she looked up into his eyes, which were even sadder than before. "You lost someone, too?"

He nodded. "A couple years ago."

"It still hurts?"

"Yes, it does," Kampov said. "But you're going home."

"Thanks to you and Ev," Patti said. Her eyes were filling but she didn't give a damn.

"Just keep in touch," Kampov said, and he held her close again for a long time.

When they parted she looked up into his eyes, which were glistening. "I will," she said.

Kampov and Greenwalt shook hands again. "Safe trip."

"Thanks," Greenwalt said. "What's next for you?"

Kampov smiled bitterly. "I'm going to see some Mafia guys about an old friend of mine."